AUSCHWITZ PRISONI

Producer & International Distributor
eBookPro Publishing
www.ebook-pro.com

AUSCHWITZ PRISONER NO. 31119
YITZCHAK BOROWSKY

Translation: Sara Davis

Contact: yitzchak1010@gmail.com
ISBN 9798363455865

Auschwitz Prisoner 31119:

The Shocking True Story of a World War II Holocaust Survivor

"For God called the Spring and the Massacre – together,
The sun shone, the acacia tree bloomed and the slayer slew"
From: The City of Slaughter, Chaim Nachman Bialik

A Document for Human Beings Whoever They Are

In Memory of her Parents, Isaac and Sheine Reisel (nee Horwitz) Plaskovsky
May God Avenge Them
And of the brothers Haim and Zvi Plaskovsky
May God Avenge Them
And Fruma Horwitz
May God Avenge Her

Bluma

Sheine Reisel Plaskovsky, Bluma's mother and Zvi Plaskovsky, Bluma's younger brother

IN MEMORY of our beloved family members who supported Bluma's broken soul and passed away.
Sheine Reisel's siblings Sol, Sam, Mendel Horwitz & Fannie Chester.

The deceased Cousins:

1. Elaine & Harry Wayne of Skokie Illinois.
2. Beatrice (Bluma) Turetzky of Boston Massachusetts.
3. Jack & Nancy Horwitz of Brooklyn N.Y.
4. Herbert Horwitz of Los Angeles California.
5. Irving Harvin (Horwitz) of San Diego California.
6. Nathan Horwitz of Tijuana Mexico.
7. Saul Horwitz of Mexico City.
8. Philip Horwitz of Chicago Illinois (Fruma's brother).
9. Ida Horwitz of Chicago Illinois (Fruma's sister).
10. Ann Horwitz of Chicago Illinois (Fruma's sister).
11. Isadore Horwitz of Chicago Illinois (Fruma's brother).
12. Annette Horwitz of Hadassah Organization in Chicago Illinois who was as a sister to Bluma.
13. Dr. Morris Finsky, a leading surgeon in the South Side Chicago Hospital.
14. Ethel Mayer of Milwaukee Wisconsin.
15. Paul Lipton, Attorney at Law, Milwaukee Wisconsin.
16. Sam Lipton, A proteins Researcher of Burlington Wisconsin.
17. Ruth Stein of Milwaukee Wisconsin.
18. Laurence Weinstein of Madison Wisconsin.
19. Harry Philips of Dumas Arkansas.
20. John Platt (Plaskovsky) of Los Angeles California.
21. Haim Platt (Plaskovsky) of Silver Spring Maryland.
22. Chanan Ayalti (Kleinbort), Author & Editor in the Yiddish Newspaper Forverts of N.Y City.
23. Nathan Stone of Los Angeles California.

Bluma's Deceased Relatives in Israel:

1. ehuda & Tamar Ayalti, Founders of The Ayelet Hashahar Kibbutz, Israel.
2. Zehava & Reuven Paikovsky of Israel.
3. Moshe Plaskovsky of Givataim Israel.
4. John Mayer, A Musician who made aliya to Israel.

Our deep love and thanks in the process of writing this book to our dear cousins, who encouraged, supported me.

First, our deepest appreciations to the Noble Cousin Frances Weinstein of Madison Wisconsin, who supported Bluma through the difficult years of her sickness. Her dear sister, Esther Lange of Barabo Wisconsin, Dan & Yael Weinstein and Harold B. Stein. Esq.

Contents

Introduction

This book is about the life story of our mother Bluma (Plaskovsky) during and after the Holocaust, and its ramifications and impact on the whole family.

My mother Bluma, of blessed memory, was born in Sopotzkyn, in the Volhinya District in north-eastern Poland (today – Belarus) on January 15, 1925, and died in Israel on August 25, 2016. My father Hanan Borowsky, of blessed memory, was also born in that town on August 22, 1911, and passed away in Israel on September 29, 1978.

My mother experienced the horrors of the Holocaust as a teenager – between the ages of 16 and a half and 20. Afterwards, she raised a family in Israel, although she was suffering emotionally from post trauma. In the last ten years of her life she developed Alzheimer's disease, as a direct causal effect of the post trauma.

It is important that my mother's life story be told. It is a personal story, being an authentic historical, psychological and legal document of a struggle for survival.

It is the story of a young Jewish girl from Poland, on whom and on whose family the horrors of the Holocaust left their mark for all eternity, deciding her fate – to be stricken with post trauma[1] – and that of her children, who lived with her under the same roof, and suffered the ramifications of that condition.

The story of my mother, who was a gracious woman with a great

---

1 A study was recently published by Dr. Dale Bardsen, a Neurologist at UCLA, in which he establishes the thesis, which was eventually proven correct, that strong post trauma and its anxieties are the basis for the occurrence of Alzheimer's Disease.

personality, is that of her struggle, as a young girl, woman and elderly lady, against evil and injustice, the results and implications of the actions of human beings during and after the Holocaust.

It is intended for whoever believes in the search for the truth, and in the right of every person, every human being, to live a good, decent, respectable and happy life.

The book describes the events, as they were told to me by my father and by my mother. It relies on the study of official documents concerning the events, which I obtained from the Nazi Archives in Bad Arolsen, and other documents written at the time, and from affidavits given by my mother. Prior to publication I decided it was my duty to visit the places mentioned. There is nothing better than seeing for oneself.

My mother's personal story tells of survival in impossible conditions, under the constant threat for her existence. This personal story reflects the effects of the Holocaust on European Jewry and demonstrates the manner in which the survivors who arrived in Israel integrated into the life of the State, and how the State dealt with them and their difficulties.

Our mother's experience with the Holocaust remained with her all her life. Dr. Asher Bar Halperin [2] contends that she fell into a situation in which the traumas were revived and came flooding back, thereby exacerbating her post-traumatic responses, and creating a vicious circle which fed on itself and from which she was unable to escape, leaving her, in fact, trapped for ever within her past.

At the age of 82 she was diagnosed with Alzheimer's disease, and then all the events of the Holocaust returned to her as if they were real, and she again experienced the situation as if it were occurring right then. At the "Gan Shalva" Institution, where she was hospitalized due to her condition, she would tell the staff that German soldiers were pursuing her, and that she was being taken to labor camps or that she must pack her belongings quickly because she had to leave the place. [3]

---

2 Dr. Asher Bar Halperin, Chief Psychiatrist of the "Amcha" organization, the Israel Center for Emotional and Social Support of Holocaust Survivors and the Second Generation.
3 A publication by the U.S. National Health Institute, citing the research by Prof. Rachel Yehuda and her colleagues from the School of Medicine of the Mt. Sinai Medical Center, and the James Peters Veterans Medical Center in the Bronx, New York, argues that Post Trauma is inherited genetically.

My mother often shut herself in and sat silent. Her demands of myself and my brother were quite spartan: make do with very little, which she considered a means of survival, thorough and methodical study, integrity and help to others.

I was afraid to bring friends home – I did not want them to witness her sadness. My mother did not envelop us in love, she did not embrace or kiss us, she did not compliment us, and did not express emotion.

My father balanced the home atmosphere a little. He had also survived the Holocaust, but he was a joyous person with a charismatic personality. He was immediately noticeable in a crowd. Our home was open to residents of the town. From time to time friends from Sopotzkyn would get together, and would listen to stories from my mother and father about their dear ones who had not survived. The conversations often concerned the Israeli scene, the establishment of the State and the faults of its government.

My father would tell humoristic stories that were aimed at changing the atmosphere and extracting some laughter from those present, mainly our mother, who was always quiet and serious. I would imitate my father, and I also endeavored to make my mother laugh as far as I could.

Our mother demanded of me and my brother to serve in significant positions in the Military. When I transferred from a combat unit to a service unit, she expressed strong criticism. She was a Zionist in every bone of her body. She was concerned about the fate of the Jewish State, especially in light of the moral and governmental carelessness of the politicians, and the preference given to wealth and money over the values of mutual responsibility and help to others.

Unlike my father, my mother never told us her personal story. Only after his death did she begin to share with us the events of the Holocaust, and even then only grudgingly. Eventually, when I began dealing with the legal issues concerning the reparations due to her, I discovered that she had been taken to participate in the experiments made by Dr. Mengele, of which she never spoke directly.[4]

My mother and father were two out of the four survivors of the town of

---

4 I shall refer to that later on.

Sopotzkyn, and the only ones who came to Israel. From my room I used to listen to the conversations at the meetings held in the living room of our home. My mother would continue to weep many more days after those meetings had ended.

In 1977, aged 66, my father was diagnosed with aggressive malignant lymphoma. Our mother devoted herself to looking after him. About one week prior to his death, on the eve of Rosh HaShana 1978, when I visited him in the Oncology Department at the hospital, he made me responsible for the family. At that time, my younger brother Emanuel was studying for his MA in software engineering at the Santa Barbara University in California. I was then a young attorney, serving as Deputy District Attorney for Tel Aviv. My father's death was a serious shock for us all. He was my mother's main support, and now she was 54 years old with no emotional help and no apparent source of income.[5]

Upon my brother Emanuel's return to his studies in the U.S., after the period of mourning in Israel, the relationship between my mother and myself became closer. She began to share with me the events of the Holocaust. The stories began coming slowly, then the flow broadened and intensified. It was hard for me to listen to them, and mainly to digest them. I could never understand how a young, slim, fragile girl, was able to survive alone in a cruel world, after all her family had been murdered. As the years passed, and she grew older, she added more and more details. Her long-term memory became stronger and more active as her short-term memory gradually disappeared, but the Alzheimer's disease erased all the horrors after four years.

After my father's death, my mother told me the story that had been kept secret, that my father Hanan, of blessed memory, had been married and was the father of a little girl, who had also been murdered, as were the remainder of his family. So long as my father was alive, they never shared this story with us (on that I also obtained documents from the Bad Arolsen archive).

As the descriptions continued to become more detailed, I began adding

---

5 Eventually, after a legal struggle which I conducted in Germany, it emerged that there was such a source, but she had not utilized it because, due to her post trauma, she had refrained from applying to Germany for fear that their response would be to take from her what she had already received.

one to the other and I understood that <u>one of the reasons why my father married my mother was also out of a sense of personal responsibility and obligation for one of the only survivors from the town</u>. She had looked after his wife and little girl at the Kielbasin trenches (presently a south-western neighborhood of Grodno. In the past it was a tractor farm outside Grodno). At the end of the war he was 34 years old and she was 20.

I often considered recording my mother while she was telling me her story, but I was concerned that the recording machine would prevent her from telling the story. Recording was also not possible because her stories came out spontaneously as bits of information or associative flashes. In addition, she was afraid that the load would be too much for me, so the stories were told in no chronological order, and from time to time.

The first time I heard a continuous statement from her was in August 2006, when I brought my friend, psychiatrist Dr. Valdmar Viborsky to get an impression of her mental condition. He sat with her for about eight hours, and wrote down a detailed anamnesis.

Her statement constitutes a living testimony to the importance of preserving the memory of the Holocaust, although it was not recorded for that purpose. Preserving the memory of the Holocaust by means of the voices and through the eyes of those who experienced it is the best way to mediate between the trauma and the listener. Listening to the survivors is the only possibility: "To erase the distance between the past and the present", [6] the study by Prof. Amit Sharira, states that post trauma is also transferred to the sympathetic listener by the giving of testimony. [7]

I had the great privilege of hearing the testimony dozens of times from someone who had been saved from the inferno and the depths of hell, while each time the description became more detailed. I feel it is my duty to bring this to humanity. It is too heavy to bear alone.

---

6 Claude Lanzman

7 Prof. Amit Sharira, Clinical Psychologist, expands on the significance of examining the effect caused by exposure to this testimony over a long period of life, which results in the listeners themselves suffering from post-trauma. See his article: Aging and Mental Health 11/2015 Routledge Taylor & Francis Group.

Bluma of Sopotzkyn and her Family

Dozens of small towns are scattered along the road leading from Minsk (presently the capital of Belarus) on the way to Grodno, which is also in Belarus today, where the Jews of East Poland settled on the border between Lithuania and Belarus.

It is a beautiful region. I saw it recently in the fall of 2019, when I made a special visit there just before this book was published.

For more than 350 km along the road there are beautiful forests of trees with white trunks, which is why this country is called "White Russia [Belarus]". Not only did the cream of Jewry live in the region, but in the Second World War it had decisive implications on the fate of both the Russian and the Jewish peoples, who should have enjoyed a close relationship between them.

In the autumn the trees shed their leaves, and this creates a kilometer-long scene of red, orange, yellow and gold. Also along the roadway are bushes on which various kinds of berries grow. The forests are full of mushrooms, which is the basis of a soup eaten with gusto by the residents of these regions.

In the many kilometers of open fields along the road, the like of which I had never seen before, grow various crops in unimaginable quantities: there are many fruit trees, fields of wheat, oats, cabbages, potatoes, carrots, and beetroot, which is the most widespread food among the residents of the area, used in various dishes – borscht and beetroot salad, among others. The region is well watered with streams and rivers.

The air is perfumed with the aromas of the fertile land and the variety of its produce from trees, bushes, flowers and earth. The colors of the ears of wheat are darker than the golden wheat I had grown up with. This is the most fertile of lands, and the blessing of God is on any people and human being who consumes of its produce, who lives and develops on it.

Along the road one encounters the names of towns, whose wonders my late father, Hanan, never tired of sharing with me, and of telling me how often he had visited them. Their names were engraved on my memory from his stories, and now I was passing alongside them. Volozhin, with its famous Yeshiva, at which my uncle Shemaryahu Borowsky (may God avenge him) had studied and was ordained as Rabbi. The towns of Slonim, Nowogrodek, Skidel, Novidvor, Lida, Radin, Yazuri (the birthplace of Bluma's cousins who emigrated to the U.S. before the Nazis came to power).

The town of Grodno is crossed by the River Neman, and there, also, is the Augustów Canal, which connects the streams to the river which enters Lithuania and flows into the Baltic Sea. This canal passes close to the town of Sopotzkyn.

In this region, especially at the convergence of the borders between Poland and Lithuana, lived the "Misnagdim" and educated Jews who, in addition to Jewish religion and tradition, expanded their education to the knowledge of secular subjects. Many of them sent their children to universities, and supported them when they joined the youth movements, whose ideals were Zionism and emigration to the Land of Israel.

Although the languages spoken here were Russian, Belorussian and Polish, the Jewish families spoke Yiddish as their first language. The communities who supported the "Haskala" movement and the expansion of knowledge, built the "Tarbut" network of schools, which gave the Jewish children an education in general secular subjects, and particularly in Hebrew.

Bluma, Hanan, my aunt Esther and many others of the town of Sopotzkyn and the region spoke and wrote fluently in a Hebrew which was incomparably richer than the Hebrew presently spoken by Israeli children in their free country. The language of those Jewish children in Poland was saturated with expressions from Jewish sources and the writings of the scholars from the region's Yeshivot, outstanding among them being the Yeshivas of Volozhin, Kovno and Grodno.

Hundreds of thousands of children and youths, fluent Hebrew speakers, from this region and especially from the town of Grodno, were prominent in the establishment of the State of Israel, among them the first President Chaim Weizmann, of blessed memory, Prime Ministers Yitzchak Shamir and Shimon Peres, of blessed memory, the Palmach Commander Yigal Alon (Peikowitz), whose parents came from Grodno; also – Prof. Laurence Marvik, who was born in Sopotzkyn, and was Director of the Department of Semitic Languages at the Library of Congress in Washington, and Dr. Morris Finsky, Bluma's first cousin, who was a surgeon in a Chicago Hospital.

The majority of the Jews in these regions and in Sopotzkyn worked for their living in various occupations or as medium and small merchants.

Because of the events and political consequences of World War II, Grodno and Sopotzkyn, and other places that had been Polish before the war, were transferred to Belarus. From the Jewish national viewpoint, this is a uniform region.

The reader is invited to view photographs from the region, both those that came into my possession from the remote past, as well those I photographed recently myself. The marketplace where my mother and father, of blessed memory, used to live is now in the form of a square, not a circle. The Soviets decided that the residents of the town must bow to Lenin, so his statue stands in the middle of the square, with benches placed around it.

The square and the houses where the Jews lived, who constituted more than half the town's population, looked much more impressive in the past than they do now.

I found Teholin Street, where there is a local Eastern Orthodox church, with a large adjacent yard in which was the Ghetto where the Jews of the town were concentrated prior to being transferred to their next stop – Keilbasin.

In particular I found the Jewish cemetery of the town. It is located on the side of a hill up the road rising from the marketplace to the exit on the left side. The priest gave me instructions on how to find it. I climbed up the hill and found the gate with the Magen David. I immediately noticed gravestones with Hebrew writing, some of which had fallen and some were still standing, but all needing to be looked after. In this cemetery my grandfather Yitzchak Tanhum Borowsky, of blessed memory, was buried. He died soon after his return from Montana, U.S.A. in 1925, where he had gone in order to meet his brother who had emigrated there. He had returned to Poland, planning to take his family to the U.S., but died at a young age. His plan was foiled by his death, and his family fell victim to the Nazis' rise to power.

At the back of the town, in the direction of the Augustów Canal, there are recreation areas, as well as a beautiful lake surrounded by forests. Around the town are low hills covered in forests and woodland with bushes bearing raspberries and wild strawberries.

On January 15, 1925, Sheine Reisel Plaskovsky, nee Halevy Horwitz, delivered her daughter Bluma into the world, in the city of Grodno, Poland. This was her second child, after the birth of her elder son Haim, two years earlier. Her husband, Isaac Plaskovsky, was a merchant dealing in grains and cereals, a business which he managed from the yard of his large house in the town of Sopotzkyn, half the residents of which were Jews.

Sopotzkyn lies about 17 km north-west of Grodno, the ancient capital of Lithuania, built close to the banks of the Augustów Canal and the Neman River. The city is surrounded by low hills, green forests and streams of water, where the Jewish youth would go out to strenghten their friendships, to develop and realize the dream of the return to Zion – by emigrating to Palestine.

This region of Grodno and the town of Sopotzkyn contains within it many more towns, such as Skidel, Yizuri, Augustów, Sovleky, Beranovich and Droskiniesky, where there were many ancient Jewish communities.

The Augustów Canal was used to float rafts carrying logs and merchandise. At the center of the town, on the market square, the peasants and farmers would come from the surrounding villages to sell their wares. The street that surrounded the market was called Market Square. Isaac Plaskovsky lived there with Sheine Reisel, Haim and the baby, Bluma, who was born on January 15, 1925 at the maternity hospital in Grodno. The home of the family of my father, Hanan, was also on Market Square, with its metal goods store and the machinery repair workshop established by my grandfather Tanhum, of blessed memory.

The birth of the baby Bluma brought great joy to her parents Isaac and Sheine Reisel and her brother Haim. Their house was surrounded by a high fence, which was covered by bushes bearing raspberries and blackberries, and cherry trees. Behind the house there was a green field and a well. Isaac was a good businessman, and he was quite wealthy. My mother said of him that he spoke little and acted a lot. Bluma inherited these two traits – she spoke only when necessary and never gossiped.

My grandmother Sheine Reisel was a beautiful woman, originated from the Horwitz family which was scattered among the nearby towns Yezori, Suvalki and Beklarova. Sheine Reisel loved to sew, and also tried her hand at acting in the local Yiddish theater. She was known among the Jews of the town as "The Angel". She would quietly and secretly investigate and inquire who was in need of help in the form of food, medicine, money and nursing. She devoted her time and money to helping others and donating in secret, according to Jewish values. She never told anyone about it, and never boasted of her gifts, so as not to shame or embarrass those whom she chose to benefit from her help. People who knew her in her short life were not stingy in their praise of Sheine Reisel the Angel, who would go among the poor people of the community and help them, without anyone knowing in what way or how much.

Isaac loved his daughter Bluma very much, as well as his firstborn son Haim, and his younger son Zvi, who was born about five years after Bluma. There was an active synagogue in the community, with educated and enlightened Rabbis. The Jewish youth belonged to traditional Zionist youth organizations that had been established in the town, among them HeHalutz, HaShomer HaTza'ir, Beitar and Mizrahi. Bluma did not go to any of them. The youth movements designated and directed the young people of the town to emigrate to the Land of Israel. Rabbi Tchernovich, the Rabbi of the town, the grandfather of the writer Yemima Tchernovich, issued a Zionist manifesto long before the first Zionist Congress in Basel was convened by Dr. Theodore Herzl.

Isaac used to pamper Bluma his daughter with fresh cream on the various kinds of berries from the bushes that grew on the fences of the house. My mother told me that her father almost never spoke, but when he did, his words gave her much warmth and devotion. She also emphasized his talents as a wise, shrewd and efficient man.

My mother told me that she kept the company of her mother as much as she could. She would help in the housework, sewing and assisting in the arrangements for her help to others. She often asked her mother: "But so-and-so should have repaid the "charity" you gave him, so why do you continue to give him more?" Her mother would reply: "Blumkeleh, where charity and help to others is concerned, one does not manage accounts like merchants. They will repay."

Between Bluma and her brothers there was a relationship of love, devotion and friendship. Haim turned out to be an exceptional student, and had registered to emigrate to the Land of Israel, where he was to study at the Ben Shemen Youth Village. Bluma was also an outstanding student. Her father rented a room in Grodno for her, so that she could study at the excellent Russian Gymnasium. Bluma went to live in Grodno and attended that school, where she managed to study for two years until the Nazi occupation, which caused her whole world to collapse when she was just sixteen and a half.

The brothers and sisters of her mother, Sheine Reisel, of the Horwitz family from the towns of Yizuri and Beklerova – Sam Horwitz, Shlomo Horwitz, Mendel and Fannie Horwitz, and her cousins of the Lipchek and Finsky families from Sopotzkyn – joined the millions of Jews from Eastern Europe who emigrated to the United States of America many years before the rise of the Nazis. The majority settled in Chicago and Wisconsin, where the climate is similar to that of the country of their birth.

Shlomo Horwitz settled in the city of Chicago, Illinois, where he established a Jewish bakery on Roosevelt Avenue. Mendel Horwitz, who eventually became blind, also arrived in Chicago, and from there continued on to California. He established a wholesale business in Los Angeles, where he sold tobacco, candy and cigarettes. After him, his only son, Herbert Horwitz, of blessed memory, built up the business into an empire. Fannie Horwitz went to live in Los Angeles. The members of the Isaac Lipchek family moved to the town of Burlington in Wisconsin, and there they raised a glorious family with many sons and daughters. Elaine Wayne, the daughter of Max Zeilin, was my mother's first cousin, and her eldest daughter Corky, was named after Grandmother Cona, of blessed memory, whom my mother saw, at age four, lying dead on the floor of her house before her burial, surrounded by memorial candles. This sight was engraved on Bluma's memory, and she repeatedly told me of it as her first memory. How sad that the element of death accompanied her throughout her life.

Before my mother's uncles of the Horwitz family of Beklarova, Poland, emigrated to Chicago IL, they faced a very cruel hurdle. The US immigration laws did not allow entry to family members of immigrants who were mentally defective.

Fruma Horwitz, Shlomo's daughter, and the sister of Ida, Anne, Philip and Isadore Horwitz, was unfortunately born retarded. Shlomo asked his sister, Sheine Reisel to agree to take Fruma into her home as she had not been allowed entry to America. With a broken heart and choked with tears, they told Sheine Reisel that they would cover her living expenses each month. They were certain that Sheine Reisel, my grandmother, was the most suitable and reliable person to look after Fruma. They hoped that one day the immigration laws would be softened, and would no longer condone such a terrible wrong as tearing a wretched soul from the bosom of her family.

Fruma was a few years older than Bluma. My grandfather was party to the agreement to keep Fruma with them. Bluma helped in looking after Fruma, she loved her, gave her attention and warmth, like a most devoted sister. She took her to participate in the meetings of the Jewish youth and other events. My mother told me that Fruma used to call Sheine Reisel "Mother", and Bluma "my sister". My mother kept her amused, she picked berries for her, sang to her, made her as happy as she could, with great sensitivity.

When letters came to Fruma from her parents and brothers in Chicago, Bluma would sit and read the contents to her again and again. At first Bluma's contact with Fruma was only when she came home for weekends from her studies in Grodno. Afterwards, the relationship grew closer. My mother risked her own life to conceal Fruma and save her from the Nazi oppressor.

It was the outstanding teacher Esther Shapira, of blessed memory, who taught Bluma Hebrew in Sopotzkyn. Esther was the sister of the Mizrahi movement's leader, Haim Shapira, of blessed memory, who eventually became the first Minister of the Interior in the State of Israel.

My mother spoke Yiddish, Hebrew, Russian and Polish fluently. She had a great talent for languages. It is amazing how, during the initial phase of her Alzheimer's disease, she spoke Russian with the nurses as far as she could. She avoided speaking Polish all her life, and endeavored not to speak with people who used that language. Both she and Hanan bore great anger in their hearts against the Polish people, aside from a few exceptions. In Yiddish she was fluent on an excellent literary level, with a fascinating ability to express herself. Hebrew also flowed easily for her. Her handwriting was very impressive.

My mother had many friends. Their relationship with her was that of sisters. The ones most dear to her were Bella Vinitzky (eventually – Pollak), who passed away in San Diego, California; Hassia Bornstein, who also came to Israel and became a member of the ultra-orthodox (Haredim); and Esther Yellin who remained in Warsaw, and was one of the major translators for the Red Army Commander who defeated Hitler, Marshal Georgy Konstantinovich Zhukov.

My mother made many friends, both male and female, in Sopotzkyn. She was a good listener, and with her great delicacy and good mind she acquired their love. Avraham Shadzonsky, Bella Pollak and Yehudit Goldman were her closest friends. In her social circle she impressed all those around her by her quiet, calm and sympathetic, loving and supporting attitude which never contained any kind of criticism.

Her parent's home and environment gave my mother a splendid education and culture. From her home she absorbed the love of books and learning and the aspiration for study and knowledge until, at the age of sixteen and a half, fate overtook her and her family and caused her to face intolerable ordeals.

Old marketplace where Bluma's and Hanan's were located

Old Jewish Cemetery Sopotzkyn   Jewish gravestone at Sopotzkyn Jewish Cemetery

New Russian Orthodox Church of Sopotzkyn –
built on ruins of Jewish Ghetto

RSHA, the Reich Security Head Office and the Wannsee Convention

The Reich Security Head Office was in charge of the security of the Third Reich, similar to the general security services that are customary in every country. This office was managed by Reinhard Heydrich, with entities such as the S.S., S.D, the Gestapo and others being subject to it.

The Jewish people everywhere, but especially in Europe, was declared by the Nazi platform to be the greatest enemy of the Third Reich. The Jews were inferior to the superior German Arian race. They were located within Germany and around its borders and constituted a danger to the existence and security of the Third Reich. Therefore, the only way to deal with them was – physical extermination. Since the aim of the Third Reich was to achieve "lebensraum" for the German people on European soil, the Jewish people had no place in this "living space" where they endangered the German Arian race.

This doctrine had been developing at all levels of the Nazi regime since the 1930s. Now, after Operation Barbarossa (the attack on the U.S.S.R. on June 22, 1941), due to the fact that the Third Reich's armies ruled all over Europe in places where the majority of the Jewish people were to be found, the time and the opportunity had come to execute the "final solution" – a physical extermination of the Jewish people.

So long as the Third Reich had not yet formulated an operational plan for the extermination of the Jews of Europe and of the entire area of German occupation (which eventually included Africa), there was still a glimmer of hope that the massive extermination would not be executed in the absence of a military presence, an operational plan and a toolbox for its implementation.

Bluma and her family, and millions more Jews, remained in their towns and villages, wearing the yellow patch, while the majority of them were concentrated in ghettos. After the Wehrmacht's conquest of all of Poland and large parts of Russia, Ukraine and the Baltic Republics, Heydrich, the commander of the Reich Security Head Office, requested Adolf Eichmann, head of Section IV B4, to set up a conference that would deal with implementation of the idea of the extermination of the Jewish people. The tragic fact was that the majority of European Jews were already under the control of the German occupation army in significant regions of Europe, especially in the east, so now the plan could be carried out.

On January 20, 1942, a conference was convened at the Wannsee Villa in Berlin, on the promenade of the Wannsee lake in south-western Berlin, at which executive coordination and decisions were made concerning the final solution of the Jewish problem who were a danger to the security of the Reich. The conference was attended by all the most nefarious entities of the Third Reich in the Security Head Office – the Gestapo, the S.S. and the S.D.

The decisions taken at the Wannsee Conference were operational. They directed the establishment of extermination camps on Polish soil, the purpose of which was the physical extermination of the entire Jewish people in Europe and in all areas occupied by the Wehrmacht forces. The killing would be performed by using Zyklon B gas and the bodies would be burned in crematoria in places that were camouflaged and hidden from view. Burning the bodies out of sight would constitute an effective solution, would save the effort of burial and would also destroy most of the evidence of genocide.

On September 1, 1939, Germany invaded Poland, but was not yet prepared for the encounter with Stalin's Russia in the east, where the Germans aspired to expand their "lebensraum". Poland was overrun by the Wehrmacht in three weeks, but Germany compromised with Russia under the Ribbentrop-Molotov Pact that was signed about one week after the conquest of Poland.

The agreement was essentially a non-aggression pact between Hitler's Third Reich and Stalin's U.S.S.R. In order not to waken the Russian bear from its slumber, although the whole of Poland had been occupied by the Germans, the Russians and Germans agreed on the division of Poland. The Red Army moved a little westward, while the German Wehrmacht retreated a little more to the west, and set up a government from the outskirts of Warsaw westward, which was called the General Government. This movement of the Red Army in a westerly direction saved Grodno, Sopotzkyn and the surrounding towns for 21 months, and left a large part of the cream of Jewry from September 1939 to June 1941 outside the control of the Third Reich's army.

At the time of the Wannsee Conference in January 1942, Germany controlled Warsaw, Lublin, Wroclaw, Lodz, Czestochowa, Katowice, and others. At the disposal of the executors and planners of the final solution stood the military and civilian government over the majority of the Polish people, among which, in the areas of the General Government, were also about two million and two hundred thousand Polish Jews. The Wohlin District was not yet under German control. In the districts of Bialystok, Wolin and Belorussia there were another one million Jews.

The final solution for the Jewish problem was designated to be carried out in extermination camps, the function of which was to annihilate the Jews in the General Government, to erect and operate the Treblinka, Majdanek and Sobibor camps. Treblinka was intended to exterminate the Jews of Warsaw. Majdanek was intended for the Jews of Lublin and its environs. Sobibor was to get rid of the Jews of Lvov in the West and Ukraine.

The majority of the decisions made at the Wannsee Conference from the aspect of the extermination of European Jewry – the "danger to the Third Reich" – focused on collecting, concentrating, deporting the Jews and operating the extermination camps with a minimum of manpower. For that purpose, it was decided that the Jews in the occupied areas under Wehrmacht control, would be uprooted and removed from their homes and property, and concentrated in Ghettos in the places where they lived. They were obligated to wear a yellow patch with the "Magen David", and their movements were limited to the Ghetto and its immediate vicinity. Men were permitted to move about in the adjacent area for the purpose of obtaining minimal financial means and a supply of food.

The Ghettos were operated under the auspices of the S.S. and the Gestapo, while "Judenräte" – Jewish Councils – were also established in the Ghetto for the purpose of liaison between the Nazi authorities and the Jewish population. The Judenräte received demands and orders from the German commanders, to whom they presented its own requests, to the extent they felt brave enough. The responses to these requests were often punishments and executions by firing squad for members of the Judenrat, in order to terrorize its members.

The crowning glory of achieving the goal of extermination was to bring the Jews of Europe to the Zyklon B gas chambers and, after killing them, to burn their bodies in crematoria in order to conceal the evidence of genocide.

The task of bringing the Jews to the camps was given to a special system of trains that were allocated for that purpose. The trains were equipped with freight carriages designated for carrying goods in bulk, animals and the like. The trains would arrive at the next place for concentrating the shipment, with orders to deport the human load on them to their destination, the designated extermination camp, regardless of the situation on the battlefronts and without any delay. The extermination of the Jews, the enemies of the Third Reich, must not be held back. It must be executed "in all military weathers".

The logistical trains system that supported the Wehrmacht over the long supply lines into Russia and Ukraine was not more important that the trains system of the RSHA – the Reich Security Head Office. Supreme preference was given to exterminate the Jewish people so as to achieve perfect execution of the decisions taken at the Wannsee Conference.

Even before a deportee was killed at the final destination, the gas chambers at the extermination camps, he had already been separated from his property and his home, and he was permitted to carry with him only a small bag containing clothes. The uprooting, separation from property, acquaintances and relatives into the cattle carriage that awaited him, constituted a road of no return for each and every one, among them Bluma, Sheine Reisel her mother, Zvi her younger brother, and Fruma Horwitz, even before their death at the final destination. People were erased from the basis of their existence.

At the Majdanek and Treblinka camps the pace of extermination reached about 20,000 Jews a day, but the "supply" to the furnaces dried up, since in the vicinity of Warsaw and Lublin lived nearly one million Jews.

The RSHA trains system had to be made more efficient if the maximum results of exterminating the Jews of Europe were to be achieved. Five million more Jews still remained to be exterminated, the major part of which were the Jews of East Poland in the Bialystok District, where the town of Sopotzkyn was situated, and many other well-established communities: the towns of Belorussia, the Baltic republics, the Ukraine, Hungary, Czechoslovakia, France, Holland, Greece, Italy and even North Africa. The system was also subject to developments on the various fronts.

On June 22, 1941, the lot fell. Germany violated the Ribbentrop-Molotov pact and commenced an all-out attack on the U.S.S.R. with three groups of united armies consisting of about three million soldiers. The day on which Operation Barbarossa commenced – Nazi Germany's attack on the U.S.S.R. – apart from being the day on which Bluma's fate was sealed, it also sealed the fate of another six million Jews to die, and eventually led to the fall of Hitler's Third Reich, since the major cause of that was the soldiers of the Red Army who fought heroically for their homes.

As soon as the German armies seized control of parts of European Russia, Ukraine and the northern front, in the direction of the Baltic states, the erection of the extermination camps of Majdanek, Treblinka, Sobibor, as well as the Auschwitz camp next to the town of Oswiecim, west of Krakow, could take place.

The Auschwitz camp was built in the south-east of Poland, near the town of Oswiecim, about half an hour's drive west of Krakow, and it was deliberately placed there. It was close to Hungary, Czechoslovakia and Ukraine, and one day's journey by train from Bialystok, a district where there was a large well-established Jewish population. At first only one crematorium was used for extermination purposes at the Auschwitz camp. At that camp, fit and "productive" Jews were sent to work for the needs of the German army, and professional Jews were transferred to military and civilian factories serving the German war effort.

The Germans understood that the depth of the Wehrmacht's penetration into Ukraine and Russia would enable them to exterminate the Jews of Poland, Ukraine, Hungary, Czechoslovakia , Romania, Bialystok District, Belorussia and the Baltic republic in the south-east of Poland massively and rapidly, from both the aspect of deportation via the RSHA rail system and the time at their disposal to complete their mission. The same went for the Jews of France, Belgium, Italy, Holland and the western front.

The Germans preferred the extermination of the European Jews to take place as much as possible on Polish soil, since the countries and regions close to Poland, to the south, west and east, contained the majority of the Continent's Jews. The Jewish population of Ukraine, the Baltic states, Czechoslovakia, Hungary, Holland and France were significant in the course of the extermination process.

The Auschwitz camp was surrounded by high electrified fences, watch towers, ditches and internal partition areas. Watchdogs were chained to posts and in passages, and projectors illuminated the camp at night. There was separation between men and women.

At places like Babi Yar, the Ponar forest in Lithuania and in dozens more places where there were no camps at the time of the German invasion during Operation Barbarossa, Jews were massacred by massive shootings in concealed places. The bodies of the murdered had to be buried in large mass graves, which forced the S.D. and "Einsatzgruppen", who performed this murderous work, to employ a great deal of manpower in digging and covering the mass graves.

The Nazi directors of the murder operations understood well that the work of shooting men, women and children would cause a conflict for the soldiers, between their education, that was based on the works of Schiller, Goethe and Bach, and the "values of the Third Reich", and might have an adverse effect on them.

This method was not efficient enough in their opinion, and did not promise the desired outcome. This use of shooting in mass graves in random places wherever the Wehrmacht arrived during their invasion into east Poland, Russia, Ukraine, and the Baltic states, could not assure the achievement of the Reich's goals and implementation of the decisions of the Wannsee Conference. Collection of intended victims was not methodical, it prevented the supervision by the Reich Security Head Office over the progress of the process to realize the goal, and left behind incriminating evidence.

Accordingly, the Reich Security Head Office decided to set up Ghettos in the towns which came under Wehrmacht control after the eastward invasion, into which all the Jews of the town were herded, while threatening the local populace that whoever concealed or supported the smuggling of Jews would pay with his life as well as that of his dear ones for that activity. The Jews were forced out of their homes and crowded together in the restricted area of the Ghettos, in which they had to conduct their existence and that of their families. The men were allowed to go out to work within the confines of the town, or the villages in the vicinity, to help in the operation of the local civilian administration, for which they received food and items of clothing from their employers in the towns and villages.

The Sopotzkyn Ghetto and the Murder of Bluma's Father and Brother

Since the town of Sopotzkyn was close to the armistice line under the Ribbentrop-Molotov agreement, it was one of the first to suffer from German air raids and artillery shells on the morning of June 22, 1941, the day on which Germany attacked the U.S.S.R. at the commencement of Operation Barbarossa.

The home of the Plaskovsky family, like dozens of other houses, was destroyed and burned. Both Jews and non-Jews of the town fled from their homes to the fields. Isaac Plaskovsky, Sheine Reisel, their three children and Fruma also fled to the fields to save their lives. When the raid ended they returned to their homes, where they discovered a horrific scene.

Hundreds of people lay dead and wounded in the yards of the houses, on the roads and sidewalks, bleeding, groaning and screaming with pain and crying for help. Some had lost limbs, parts of their faces were gone, all mixed up with body parts of horses, cows, sheep and chickens.

These terrible sounds and sights were accompanied by fires running wild all over the town, from which the smell of burned flesh reached their nostrils, of both people and the animals who had been kept in the yards of their homes, and were now burned and charred in the hellfire.

Up to the 22nd June 1941, Bluma had been just like any young girl aged sixteen and a half. A day or two before, she had come home full of the joy of life from the gymnasium where she had been studying in nearby Grodno, dreaming of a future full of happiness and promise, as a girl and young woman. Now she found herself at the bottom of hell, which continued to become deeper as time passed on and never stopped.

No more than a few hours passed and the Wehrmacht entered the town. The soldiers rounded up groups of residents, and employed them in collecting the body parts of people and animals and burying them or burning them, depending on their condition. The residents were also made to put out fires and repair damaged infrastructure, such as water pipes and telephone lines.

Many families, both Jews and Poles, remained with no roof over their heads. Their homes had burned down, and some not only lost their property, but also some of their loved ones. Bluma witnessed the events. She saw all the horrors and could not forget how she suffered with anxiety until she found her mother, Sheine Reisel, and afterwards the other members of her family in the surrounding wheat fields.

Dozens of families remained homeless. Some of the Poles moved to nearby villages in the region, where they had relations or acquaintances. The Jews had nowhere to go.

In Teholin Street in Sopotzkyn stands a church. Near it stands the Jewish synagogue, and next to that is the "Hekdesh". I find it necessary to explain to the reader the meaning of this word, the existence of which I heard for the first time when Bluma's experience with Alzheimer's disease started. The first time she began mentioning this term was when her condition deteriorated in 2006. It was the custom among the Jews of the small towns, whereby if a Jew was on the road in the evening or at night, and he was unable to continue on his journey until the next morning, this place would serve as a "motel" set up for him by the local community. Here he could sleep for the night, wash, make a cup of tea or coffee with some biscuits, and then he could go on his way the next morning. This Jewish "wayside inn", which was intended solely for Jews on their journeys, was called "Hekdesh". It was set aside by the local community for Jews who were on the road.

The Wehrmacht commander in the town ordered all the Jewish families who remained homeless to gather in the synagogue on Teholin Street and the Hekdesh close to it, on a very restricted area, so that they could lay down their heads under a roof to protect them from the rain and snow, in a place where they could prepare food and wash themselves. The Plaskovsky family had no choice. They occupied a small area in the Hekdesh on Teholin Street. From their home and its contents nothing remained. Subsequently, all the Jews of the town whose houses remained standing, were ordered to concentrate in the Hekdesh on Teholin Street, which became the Sopotzkyn Ghetto.

There was a doctor in the town, and in view of the number of wounded and sick he opened a clinic in the place. The clinic treated those whom it could help medically by the means that were available. At that time, Bluma understood that her studies close to the end of the second academic year at the Gymnasium had been cut short, and that together with the loss of their home and the disaster that had overtaken them, she must busy herself with something immediately. So she volunteered to help the doctor – bandaging wounds, spreading ointments to the extent they were available, changing bedclothes, sterilizing the doctor's instruments and many other ways to help in the clinic, and obtaining nutrition and types of food that could help the needy.

Not long afterward, the German military governor of Sopotzkyn advised the Jews of the town that they must all stay close to the synagogue and the Hekdesh in Teholin Street, and that the Third Reich had ordered them to wear the yellow patch on their sleeves with the Magen David, so that their identity should be visible for all to see. A Jew who was not wearing a yellow patch would be shot. This was the statistical method by which the Reich Security Head Office obtained the number of Jews to be borne to the slaughter.

Bluma and all Sopotzkyn Jews who had not been killed in the shelling and bombings, including Hanan and his family, lived in the Sopotzkyn Ghetto from now until the end of September 1942 – fifteen months. All the Jewish population that remained alive were held under guard in the Ghetto. At the same time, next to the town of Oswiecim in south Poland, the Germans began to erect the Auschwitz 2 Birkenau extermination camp.

The Germans enabled the men who could earn a living to go out to work in the vicinity, while they, as the military government, were interested in and obligated both regarding the logistical needs on the eastern front and fulfilling the needs of the population regarding basic products such as wheat, flour, water, electricity and other elementary needs. A number of weeks after opening the Ghetto it was transferred to the supervision of the S.S. Men who went out to work in the vicinity would return with products, necessary supplies, clothes and shoes, to the extent they could obtain them.

Bluma told me: "Yitzchak, a few weeks before evacuating the Ghetto and transferring those who remained there to Kielbasin, my father Isaac Plaskovsky and my elder brother Haim were taken to Bialystok prison". Sheine Reisel, Bluma, Zvi and Fruma never saw them again. Bluma told me that, from inquiries she made, it emerged that they had been killed in the Treblinka extermination camp, located about 111 km north – east of Warsaw, on the road from Warsaw in the direction of Bialystok.

The seventeen-and-a-half year old girl was left without her father and elder brother, her house had burned down, her relatives murdered, she was under guard by the S.S. and the Gestapo, and the campaign of fear, terror, pain, suffering and torture were only just beginning in September-October 1942.

Transfer to the Kielbasin Trenches

The Jews of Sopotzkyn and other towns at the north-eastern side of Poland in the district of Bialystok and White Russia, groaned under the life in the Ghetto and the fear of the unknown. At that time, subcontractors of the RSHA, under the command of Heinrich Himmler, the Gestapo Commander, were engaged in the erection of the largest camp for the extermination of humans in the world, Auschwitz 2, Birkenau, where four crematoria were to be operated in one place, as it was in the preceding camps: Treblinka, Majdanek, Sobibor and Auschwitz 1.

The RSHA was about to open the Birkenau extermination camp around the time of Bluma's eighteenth birthday, on January 15, 1943. The first victims designated for extermination were the Jews of Wolin from the Bialystok district, among them the Jewish community of Sopotzkyn.

In Sopotzkyn and other nearby towns where there was a Jewish population, there were no train stations, and the Wehrmacht and the RSHA were certainly not planning to build more railways and stations in each and every town.

In 1939, when the agreement on the division of Poland – the Ribbentrop-Molotov agreement – was signed, the Russians knew that the German army was only buying time to prepare itself thoroughly for an attack on Russia. The Russian high command understood that the contiguous area of Poland and White Russia was a critically strategic region for the German forces' future plan to move in the direction of Ukraine, Moscow, St. Petersburg and the Baltic States.

Not far from Grodno, at its southern corner, in the direction of the railroad's exit from Grodno and the road leading to Bialystok, there used to be a large tractor farm, called Kielbasin after its owner. The Russians decided to dig long, parallel ditches in that place, about ten meters wide, three meters deep, and 200 meters long. They would serve as a line of defense against a German armored attack.

While I was writing this book, it was absolutely clear to me that Kielbasin was the most shocking site in the history of the Jews of Grodno and the surrounding villages in the context of the extermination of the local Jewry and their transfer to Birkenau.

But although I examined many maps and other documents to find the location of this site, I could not find it. I was not happy with that. Seeing with one's own eyes is always better than hearing about it. Especially, with regard to the description and execution of the process of collecting and exterminating the "Jewish material" in the gas chambers and burning them in Birkenau's new crematoria. On my visit in October 2019, I inquired of the driver, Pavel, if he knew of the place called Kielbasin.

To my amazement, Pavel replied that he knew where the place was. It was a village or neighborhood which was then outside the town, remote and cut off from Grodno, on the south-western side, where the road and railway lead away from it to Bialystok.

Our American Jewish brother, Harold Gordon, born in Grodno, currently a resident of Salinas, California, who wrote the book "The Last Sunrise", testifies extensively about Kielbasin as an outstandingly cruel transit station for collecting all the Jews of the towns in the vicinity and the Jews of Grodno.

The driver Pavel and I arrived at Kielbasin, today on the outskirts of the town of Grodno, spreading over the hills east of the Neman river that crosses it on its way to the Baltic Sea. Kielbasin is currently a neighborhood on the south-western side of Grodno, on the slopes of the hills. At its center lies the main road from Grodno to Bialystok, and parallel to it, on the left, at a distance of half a mile, passes the railway from Grodno to Bialystok. The whole region from the road to the railway, on the left side, is populated with one-story homes. I explored around and found nothing.

Luckily, a very elderly Polish man emerged from one of the houses. By his appearance I could see that he was a local and, therefore, there was certainly a chance that he would know the location of the Kielbasin trenches. And I was right. The pleasant-faced man told me that, on the right-hand side of the road to Bialystok (not the left-hand side where we had explored), there was a memorial site, and that every year on May 9th, the day of the victory over Nazi Germany, a state ceremony is held there by the residents of the region. I was so happy, I embraced the Pole, and thanked him with a gift of money which surprised him.

Pavel drove to the place as the man had directed us. We crossed the main road from Grodno (today Belarus) to Bialystok in Poland. On the slopes of the hills under the trees, I saw remains of the trenches along them from the top of the slope to the bottom, looking like a grave before the gravestone is set, i.e. covered by a mound of earth about 20 cm high, the length of all the parallel ditches, with beautiful flowers growing on them, and wreaths laid on them.

On the top, southern part of the trenches, there is a large white memorial stone, on which, as was explained to me, the following was engraved in Russian: "So long as the heart beats, do not forget. Here were murdered by the Nazis fourteen thousand soldiers and civilians."

And who are the civilians who were murdered? Jews of Sopotzkyn and the nearby towns, who were brought to Kielbasin and thrown into the trenches in November-December 1942, before being deported for extermination. Jewish men, women, babies and old people, died of cold, hunger, disease and shootings, together with the bodies of the Red Army soldiers who had been murdered by drowning them by the Wehrmacht and the S.S. fifteen months earlier.

My father, Hanan, told me that, for him, those trenches in Kielbasin were the worst place of all. I have the feeling that his first wife and daughter (my stepsister), and perhaps also my Grandmother Dvora, did not survive the Kielbasin trenches. Here Bluma helped my father and his first wife, Yochi, and his daughter whose name I shall never know. That is the reason why my dear father, Hanan, who was a man of supreme moral values, decided to search for Bluma after the end of the war in Germany.

As part of their concealment plan, the Nazis hid the Jews who had been uprooted from Grodno and the surrounding towns outside the town in a secluded place, so that the population would know nothing of their deeds, and that they had uprooted the Jews from their homes. Concealment and suppression of evidence accompanied them every step of the way.

I feel compelled to shine a spotlight on Kielbasin. The Red Army soldiers were buried in Kielbasin in a mass grave, together with the Jews of the towns in the Wohlin district. Ten percent of these soldiers were Jews. Subsequently, the Red Army liberated Auschwitz and Birkenau, and saved five hundred thousand Jews from extermination. We must not forget that, and whoever leads Israel must not cease reminding the leaders of Russia of that fact. It is a pact between peoples. The bodies of murdered Jews lie on a bed of the Red Army soldiers who were taken prisoner and murdered.

In June 1941, in the first days of Operation Barbarossa, the soldiers of the Red Army had fled from their trenches to escape air bombings. The trenches were seized by the Wehrmacht and eventually served them for drowning about ten thousand Russian soldiers who had been taken prisoner, and were brought there to be drowned.

The RSHA decided that the Kielbasin trenches would be the place closest to the Grodno railway station where all the Jews from the Jewish towns in the vicinity would be concentrated until their evacuation to the Grodno Ghetto, in accordance with the operational plan. From Ghetto Grodno, each town, one or two a week, would be deported for extermination upon the inauguration of the Birkenau camp. I learned of the Kielbasin trenches both from my mother, and mainly from my father, who described to me the horrors that took place there. For him, Kielbasin was the worst of all, since due to the essential nature of his profession for the S.S. officers, he was at Auschwitz for only very few days, so Kielbasin had been engraved on his memory as the greatest atrocity. This was understandable. At Kielbasin whole families lived in open graves in the earth, in the winter of eastern Poland, in the rain and snow, with only branches of trees for a roof.

At the beginning of October 1942, all the Jews who lived in the Sopotzkyn Ghetto were ordered to pack their personal belongings in sheets, and the Wehrmacht put at their disposal carts with horses taken from the farmers of the town and villages in the region. Two or three families were put on each cart, and the horses drew the carts with the people on them to Kielbasin. The days were very cold and snow fell from time to time.

Each town brought to Kielbasin was designated one trench. When the carts arrived, they were placed so that their rear faced the trench. The deportees were ordered to throw their belongings into the trench, and after they had done so the horses were pulled back and the people were thrown like inanimate objects onto the layer of their belongings that lined the floor of the trench.

Into these trenches were thrown more than two thousand of the Jews of Sopotzkyn who had survived the bombings of June 22, 1941. They were forced to construct platforms for themselves on which to lie down, to enable people to pass along the trenches, to build a roof of branches in order to protect themselves somewhat from the snow and rain, and to enable the heating of food and water on oil stoves for those who had them.

The Germans permitted professionals in essential jobs to go out to work. My father told me that he was allowed to go out, because in the Ghetto he had served the Wehrmacht officers as maintenance man for the flour mills on the Wilchinsky estate, which owned the mills. My father had served as mechanic and was responsible for repairs there even in the days of the Sopotzkyn Ghetto, which had just ceased to exist, due to the evacuation of all the Jews of the town to the Kielbasin trenches.

Bluma told me after Hanan's death that my father's first wife, Yochi Umansky, of blessed memory, had died in the Kielbasin trenches, together with her two-year-old daughter, may God avenge them. My mother often told me that her younger brother, Zvi, who was 10 or 11 years old at that time, became very sick there. Sheine Reisel, his mother, held his head on her knees, and did everything she could to provide him with a little warmth and softness in those horrific conditions of cold, darkness, starvation, mold and damp.

Bluma undertook to take care of the needs of Fruma Horwitz in the trenches. She volunteered to work in her place, and even saved food from her own mouth in order to keep Fruma alive.

Afterwards I understood that there had been an agreement between my parents, that my brother Emanuel and I would not know that my father had been married and had a daughter, as long as he lived. I put together a few facts that I had heard from both my father and my mother, and I understood that, due to my father being allowed to work outside, he made sure to bring them supplies of food, medicines, cleaning materials, shoes and anything else that could help to maintain human life. I understood that Bluma was of great help to my father's wife, Yochi, and his little daughter while he was away at work, and that the very fact of his work was also good for Bluma, Fruma, Sheine Reisel and her son Zvi.

In the Kielbasin trenches, many died of cold, hunger, weakness and mold. My father said not once that, comparing the stone buildings of Auschwitz with Kielbasin was like comparing hotel rooms with pig sties.

For three months in the winter of 1942 the Jews of Sopotzkyn were buried in the Kielbasin trenches. Some succeeded in burning lanterns at night, some managed to obtain another piece of clothing or other object from a person who had died, in order to ease their suffering from the cold and hunger.

My younger brother Emanuel David Borowsky has been a resident and citizen of the U.S. since 1977, and lives in California. About ten years ago he studied mathematics in the city of Salinas, CA, the home town of one of the greatest American authors, John Steinbeck. My brother told me that, one day, he bought a car from an American priest, who told him that the garage where the car had been serviced was owned by a nice Jewish man, born in Poland, who had survived the Holocaust.

My brother approached the man, and it turned out that the name of this dear Jew was Harold Gordon. Mr. Gordon had been born in 1931 in the town of Grodno, had survived the Holocaust and had described his memoirs in the book "The Last Sunrise", I mentioned earlier.

Mr. Gordon sent me his book, in which a number of chapters describe the Grodno Ghetto and the affair of the Kielbasin trenches, where whole Jewish towns were sent to live before extermination. In his book he says that every week, about two thousand Jews were collected for extermination at Kielbasin and the Grodno Ghetto. It must be remembered that Mr. Gordon was describing his memories of when he was 11-13 years old.

The inauguration of the Birkenau extermination camp was approaching. At the beginning of 1943, all of the Sopotzkyn Jews who remained alive in Kielbasin were transferred to the Grodno Ghetto, which had been set up in the central synagogue of Grodno and the adjacent yard. The murderous S.S. officer, Kurt Weise, was the commander of this Ghetto. The extermination of the Jews of Sopotzkyn was about to begin, and would be integrated with the planning and execution of the Wannsee Conference.

The three attached photos are of the Kielbasin site. It is a tract of land located on the slopes of the hills south-west of Grodno, close to the road leading to Bialystok and the railroad leading to the south-west of Poland.

These miserable people made all possible kinds of protection against the rain and snow out of branches, fabrics and wooden supports. Sopotzkyn – the community of Bluma and Hanan – had been sent to one of the Kielbasin trenches in November 1942.

Many Jews, women, old people and children, died there of cold and starvation. S.S. Officer Karl Rinsler, the murderer from Romania, who was the Commandant of the place, also personally shot many of them. In these trenches, were also my grandmother Dvora Borowsky, my aunts Rachel and Leah, my uncle Shemaryahu, Zvi, my father's first wife, Yochi and their little two-year-old daughter, whose name I shall never know.

When the time came for the Jews of Sopotzkyn to be deported for extermination at Birkenau, they were transferred at the beginning of 1943 to the Grodno Ghetto in the synagogue yard. From there they were taken about 10 days later by train on the Grodno-Birkenau line about 500 km to the south-west.

When I visited the place, I found the remains of the trenches along the slope, under trees and flowers; wreaths of flowers decorated the mounds of earth covering the trenches. On the higher ground stands a large stone memorial.

Kielbasin Black Stone Memorial – Stalag 324 (Prisoners Camp

Underneath the green grass was one of the trenches in which
Russian soldiers and Jews were buried

Memorial at Kielbasin saying:
People, as long as hearts beat, don't forget

Ghetto Grodno

Seventeen kilometers south-east of Sopotzkyn lies the city of Grodno, called Horodna in Russian. The city is divided in two by the river Neman, with its bridges and fortress. In the past, the city was the ancient capital of Lithuania. It was annexed to Poland in the period of Poland's independence after World War I, when it was governed by General Jozef Pilsudsky. The city is currently located in the western part of Belarus at the junction of the Polish and Lithuanian borders.

This city, apart from being a beautiful place, surrounded by lakes and forests, served as a Jewish center, rich in culture and knowledge, glorious Yeshivot, leading, educated and learned Rabbis, and a variety of Zionist movements, whose aim was Zionism, preparing and training Jewish youth in the city and surrounding towns to emigrate to the Land of Israel.

From the town of Sopotzkyn and the surrounding towns and villages where there were lively and developed Jewish communities, there were bus lines to Grodno, and there was also a railway station. One of the leading sons of the new State of Israel, Yigal Alon, of blessed memory, Commander of the Palmach, which established the country's present borders, was the son of parents who came from Grodno.

In Grodno there was a general hospital and a maternity hospital, and the majority of the Jews of the region, although living in neighboring towns, entered this world via the Grodno maternity hospital, among them both my mother, Bluma, and my father, Hanan.

The city also boasted a beautiful synagogue and a Jewish community famed for the cultural and educational standard of its Jews, who were known as "Litvaks". The religious and observant Jews lived in friendship and brotherhood with their neighbors.

The German forces in Russia had already suffered a number of defeats, among them at Stalingrad. While they were occupied with battles with the Red Army, the RSHA was also busy with implementing the "Final Solution" program and completing the Birkenau extermination camp towards its opening in January 1943. The region of the communities around Grodno, which was outside the General Government, under the command of Otto Frank in Poland, was the target for immediate extermination, the method being – from the outside, inward to the center: the remoter places first, the nearer ones at the end.

At the beginning of January 1943, just prior to the inauguration of the Birkenau camp, the decision was taken in the offices of the RSHA to concentrate all the Jews of Grodno and the surrounding towns in two ghettos in Grodno, which would serve as launching stations for the "Jewish cargo" to Birkenau: one ghetto for non-productive Jews, under the S.S. commander Otto Streblau, and the other, in the synagogue building, for productive Jews, from some of whom it was still possible to derive some benefit before killing them (see the letter below from Dr. Suzan Urban, Director of the Archives at Bad Arolsen).

The "productive" Jews were brought to the Ghetto in the synagogue from Grodno and the vicinity, whose commander was the S.S. officer Kurt Weise, a cruel, two-legged animal of a man. They had been taken out of the Keilbasin trenches and had been transferred to the command of the murderer Kurt Weise in November 1942, to be held there until the arrival of the RSHA's cattle train which was to transport them for extermination in Birkenau.

Old men and women, women, children and handicapped persons were thrown on to the floor of the synagogue. Some of them were already in critical condition after the damage caused by hunger and cold which they brought with them from the Keilbasin trenches. It was desperately cold. The little food that was supplied or brought in by the men who were allowed to go to work was snatched up by the starving people, who engaged in "catch as catch can".

When anyone disturbed Kurt Weise by his screams, weeping, pain or hunger and was unable to curb his emotions, Weise would walk among these miserable people and shoot them in the mouth, causing parts of their brains to be splattered all over the synagogue floor.

Bluma, her mother Sheine Reisel, her brother Zvi and Fruma Horwitz, saw untold times a day how the Satan Kurt Weise would shoot his pistol into people's mouths or heads or beat them murderously with whips, causing some to lose control so that they defecated and urinated on themselves and the floor of the synagogue, while into that excrement on the synagogue floor in Grodno fell the bodies of the people who had been shot, and lay bleeding in the faeces and urine.

Bluma, her mother Sheine Reisel, her brother Zvi and her cousin Fruma Horwitz, together with another 2,050 Jews of Sopotzkyn, were loaded at the Grodno railway station onto the freight train for the planned destination where "Work sets you free" – the Auschwitz 2 Birkenau extermination camp. Behind them they could see the corpses of children, the elderly, the sick, lying in urine and excrement on the floor of the Grodno synagogue.

The Jews of Sopotzkyn stayed in the Grodno Ghetto for a very short time. The Ghetto "accommodated" many other towns which had been evacuated from the Keilbasin trenches, in accordance with the pace of the freight trains provided by the RSHA for that task. The "operation" of the Grodno Ghetto for the purpose of transferring the Jews of the Grodno district and the surrounding Jewish towns for extermination lasted a very short time, since in the second half of 1943, the first Belorussian front of the Red Army caused the Wehrmacht to collapse in that arena. However, unfortunately for the Jews of the region, it was too late – they were already in the hands of the RSHA.

Inside the synagogue of Grodno, which not long ago had been the shining home of the cream of Jewish communities, whose youth had all studied and spoken Hebrew, the achievements of the human spirit became in a moment submerged in the mire of other two-legged souls. Good and bad lie among theapes, who rose and emerged into the world from the family of the primitive mammals. As written by F. Schiller in "Ode to Joy", adopted by Beethoven as the final movement in his Ninth Symphony: <u>"All the good and all the evil drink at Mother Nature's breast"</u>. In the Creator's universe, alongside the giants of the spirit and of the heart, two-legged human animals also exist, the majority of whom are or aspire to be the rulers. For the thinking reader, it is demonstrable that all the great murderers in the history of humanity came to power from a satellite country – Alexander of Macedonia, Napoleon, Hitler and Stalin. Whoever seizes power in the parent country, from the satellite country, is a murderer. The evidence shows that Kurt Weise the murderer also found an outlet for his murderous tendencies by serving the Reich in north-eastern Poland.

In Grodno, Bluma had been living, up to about eighteen months ago, as an outstanding student at the Russian Gymnasium, in an apartment rented by her father, holding in her soul the same hopes, joy, optimism and rosy dreams as every 16-year-old girl. She had a warm and rich home. Her mother's relatives had established themselves in Chicago. She spoke fluent Hebrew. Her road to the top was well-paved.

All the human values accumulated by Bluma from her home, her glorious community, her studies and education evaporated after the horrors of the conquest of the town, and once again in Keilbasin, and now by the animal Kurt Weise, who joined the S.S. in order to find an outlet for the bestial soul within him, before sending the Jews from the Grodno synagogue in January 1943 for physical extermination. Brilliant minds and wonderful souls were cruelly murdered by shots to their mouths from the pistol of Kurt Weise.

My father, Hanan Borowsky, of blessed memory, who was a reliable witness for the German authorities' legal inquiry under the Nazis and Nazi Collaborators Punishment Law, also testified against Karl Rinzler, the commander of Kielbasin. He was sentenced to life imprisonment by the German court at Cologne, which was very lenient.

Entrance to Grodno Ghetto behind the Synagogue

Memorial Plaque saying: 29 Thousa
Jews from the Grodno Ghetto were
taken to their death

My visit to the Sukka of Grodno's Synagogue

Grodno Synagogue's Entrance

Grodno's Synagogue in which premises Ghetto Grodno was located

Grodno Synagogue's beautiful interior

Deportation to Birkenau

Three days after her eighteenth birthday, on January 18, 1943, Bluma and her mother Sheine Reisel, her brother Zvi and her cousin Fruma Horwitz, were loaded onto the freight train waiting at the Grodno railway station. With them on the train were 2,050 Jews of the town who had survived the bombardment on June 22, 1941, after the executions and deaths in the Sopotzkyn Ghetto, at Keilbasin and in the Grodno Ghetto.

The normal understanding of a reasonable passenger train is that the carriages are built to comfortably carry twenty-five to thirty people. There are toilets, and the best trains also have a buffet and restaurant.

In the freight trains there are no seats and no toilets. About one hundred persons are crammed into each carriage like sardines. If an elderly or handicapped person needs to sit or be supported, he depends on the mercy of the other crammed people. Everyone gets into the carriage with his small bag, in which there is usually a coat, shoes, a change of underwear and socks, for protection against the extreme cold. Some have a few gold and silver coins, in which they naively place the remnants of a tiny hope to survive in a time of distress.

When the carriage has been filled to bursting, the guards close and lock and bolt the doors from the outside, and the rolling dungeon is ready to move. The carriage has no windows like a regular passenger carriage. If you were lucky, you found yourself on a carriage with a small hatch, or with spaces in the walls, enabling you to breath to a limited extent.

The Germans counted the people loaded onto the trains for their statistical needs. Their aim was to examine subsequently the success of the "final solution" and capacity vs. planning.

The destination of the RSHA train was the Birkenau camp near Auschwitz, about 500 km south of Grodno. It did not travel continuously, but kept stopping to make way for the military trains on the railroad, which were bringing supplies to the extended Wehrmacht forces. The German High Command was slowly beginning to understand that the soldiers of Ivan the Terrible were physically and emotionally strong and were anything but pampered, and that they and the German armies, who were used to comfort, were not similarly resistant.

The train keeps stopping, and people are defecating and urinating in the carriages. The stink and fumes rise sky-high. The cold is biting, although the crowding helps a little. Every half day or day the guard soldiers throw the "precious cargo" a few loaves of bread into the carriage. Those who succeed in getting their hands on a loaf – eat, and those who are unsuccessful – remain hungry. Those who managed to smuggle some food, or a few apples, into the carriage in their bags, have done themselves a favor.

If that were not enough, it is not possible to shower or maintain personal hygiene in the carriage. The stink and foul odors from the excrement which is uncontrollable beat down the soul and the nostrils with full force. There is no separation in the carriage between men and women – they are all together. After four days on the railway, the train slowly enters, with the men, women and children inside it, exhausted, starving, in pain, sick and dead, in a stinking mire, to the platform where "Work sets you free" – the Birkenau extermination camp. They do not know it, but the execution would take place in a matter of a few hours. There would be no verdict, no appeal, no pardon. The sentence: You are guilty of being born a Jew. That was the decision of the Third Reich, which had passed the planning thereof on to the Wannsee Conference. The entire Reich would be "clean" of Jews – Judenrein.

Arrival at Birkenau

The sky is dark and grey, and the guards of the S.S. and the Gestapo open the screeching bars, and order the people to exit the carriages. Some can still go out under their own steam, some fall onto the concrete platform, the muscles of their legs cramped and frozen. Some are taken out and laid on the cold surface. Many corpses are removed from some of the carriages.

The human cargo that arrived at the platform – the Jews of Sopotzkyn – did not know that the camp management was in need of workers at its inauguration, who would perform various jobs as prisoners. A people like the Germans would never employ soldiers, graduates of the high schools in Hamburg, Berlin, Leipzig and Heidelberg, in the jobs to be carried out in this large new facility. They would suffer emotional collapse. Those who were to perform this dirty work were the men and women of the cargo itself, and they would be supervised by the older S.S. and Gestapo personnel, who had a sufficient measure of evil and cruelty to deal with the murderous job imposed on them by the Third Reich by means of the RSHA.

The medical committee of Dr. Josef Mengele and his henchmen convened on the platform of the train bringing the Jews for extermination at Birkenau. Upon unloading the miserable human "cargo", the Jews, "the enemies of the Third Reich", were ordered to lay down their little bags onto the platform, and the S.S. and Gestapo personnel, Jewish men and women prisoners under the orders of the Gestapo or the S.S., would collect them from the women and men, who had been separated, the children being with the women, in order to transfer the loot to the possession of the Third Reich. Those who brought with them gold, silver and jewelry were separated from them forever. They would never purchase with them any momentary alleviation from their fate.

Dr. Mengele's "Objective Medical Committee" had nothing to do with medicine. The majority of the people sent to the gas chambers, who had been healthy before the June 22, 1941 Operation Barbarossa, or before setting foot on the Birkenau platform, were set to work – and worked very hard.

The aim of the "medicine" applied by Dr. Mengele and his henchmen was for the needs dictated by the camp command, in order to fill the quotas required as an auxiliary force from among the potential victims. They would be employed in collecting the spoils, the clothing, gold, money, hair, shoes, the human ash which was used to manufacture soap, and other needs of the Wehrmacht, such as inserting bullets into machine-gun belts, or other accessories for the Wehrmacht soldiers. They were also employed in filling quotas as "guinea pigs" for experiments conducted in the Waffen S.S laboratories. The purpose of these experiments was to create effective vaccinations for the Wehrmacht soldiers on the one hand, and chemical and biological warfare against enemy soldiers on the other.

The quotas were set beforehand by the camp command and management, and as soon as they were filled, there was no more medicine. Accordingly, those who were selected for work were usually the youngest and strongest.

Those appearing before the medical committees were completely naked. Dr. Mengele and his assistants would examine the fitness of the men and women for work, and whether they were in a condition in which the Third Reich could derive any benefit from them as auxiliary personnel in operating the extermination in the camp. Dr. Mengele would personally decide the fate of each one – who should live and who should die. To the left – death, to the right – commando (work group). Those who were not chosen to work were transferred directly to the gas chambers to die. From the death chambers the corpses were transferred to one of the four crematoria in the largest extermination camp erected by the German people, who murdered and burned the bodies of the millions of Jews who were taken there.

Some of those examined by the medical committee were taken directly to Block 10. There human experiments were conducted in order to test chemical substances, bacteria and scientific theses, such as the "Mengele twins" experiments, and more. The experiments were conducted by a unit of the Waffen S.S. which was responsible for manufacturing biological weapons and biological defense for the Wehrmacht combat soldiers.

Initial selection was made on the platform by Dr. Josef Mengele and the doctors who accompanied him. Elderly persons, children and the disabled, according to their appearance and other criteria, were sent immediately for extermination in the gas chambers and from there to the crematoria. People whom the doctors considered had potential for productive work, both men and women, were ordered to remove their clothes and to stand in the fierce cold naked as the day they were born so that the doctors could examine them. Sheine Reisel, Zvi and Fruma Horwitz were sent to the gas chambers within less than one hour after they got off the train. Bluma remained bereft of her family, on the platform in Birkenau, the largest slaughterhouse in human history.

Bluma's standing naked on the freezing platform in Birkenau on January 23, 1943 was the most seriously horrific and monstrous moment which a human being could be required to face emotionally.

She had lost everything dear to her in the world: her parents, her brother and cousin, her home had burnt down and there was nothing she could see but God's dark sky above her, her heart turning to stone because of the pain, the freezing cold, the growling and distressing hunger and the brain of an eighteen-year-old girl who felt that her life, her emotions and her mind were in the deepest hell flooded with boiling lava. The brutal cold and the gloomy sky at least enabled her to breath.

Her dear parents, wonderful and beloved brothers, and sweet Fruma, the warm Jewish home, the education, values, strawberries and cream which her father Isaac used to give her – all evaporated, as if they had never been, erased and gone from her life. Her internal and external world was destroyed, and what hope did she have in that situation?

As if turned to stone, Bluma stood naked before Dr. Mengele, and he decided that she would join the Women's Commando 105, which engaged in the hard work of demolishing buildings with wooden rams and clearing mud from ditches. That was the "Blue Kerchief" women's commando.

In the dark of night the horrors could be faced emotionally. In the daytime no feelings must be shown to anyone. One had to remain stone-faced. To think. To think. "Everything I had been educated to believe was as if it had never been. The existence of the world of which I had been taught was a daydream."

We are dealing with a shocking and blood-curdling moment for any human being, and I often asked myself how I would have responded or how another person would have reacted to these calamities raining down on him at the start of his life, on the threshold of adulthood. The most certain replies of people to that question was – I would have burst into bitter weeping, I would have attempted suicide, I would have impulsively given way to a towering rage.

However, in everything bad there is some good. If Bluma had stood weeping on the platform in front of the S.S. guards, the Gestapo and Dr. Mengele, they would have shot her on the spot or they would have completed the extermination of the entire Plaskovsky family in the gas chambers. She did not weep – she defeated them by her restraint and intelligence in controlling her emotions, but at a very heavy price. She defeated them and survived, but suffered serious post trauma – a condition of which nobody was aware, nor of the extent of the damage it causes.

Bluma had already learned, in September 1939, and during the first bombardment of Sopotzkyn on June 22, 1941, in the Spotzkin Ghetto, in Kielbasin and in the Grodno Ghetto, what was happening under God's heaven, and her senses were blunted and she turned to stone. This tempering, the result of her experience of the phases of the horrors, which she had accumulated by the time she arrived on the platform in Birkenau, saved her life. The only issues that affected her emotionally in her subsequent life were her husband, her children, her grandchildren, her home, her relatives in the U.S. and Mexico, and education.

Contrary to the opinion of millions, numbers were tattooed only on the arms of those miserable prisoners selected for hard labor in the camp and in the vicinity. The tattoos were made by searing the flesh of the left forearm

with hot blue ink. Those who were killed were not tattooed. The S.S. calculated their number by subtracting the number of labor prisoners from the
total of the prisoners who had been loaded onto the trains.

After the number had been tattooed onto the left forearm the prisoners, still
naked, had their heads shaved. The women and girls remained bald, thus totally humiliating those who were "privileged" to continue living. After shaving
their heads, the prisoners were disinfected and provided with the uniform of
the labor prisoners camp, i.e. black and grey striped tunics. The labor prisoners
were sorted into groups and blocks, each group being given an "Arbeit Kom-
mando" number, and they were distinguished by the color of their head scarf.

Bluma is given the prisoner's uniform, her coal black hair is shaved, the
number 31119 is seared onto her left forearm. Under the number there is a
triangle pointing downwards, indicating that she is Jewish. [8]

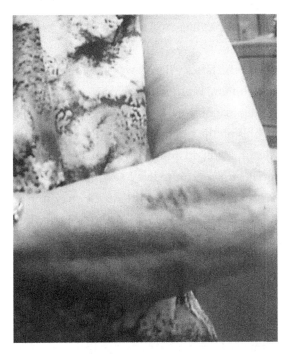

Prisoner Number 31119
The reader can find an explanation to the number
in Dr Susanne Urban's letter attached below in this book

8 A triangle pointing upwards indicates a gypsy.

A Structural Description of Birkenau

On October 15, 2019 I realized my ambition, prior to publishing this book, of standing on my own feet and seeing with my own eyes the hellish Nazi sites relating to my parents and relatives. I reached the conclusion that "seeing once is preferable to verbal testimony". I went to see the Ghettos at Grodno, Sopotzkyn and Keilbasin, and the railroad leading from Grodno to Auschwitz Birkenau.

I took a taxi from the hotel where I was staying to Auschwitz Birkenau. The weather was good and on the way we drove westward across the broad Vistula River passing just outside Kracow. We continued along the winding road, close to the hills on the right, crowded with villages, in the direction of the town of Oswiecim. After 40 minutes we came to an enormous plaza, with hundreds of tourist busses. To the left I saw the gate with the sign "Work sets you free" over it at the entrance to the Auschwitz camp and the museum there. Directly to the west I saw the famous building at the entrance of the Birkenau camp, a low stone building with a tower rising from its center and the railroad passing underneath. On these railways and in their close vicinity the murder of about one and half million persons was committed in the camp which, only when you enter it can you understand how sophisticated was its construction and preparation.

The whole complex known as Auschwitz Birkenau is located within a forest, north of which are the hills leading in the direction of Upper Silesia east of Oswiecim, to the left – the continuation of the forest, and to the south there are forests and Polish villages. A considerable part of the forest was cut down. The entire area of the old Auschwitz and the new camp Birkenau lies on flat level land.

The railway lines carrying the victims to extermination led through the building with the tower at its center into the camp. The trains arrived from the south to the west – from Kracow Oswiecim west. About one hundred and fifty meters along the railway beyond the tower inside, the edges were at the same height, but deeper in the direction of south they rose to very low platforms.

At the right-hand side of the railway to the north was the labor camp of the male prisoners. To the south was the labor camp of the female prisoners. Today, the men's camp is fenced off, and almost all its houses are built of red bricks, where the prisoners lived. On the other hand, the women's camp remains as it was, the majority of the barracks are whole, and are even undergoing renovation and maintenance.

The rows of buildings in which the male and female labor prisoners lived were numbered, beginning from the east to the west.

Bluma was most of the time in block 25, which I found, with the original two-storey wooden bunks on which the prisoners slept. Block 25 is in the last row to the west, in the left-hand southern corner.

Behind the row of block 25 is the largest slaughterhouse ever built by two-legged creatures. I shall describe it to you as I saw it and understood the planning that went into its construction.

There is a large building there, into which were brought those being led to the slaughter. Alongside the building is a trench about two meters deep, known as "the tube" (Schlauch in German). Anyone standing inside the trench could not be seen from outside it.

In the large building, the intended victims had to leave their clothes and belongings, remaining completely naked – children, women and babies. They were sent into the trench, which had no roof over it, and led directly to the gas chambers located about 60 meters to the west, and some were just a short distance from the last row of barracks in the women's camp.

The human material led naked into the gas chambers was killed there within a few minutes. The bodies were taken for burning in the four crematoria located adjacent to the gas chambers. The crematoria, the gas chambers, the trench and the building where they left their clothes were designed to dispose of the victims when they were naked as the day they were born. All clothes, property or belongings had been collected previously for the benefit of the German people.

The entire extermination and killing area was outside the labor prisoners' camps, to the west, on the edge of the forest, which was left to grow naturally. The extermination area was hidden by the forest to the west and south, and by the men's prison camp from its north to its east. No person wandering around the area could see or know what was going on there. Everything was concealed and camouflaged.

In the erection and location of the extermination camp, those executing the "final solution" had aimed at reaching the highest effectiveness possible. Their goal was the extermination of the Jews of Hungary, Czechoslovakia, France, Bulgaria, Greece, Holland, and Poland as quickly as possible, in large masses and without leaving any traces, such as human belongings and corpses.

Contrary to the shooting murders committed in Russia, Ukraine, White Russia and Lithuania, where the local population could see what was happening, here they made efforts to conceal it as far as possible. At Auschwitz the murder was planned to take place together with camouflage and robbery, and the destruction of all evidence.

Bluma, the daughter of Isaac and Sheine Reisel, of blessed memory, saw and was present at the murders both by the previous method (shooting) at the Grodno Ghetto and at Keilbasin, and the more advanced method (gas and cremation) at Birkenau.

Together with all the other Jews of Sopotzkyn, Sheine Reisel, Zvi and Fruma were killed on the day of their arrival by the new method. Those who bore the numbers on their left arm were only those men and women who were chosen to serve as labor prisoners. Those who were killed immediately were not counted or tattooed.

When she began to open her heart to me in 2000, and told me of the odor of the burning flesh of our people arising from the crematorium throughout the operation of the Birkenau extermination camp, I believed her, but I could not imagine the monstrosity of it all. Now that I saw with my own eyes that block 25 in the women's camp at Birkenau was located right next to the gas chambers and the crematoria, I totally understood the horror and the magnitude of her trauma and that of the other prisoners who were with her.

Survival in Birkenau from January 18, 1943 to January 18, 1945

Bluma was set to work in the Women's Commando 105, the "blue scarves", designated for hard labor at the edge of the camp, and sometimes outside it. Women's Commando 105 was housed at first in Block 25, and was subsequently moved to Block 6. They had to do the hardest work of all.

The blocks were built of stone, with wooden bunks stacked one above the other, and they served as the living quarters of the hard labor prisoners. There they lay when they returned from their work, hungry and shivering from the cold. One of the ways for the girls to fight the cold and frost in these blocks was by lying huddled together.

The work of the Women's Commando 105 was the hardest of all. This group of young girls was engaged in removing mud from waterways and puddles, and in demolishing buildings in order to expand the area of the camp in what was called the "Canada Area". The plan was to erect additional buildings there, and perhaps more gas chambers and crematoria to increase the pace of the extermination and cremation.

Another women's commando had to remove gold teeth from the mouths of the dead bodies before they were burned in the crematoria. Each commando group was supervised by male or female S.S. officers.

Other groups were employed in various lighter jobs inside the buildings – washing prisoners' clothes, inserting bullets into machine-gun belts for the Wehrmacht, or filling kits of other equipment for German Army units.

There were groups employed in the kitchens and in distributing the meagre bread ration to the blocks, and collecting the clothes and shoes of the victims.

The Birkenau camp was surrounded by electrified barbed-wire fences, with guard towers every few dozen meters. Electrified barbed-wire fences separated the men's camp from the women's camp. In other places within the camp there were electrified barbed-wire fences, barricades, guard dogs and projectors which illuminated the camp all night.

On the next few pages, a number of photographs are presented to the reader. They were taken by the Red Army when they entered Birkenau in January 1945, and describe what they saw. "Yitzchak" Bluma would sit and tell me when we met, the two of us, in the kitchen of her home, "that is the easy part of the horrors. What is shown today to visitors by the government of Poland is after the place had been renovated."

Not every girl who became a labor prisoner with a number tattooed on her arm and a scarf on her head worked in closed buildings. Women's Commando 105 was employed at hard labor – demolishing buildings, breaking stones and removing mud from waterways and puddles in and around the camp. The mud was loaded onto wagons which were pushed by the prisoners to the place where they were to be emptied. In addition, from time to time, Women's Commando 105 went out to abandoned Polish villages in the region, with orders to flatten them to the ground for various reasons decided by the exterminators.

Each morning they would get up early at four o'clock before going out to work. This was called by the Nazi jailers "Zahlappel", or "roll call". The purpose was to ensure that no one had disappeared or was missing, whether because she was sick or for any other reason. The immediate result of a prisoner's absence from the roll call was severe punishment, whether for her in person or for the whole group.

After roll call, a large pot with opaque hot water was brought in. Each of the prisoners, whether or not she had managed to obtain some container, endeavored to get a little of the hot water to drink as morning "coffee" before leaving for work. Other prisoners distributed half a slice of bread with jam or sausage. This meagre ration of calories together with the turbid hot water was supposed to provide the energy for the hard labor. Then the gates and fences were opened for the prisoners who were marched out in rows of five.

The group was accompanied by male and female S.S. guards, all bearing weapons and equipped with rubber truncheons. These were in constant use from morning to night, when the prisoners returned from another day of hard labor.

Imagine the situation: a column of young women wearing head scarves, tattered coats over thin cotton tunics and torn boots or shoes, marching slowly kilometer after kilometer, in the snow, cold, starving, breathing heavily, shivering with cold, accompanied by S.S. guards, with rubber truncheons and dogs, to the place of their daily labor.

From time to time one of the women would stumble over a stone on the road or due to weakness, and such stumble would immediately be punished by a beating with the rubber truncheon by a male or female S.S. guard, to bring her back into the line.

On arrival at the place where they had to work, the women would be divided into sub-groups, and given instructions on what they had to do. Some had to break down walls with wooden rams, while each blow would also cause a jolt to the body, mainly the skull, the retina, and the spinal column. Others had to remove mud from the stream into baskets whose weight could total tens of kilos, pour the contents of the baskets into wheelbarrows or onto wagons and take the mud from the site.

If a guard noticed that one of the prisoners had slowed the pace of her work, she would be beaten with the rubber truncheon. It happened not once that a prisoner would bleed, faint or collapse. There were also prisoners who had been injured on the way by stones, and others who dragged their feet, who were suffering from a high fever, general weakness and breathing difficulties. How could they and their lives be protected?

The guards could not permit injured prisoners to be left in the field, because the villagers might discover them and then the population in the vicinity would begin to suspect what was happening.

If the prisoners noticed that one of them was weakening and was having difficulty walking, they would hold her against them with the remainder of their strength before one of the S.S. guards could see it. They would hold her in the middle of the line, supporting her body and her movement, so as to return her to the block where she lived.

It often happened that a prisoner was killed or died on the way, at the place of work or on her return journey. From the aspect of the S.S. guards, her comrades were duty-bound to return her body to the camp to be burned in the crematorium.

The gloomy skies, the cold, hunger, beatings, depression, the injured, beaten, sick and dead women around them crushed the remnants of the soul of the beaten and humiliated prisoners into the darkest dungeons of pain.

"Yitzchak", she said, "everyone hoped that she would be able to open her eyes at dawn, at four the next morning, and would survive the roll call of prisoners ahead of the day of hard labor they were about to march to, in the snow and the cold at five in the morning."

The rollcall, called "Zahlappel" by the guards, was a kind of parade, where the prisoners were given their assignments for the day. If it concerned one assignment or one work area, all the prisoners would participate. If there were a number of sites, the prisoners would be divided up in advance and they would depart in groups according to their assignments.

The daily rollcall was also a much more dangerous event. At the rollcall it was often decided that prisoner so and so was no longer "productive". She would be dragged from the block and sent for extermination with the other victims. Lack of productivity was determined first and foremost by the prisoner's health condition, her capability of working and the injuries that were visible on her body.

"Yitzchak, these rollcalls were a death sentence to any prisoner who was no longer suited to the needs of the work dictated by the camp administration." It was like a continuation of Dr. Mengele's selections on a daily basis. Bluma told me, while we were sitting in the kitchen of her apartment in Tel Aviv: "Continued ability to work was a kind of drop of hope for life until the next day. The sword of the death sentence due to loss of the ability to work for health reasons hung over the soul of each of the prisoners in Women's Commando 105 who still managed to survive. Every evening, when I lay down on my bunk, I suffered an attack of anxiety about my assignment on the next day and whether I would be able to survive it."

"The best thing to do was to focus on the most vital aspects – physical and emotional – in order to survive."

"Yitzchak", Bluma told me, "At 04:00 in the morning I would get up for roll call, and I would be given my assignment for the day, sometimes with all the women in the block, and sometimes in a group. As soon as roll call ended, and after allocation of the day's assignments, two or three prisoners from the kitchen would come in and set a large cauldron of murky heated water on a stand, and sometimes distribute to each woman a slice of bread and jam or thinly spread butter. That was our breakfast before departing for work. How do we drink the water from the pot? After all, there are no mugs, plates or even tables. Each of us had succeeded, over time, to obtain for herself a tin can or small container with which to drink it. Those who did not manage to find a container depended on the mercy of the prisoners who distributed the water to allow them to drink from the ladle with which they gave the water to those who did have a container."

"Do you know what I did? She asked me. "You might wonder why I preferred to use the heated muddy water in order to wash my face. Yitzchak, cleanliness in these horrific conditions is the most important thing. A person who does not keep clean has a very good chance of getting sick and ending her life in a very short time. Those animals would not give us any medical treatment. Cleanliness was more important than food."

"We marched from the barracks to the destination that had been planned for that day. That was after we had received a slice of bread with jam or a piece of pork. I did not touch the pork. If I was lucky, I was able to exchange it with one of the others for her bread and jam."

"We marched five women in a row. Due to the cold we walked crowded and huddled together. We had been given a coat for work and shoes to protect from the cold, and these were items of clothing that were most vital in that fierce cold."

"We marched slowly, accompanied by the S.S. guards, some leading dogs. There was no male or female guard who did not have a rubber truncheon, and during the march, when one of the guards noticed someone who was not keeping up, she would be given a few blows with the truncheon on her head or back."

"There were usually two kinds of work. The hardest was the removal of mud from the streams in the vicinity, or from puddles both inside and outside the camp. There were metal or rubber buckets in the place, spades to remove the mud and wagons on the railway, into which we would empty the buckets. We worked from about six in the morning, upon arrival at the site. We would be divided by the guards into groups, some digging and filling the buckets, some emptying them (they weighed tens of kilos) into the wagons, and some pushing the wagons to the place where they were emptied into large mechanized containers which arrived there every few days."

"There were quite a few cases where someone who had collapsed from exhaustion or sickness would be beaten mercilessly with the rubber truncheons or the butt of a rifle. Nobody injured at work was treated, nor were those who were bleeding or wounded from the beatings. There were times when women died on the worksite, lying in the mud or the rubble of the demolition with the blue scarf on their head."

"For the demolition work, we would come to the site planned for that day, where there were old buildings of Polish villages, homes, barns, storehouses and the like, which were not being used, and it was our job to demolish these buildings, because the Nazis were apparently planning to build something else there that would make their work more efficient."

"We walked in that same formation of five prisoners to a row. On the site were heavy rectangular wooden blocks which were used as battering rams to demolish and break down the walls. The guards would stand five women on each side of the block, so that ten women would use their last efforts, in rhythm, to swing the block against the wall to be demolished. Some women would collapse at this work, or they were severely injured, or were beaten cruelly with the rubber truncheons and other means available to the guards, whenever they saw that the pace of work of a prisoner appeared lazy or too slow. In this work many women were killed and injured, and my condition was not too good, either."

"On one of these long days, an S.S. officer dressed in uniform and leather gloves, on a motorbike together with a dog, accompanied the guards. He decided that I was too slow at work, or found another excuse, and set the dog on me. The dog attacked me and tore off part of the coat that protected me from the cold. The officer also beat me cruelly on the head and I lost consciousness. Later I found myself at the barracks and luckily it was Friday, so that on Saturday and Sunday when we did not work I had time to recover." The damage from that incident was revealed and verified for the first time only in 1997. See Prof. Lerner's magnetic imaging.

"How did you get to the barracks from the worksite when you were unconscious?", I asked.

"It was our practice to carry anyone who was injured or bleeding or had fainted or died during the work for any reason back with us to the barracks. We would take the injured and exhausted women with us inside the row, with the strongest walking on the outside of the row, in order to camouflage and conceal from the guards the condition of the injured and weak ones. The guards did not object to our carrying those bodies. Apparently, their orders were not to leave even a corpse, neither outside nor inside the camp, so as to protect the health of the Nazis who committed the extermination from any disease caused by a corpse that had not been buried or burned."

"On the days we had to work at that hard labor, which was every day except at weekends or on days of heavy snow, a terrible anxiety would grow in our hearts that the guards would report that one prisoner or another was no longer able to perform the work, and the result would be clear."

"It was obvious. The transports continued to come, and it was so easy to fill our ranks with stronger replacements who had just come, with their muscle mass intact, good nutrition, and greater energy than we had.

Women's Commando 105, like all the other men's or women's commandos who were engaged in working in and around the camp, was a "job" which you had to keep at all costs, if you were intelligent enough to know what was good for you. There was nothing to replace it, and your absence from it was punishable by death. There was no alternative."

"When we returned, walking slowly, accompanied by the male and female guards, exhausted from hunger, cold, fear and fatigue, carrying the injured and dead into the camp with the remnants of our strength, the greatest horror began which will remain with me, Yitzchak, to the day I die. The odor of burning human flesh, members of my dear people, rose out of the crematoria chimneys 24 hours a day, for two whole years, from my arrival in January 1943 until I was taken on the death march in January 1945. The odor of human flesh rising from the crematoria chimneys, which were in operation day and night, the flesh of the men, women and children of our people, was engraved like scars in my nostrils, my windpipe and my lungs, and I bear them and will continue to bear them every day as burns and burning scars on my body and soul, until God in heaven returns me to his bosom forever, and then I shall ask him, Please explain, Lord of the Universe, how did you allow such a monstrosity to exist?"

"What was the transgression of the sweet little children, who had never committed a sin in their lives, who did not know how to lie, who only wanted to enjoy and study the greatness of your creation; what had the fathers and mothers done, who had worked so hard to raise those children? Did you know that some of these children and parents from the region with which I was familiar were your people who knew how to speak the holy language fluently, and were fit and good to renew the days of yore in the land of our forefathers? Did you know that a considerable number of them were scientists, doctors and scholars, who could have contributed so much to mankind?"

"Lord of the Universe, what was the sin of my father Isaac, my brother Haim, my mother Sheine Reisel, my brother Zvi, my cousin Fruma, our relatives and neighbors from Sopotzkyn and the other towns and communities, that you permitted their torture, suffocation in the gas chambers, cremation, so that I and others carry scars engraved in our souls and bodies, from the odor of the burning flesh of our people, to the end of our days?"

"What was my sin and my transgression, Lord of the Universe, that at the age of 17 and a half I had to get the bitter news that my father Isaac Plaskovsky and my elder brother, Haim, born 1923, who was a genius in his studies and was about to leave Plaskovsky for the Ben Shemen Youth Village, had been transported from Bialystok prison where they had been taken at the beginning of 1942, and had been exterminated in the gas chambers of the Treblinka camp?"

"What was the sin of my angelic and beautiful mother, Sheine Reisel, nee Horwitz, who only helped and aided needy people in secret, without boasting of it and reporting it so as not to shame them, who was an actress in the amateur Yiddish theater in the town, that she became a widow at such a young age together with the loss of her firstborn son, Haim, while she, her younger son Zvi and Fruma were sent together to the gas chambers?"

"What was my sin, I who had been given an exemplary education, who spoke Hebrew fluently from my earliest years and wrote it without a single error, who was an outstanding student, whose father rented a room for me in the town of Grodno so that I could study in the Russian gymnasium, who had wonderful parents and loving brothers, and who had a relationship of love and brotherhood with our relatives in the town and in other towns in the vicinity, even those who had emigrated to America? When I undertook the responsibility of protecting and safeguarding the life of Fruma Horwitz in the Ghettos of Sopotzkyn and Kielbasin, risking my life for about a year and a half, due to the refusal of the U.S. authorities to enable her to be united with her parents and brothers in Chicago – what was my sin against you, Lord of the Universe? Why did you permit me and millions of others to be subjected to these horrors, including the physical extermination of my family at such a young age, as well as all those who had been my neighbors, acquaintances or friends until I reached the age of 17?"

As the days passed, and as she grew older, she expanded the descriptions and questions. Descriptions which I had never heard in my life until I was fifty or sixty years old.

"Yitzchak, you must know that if the State of Israel succeeds in catching Dr. Josef Mengele, I am the first who will go and testify against him."

I asked her, "Mother, what do you have to do with Dr. Mengele?"

"Yitzchak", she replied, "I saw that monster almost every day."

When I asked her, "What did you see? What do you know?"

She replied, "Yitzchak, I have already seen everything that the eye of man has not yet seen and has not yet understood."

"Yitzchak", she said to me, "here in Israel everything is joy and gladness. A good standard of living, people celebrate, travel abroad three or four times a year, eat in restaurants, keep replacing their luxurious cars, live for the moment and do not think two steps ahead. Yitzchak, we have only just established our independence, but all the celebrants do not know that they are sitting at the mouth of a burning volcano, and I fear that when the lava overflows and endangers the existence of the State, the souls and courage of all those celebrants will be so weak, they will not be able to survive the pain and suffering of the ongoing horrors. Celebrations and a life of luxury do not strengthen a person's resistance. They only weaken it. I am very worried, Yitzchak. The leadership is irresponsible, and all its handling of the issue of the Holocaust that we underwent was very amateurish, and just to get it over and done with."

When I heard these things, I devoted most of my thoughts to the first part, concerning Dr. Mengele, and her desire to be the first witness against him as she said. I thought to myself, this is an extraordinarily intelligent woman, who certainly understands what testimony means. What could she have to testify against Dr. Mengele if she was never present to see his actions with her very eyes? I tried to get her to talk, to extract information from her, but she locked her mouth shut, and only said: "Yitzchak, I have already seen everything in my lifetime." From time to time, but not in the same conversation, I tried again and again to hear what testimony she would give if Dr. Mengele were caught, but she remained adamant, her lips were sealed on that matter. "I have already seen everything, nothing can surprise me," was all she said.

Eventually, in the context of the legal battles I conducted in Germany, things came together in light of the material evidence which reached me from the Bad Arolsen Archives, in a letter with evidence from Dr. Susan Urban, the Director of the Archives. The day on which I received that material, I was smitten by secondary post trauma, from which I had been suffering anyway, and I think that exacerbated it.

In the evening, when they returned exhausted from their work, they would be given their daily ration of food, before the block was darkened at quite an early hour. Most of the food consisted of soup, that from time to time contained a few crumbs of potatoes or other vegetables, such as cabbage or yams, a few slices of bread, one or two covered with sausage or pork or some other spread, mostly jam.

She told me, " I did not take pork into my mouth, and I permitted myself to eat animal protein only if a miracle happened and we were given some that I was certain was Kosher. I used to exchange the pork, which many other girls wanted, with something else, such as an increased ration of bread or additional potatoes in the soup."

My thoughts gave me no rest: with such "rations", morning and evening, which could hardly provide the human body with 1,000 calories a day, how could young women hold on to life at hard labor requiring at least 3,000-4,000 calories a day. One might think that on Saturdays and Sundays, and perhaps even in winter, when it was not possible to go out to work due to heavy snow, the prisoners could lie on their bunks in the block and some-what replenish their growing calorie deficit. But it is clear to any intelligent person that this was a situation of methodical starvation and weakening of their bodies to an unrecognizable condition.

But a deeper thought concerning the starvation rations of the Women's Commando 105 raises grave questions on issues that were brought to the attention of the reader elsewhere in this book. The food lacked the most important components which every human being requires, especially if he is young, as were all the members of Women's Commando 105. The rations did not contain a sufficient quantity of protein and fat, and they were completely lacking in vitamins and minerals. Would not such a deficiency cause the survivors of the horrors to develop severe acquired diseases in the future? Would not the continuous, methodical hunger and stomach pains cause an outbreak of physiological and emotional symptoms at a later date?

Hunger in ordinary conditions leads to expressions of anger, theft of food, begging, physical attacks and efforts to obtain it. That could not happen in the conditions of the Birkenau extermination camp. Here, any outburst, disturbance or attempt to obtain food, with the eyes of the S.S. guards on the inmates at every step, meant immediate death or punishment by beating or torture, as the reader will see in the facility which the Red Army found when it entered Birkenau, even before the Germans surrendered in Berlin.

Many of the prisoners would keep a part of their slice or piece of bread for another time, in order to quiet the chronic hunger pangs somewhat, before collapsing onto their bunk, whether the lower or upper bunk, into the sleeplessness of pain, fear and torment.

The constant hunger and thoughts on how to cope and how to consume the rationed food in order to reduce as far as possible the pain and suffering caused by the hunger, which would result in the collapse of anyone trying to deal with all that in normal circumstances, were theirs at all hours, day and night.

Continuous hunger undermines emotional balance. Fear accompanies those who have not yet lost their mind. They are aware of and understand their prospects of survival, and make sure to continue to be included in the Women's Commando 105, so that they will not be killed immediately. Anxiety grows and become established, spreads its roots in the soul day by day, hour by hour, night by night, in those miserable women, those wretched souls, lying on their bunks on their return from their hard labor, in the cold, their stomachs growling and hunger with all its significance rooting itself as eternal anxiety in their souls.

"Yitzchak, she said to me, "in the prison managed by the justice system of a reasonable country, the food supplied to the prisoners, although not abundant, is not intended to starve them, and it is planned by doctors and experts. Taking a person's liberty by imprisonment in a regular prison, except perhaps in the darkest dictatorships, does not confer on the government which deprived him of that freedom the right and privilege of starving him and creating in him the constant fear of death by the manner and quantity of its supply. A government sentencing its own citizens to imprisonment has no right to instill into them anxiety for life by means of poor food rations."

"The prisoners in regular prisons sit around tables on chairs, and are given plates, cups, forks, knives and spoons. But in the block where I was you received your ration from the distributor into your hand, and you ate your "meal" while sitting on the bunk or on the floor, if you were lucky and it was a summer's day."

"The only thing served at the meal was a bowl of soup, which was usually almost cold, and contained only a few pieces of potato, some cooked greens or a few root vegetables, and even then not all together – one day this and the other day that. This soup was accompanied by two or three slices of bread, on one of which was sausage or other piece of meat, usually non-Kosher, which I never touched. Only when I was convinced that it was reasonably Kosher did I permit myself to eat. I preferred to exchange the meat for a ration of jam, or to reach an exchange agreement with other prisoners, that they would compensate me on another day when the meat was edible for me."

"And how does one cope with the cold?" I asked.

"Yitzchak, there were no warm blankets. Over time, some of us obtained thin fabric covers from the girls who worked in collecting the loot from the victims. The most important thing to guard the body from the freezing cold was the clothing with which we would go out to work outside the building."

"If you did not look after your shoes, which would protect your feet from the freezing cold, something to cover your shoulders, chest and neck, death would await you, either directly or from disease. If you did not look after your coat and shoes that were provided for working in, you would end your life within days."

. "In the nights the girls would use parts of the coat as a pillow and part to cover their bodies from the cold. But we found another way to cope with the cold. In the nights we would sleep huddled together, and in the mornings and evenings, walking to the work site and back, we would hold each other close."

"During my stay at Birkenau there were three periods of very severe cold: from January to end April 1943, from November to April 1944, and from November to April 1945 I suffered freezing cold, and if it were not for the correct use of the coat and shoes on the one hand, and the solidarity and huddling together with the girls on the other, we would not have survived. Yitzchak, there were women who died from that cold. I had friends and we looked after one another devotedly, which made it somewhat easier to handle the ten months of terrible cold in the difficult winters there."

Regarding personal hygiene, except for the use of the warm water intended for drinking in the morning for the purpose of washing her face, she did not tell me and I did not ask her about it. She only told me on her own initiative that about every two weeks the prisoners would go to disinfect their bodies and clothes from lice, which would appear from time to time and would drive them crazy.

"But the worst and most fearful of all, apart from the cold, the hunger, the beatings and the hard labor, were the selections every two weeks to examine the capabilities of the prisoners of Commando 105 to continue working. The threat of immediate death hovers every minute in your thoughts and you cannot rid yourself of it. The fear of death from these selections, many of which were conducted by Dr. Josef Mengele himself, followed each of us day and night", she said. These expressions of anxiety were accompanied by the girls' behavior in the barracks at night, when each was with her own thoughts.

"The constant worry, and the biting cold, the continual hunger and the growling stomach and the odor of the burning flesh of your people, whose ash was rising in the wind scalding your lungs and nostrils, the concern that if you survive the next selection of Dr. Mengele or the closed mouths of the S.S. guards, caused the human spirit to be suppressed and repressed, contrary to the liberated human spirit."

"The seconds, moments and hours pass by slowly, time freezes with the snow, the ice and the grey skies around you, while the constant fear of death never leaves you for a moment. It is not a vague fear: human flesh is burning, and you breathe it night and day, like it or not, even in your sleep. Around you every day, the girls are dying, are injured, murdered, tortured with severe punishments in order to terrorize their friends, who do not know if they will survive the night and the next morning parade in a few hours' time. How can I manage to fall asleep with the cold, the hunger and these thoughts. It is important that I sleep, for without sleep my end draws near."

"In all this never-ending, ongoing horror, we, the survivors of Block 25 and Block 6, where I was transferred after a time, huddle one with the other like sheep in a herd, endeavoring to produce a tiny bit of additional heat in the fierce cold, and to conceal from the eyes of those ferocious wolves our bleeding wounds and bruises, so that they are not revealed to the predators on behalf of the Third Reich and their master, Himmler, head of the Gestapo, and his S.S. comrades. But my mind is still functioning under the eternal fear and terror. How must I navigate my way in this horror that is now the routine of my life," she said.

Will and ambition are the jewel in the crown of the life of the thinking person. They lead to action, to emotional and physical investment, which require the consumption of energy. Will and ambition are the basis of the human soul, accompanying it almost with certainty, whether on the highway or on dirt roads, even without the means to overcome obstacles set by other men, difficult terrain, lack of knowledge and other impediments. But the long period of her stay there repressed her will for her entire life, except for the existential desires of establishing a family, education and concern for health.

Predators in the wild, in the sea, on land and in the air, are almost totally lacking in cognition. The part of the brain shared by both humans and animals – the amygdala – is an autonomous genetic program, transmitting the desires to eat, hunt, flee and take cover, and activating the breeding and sensory systems. Hunger, fear, hunting and breeding are assimilated in a genetic program, dictated to the predator in the wild, and this function probably has a goal in the grand plan of the Creator of heaven and earth. These unthinking automatic desires do not constitute a soul.

We are witness to predators whose predatory ways are designed genetically for their survival. Two-legged humans have the privilege of receiving from the Creator a developed gadget built into their skulls, which is the thinking brain, conferring on all those who possess it the right to think independently, each person at his own level.

The legal scholars, particularly the judges of England, have taught us that it is the right of the State serving the society which elected it to sentence human beings to penalties for their forbidden acts under criminal law, including the death sentence in certain countries.

An act does not become forbidden unless it is accompanied by criminal intent. Developed human societies, therefore, examine the nature of the intent that accompanied the killer when he committed the crime of killing his victim. Did he do it intentionally, choosing to attain this result, or was it the consequence of negligence or lack of awareness?

The thinking human brain enables a person to express his will of which he thinks and decides. The expression of a person's will means that he exists. The philosopher Descartes was right when he said: "When the human will is suppressed, he no longer exists."

When the antelope is writhing in the jaws of the lioness with her last breath, the lion's amygdala does not allow her to "feel" mercy for the antelope. What she does feel is that, in the next few moments, she will be giving her body nourishment for a number of days, until she has to hunt again when her hunger returns.

But for the "thinking mind" which desires the death of his victim, any expression of emotion by the victim, such as anxiety, supplication, flattery, panic, surrender, addressing the emotions of the killer or torturer, arouses sadism in his "intellectual understanding" of these scenes, with even more murderousness and a greater desire to achieve the deadly result.

The victim's spasms, subservience, supplications, the expression of any desire, begging for mercy, charity and addressing the killer's heart, only arouse the latter's sadistic emotions and responses, and bring the supplicant for kindness and mercy nearer to his end. These human emotional behaviors have no place in the institutionalized murder arena of the sovereign state of Nazi Germany. A reasonable and normal person in his community will not totally disconnect from these emotional qualities in moments of difficulty, danger and pain, but their simple significance here, in these circumstances, is to hasten the end of the victim's life or, at least, to exacerbate his injury.

This diversion into the philosophical aspect of these scenes of horror is aimed at understanding the deeper level of the ability to survive in these conditions. Disconnection from knowledge and expression of will, creation of desire and expression of emotions are basic methods of survival in this kind of horror. However, as soon as they have been adopted, they are assimilated into you for the rest of your life, your functioning is distorted, and your life is no longer one of "I exist", but a life of "I am breathing".

In order to survive against the two-legged predators in Birkenau, you must become as a stone and train yourself not to desire. Neither to desire a valuable jewel on Place Vendome in Paris, nor to ask for another slice of bread when your stomach is growling with the hunger pangs of hours and days. If you want something and demand it – the crematorium awaits you.

In Birkenau you are forbidden to desire or ask for anything. Any request will lead to severe punishment or murderous beatings or torture on the rack. The Nazi sadist on that shift will want to teach you a lesson on the torture rack or by murderous beating, so that you will never dare to ask again. He is only doing you a favor and being good to you in not sending you to the death chambers.

So, if your mind is still operating in these conditions of hunger, freezing cold and desperation, it is absolutely imperative that you practice self-discipline and train yourself to alter your responses and your personality. You must take the early step of repressing the human desire mechanism with which you have been created and educated in your natural environment. You must become apathetic, lacking in will and emotion, and you must disconnect from vital responses – self-pity, expressions of sorrow, pain, weeping and begging for mercy. But the longer this defensive mechanism continues, it becomes a habit for the rest of your life, and creates an emotional change in your personality. And that is the death of a person's soul.

And if you thought that that is the whole extent of the emotional and character exercises required in order to survive, then you are mistaken. The greatest enemy of man is anger. Humans are born with this property – some more and some less.

The prisoners of Commando 105 were human beings, regardless of the events and of their being subject to these circumstances against their will. Each had her own unique personal characteristics. Each had her own level of anger and stimulation. One would be offended in an instant, the other would never take offense in years. One would flare up in anger in the blink of an eye, while the other would remain unmoved.

In the normal society in which we live, we become close to those we choose by our own free will. We do not relate to those with whom we are uncomfortable, and, even when we do connect with one person or another, we often find ourselves disappointed and convince ourselves in retrospect that we have made a mistake. Such phenomena occur between spouses, as well.

"Here, Yitzchak", she told me, "you find yourself among women whose company is forced upon you, whom you have not chosen. Some of them are wonderful, good, reliable and helpful, some of them are bad, cry-babies, lazy, weak, wild and angry, with whom you would have nothing to do in your normal life. On the other hand, you find yourself under the supervision of the sadistic camp guards, who are only waiting for the outbreak of a quarrel or fight between the inferior humans in the cage. It will be another opportunity for them to express their cruelty by beating or torturing anyone who finds herself in a quarrel or fight. Those will be pulled out of the barracks, or will remain in them while taking a fierce beating from the guards. The extent of the cruelty of the punishment is equal to the evil nature of the guard on duty."

She added, "And who can I trust? How can I be sure that if I share my deepest thoughts with a woman, she will not gossip about me or pass on the information to some undesirable party so as to derive personal gain? You can never tell the extent of the girls' resistance under pressure, even those whom you know, and what you can expect if you share your thoughts and emotions with them. Suspicion and mistrust accompany your every step as the moments pass. Eventually they become part of your personality."

"You must never comment, react, criticize or object to the behavior of one or another woman. Should she be offended or explode in anger, you and she will both be punished severely. It is also necessary to refrain from criticizing or objecting to those who do not burst out immediately but hold their resentment inside them for a moment of revenge which could lead to your death."

She added, "God forbid you should tell some gossip to this woman or that. You must guard your soul not only from those outsiders who actively hate you, but even those who live together with you inside the barracks."

"I understood there, within a few days, that as was said by the wisest of men, King Solomon, 'the best protection for wisdom is silence', and 'anger lies in the hearts of fools'. The directives for saving life prevail over everything."

"Assume for yourself a master, acquire for yourself a friend," as written in the Ethics of the Fathers.

Since my early adulthood, Bluma had remarked and reminded me not once that you may take offense only from someone close to you and whom you trust. Do not build plans with people based on anger. Anger and rage usually lead to an unplanned destination. Make yourself a friend and refrain from making enemies, to the extent you are able to control your feelings. If you do not control your feelings, you bring the end of your life closer.

Eventually I understood that although her advice to me was correct, the battle for her personal survival, despite her extraordinarily good heart, had stamped the suspicion of people on her personality. This suspicion disturbed and damaged her for many years, and included her suspicion of myself, since I was a lively child, somewhat disobedient and uncontrollable. After the death of my father, after she did what she did with the reparations offices, which brought down disaster on herself and on me, she understood that she had been totally mistaken in her suspicion and mistrust of me in my younger years. She suggested that we live in her home with her, not for the sake of convenience, but due to her full confidence in me. Judging a person's soul and qualities is not an easy task. "Do not judge your fellow until you have stood in his place", say the writings of our people.

As of April 1944, when Prisoner 31119 Bluma had already been 14 months in Birkenau, women began to arrive at the camp from Hungary and Czechoslovakia, a few to Women's Commando 105 and to some other work groups. That was the first time Bluma had met women who were not from Poland or Lithuania.

The arrival of the Jewish women from these countries caused shivers among the women who had been in the camp since 1943 and were by now completely exhausted. Their first thought was that the S.S. would get rid of the weakened women, and would replace them with stronger ones who had just arrived from Hungary and Czechoslovakia, who were in good strength and fit for work.

What saved the day was the fact that the work of Commando 105 outside the camp had been reduced and the camp operators preferred to place the new arrivals in other work groups, who were more essential at that time, in view of the heavy losses suffered by the Wehrmacht and its supply lines, which required large amounts of manpower to prepare light ammunition for machine-guns, according to the understanding of those who were outside the fences.

The women from Hungary and Czechoslovakia brought with them additional harsh information for the prisoners – that the Germans were apparently in control of all of Europe, so that the end of the horror was not yet in sight. The Red Army was on its way to eastern Poland, while the Wehrmacht had already been routed on its eastern front inside Russia.

Since I was busy, in the course of Bluma' Alzheimer's disease, that had been diagnosed in 2006, with tremendous struggles in Israel and Germany to obtain financing for her at the expensive Gan Shalva sanatorium, I made every effort to collect information that would help to improve the percentage of her disability due to the Nazi persecution, compared with what had been determined for her in 1956 by the Hannover-Lower Saxony Reparations Office.

In the course of these efforts, I filed two applications to the Saxony government, where my mother had been hospitalized after the abdominal surgery which I shall describe later, and another to the Nazi Government Archives, which are kept in the city of Bad Arolsen, in the State of Hessen near the city of Kassel.

The application to the Bad Arolsen Archives, was made possible by the honorable Chancellor Mrs. Angela Merkel, who directed her government that the material found in the archives about those prisoners in the extermination camps may be displayed only to their children. This decision of the Chancellor is directly related to a number of issues dealt with in this book, particularly that of post trauma.

In the months of January 2010 and July 2010, I was in Germany in connection with my legal efforts to improve the financing for keeping Bluma in the worthy institution which I had found for her terrible disease.

In July 2010 I received a letter from Dr. Susan Urban, Director of the Bad Arolsen Archives, notifying me that they had found material there concerning my mother, that had been transferred from the Birkenau camp. How was that?

Dr. Susan Urban sent me a short letter, asking me whether I was ready to receive that material, and requesting my reply. She wrote that the material contained very painful information.

Why and how did material remain concerning Bluma, my father, Hanan, and his first wife, Yochi-Yocheved, nee Umanski, and his daughter?

When the Red Army was at the gates of Birkenau, the Gestapo Commander, Heinrich Himmler and the Auschwitz Commander, Rudolf Höss are well aware that to the extent any written material were found concerning the prisoners, their history and what had happened there, it would incriminate them as having committed crimes against humanity, and they would be killed by the Red Army soldiers in their thousands, without the trial they were eventually given by the British, Americans and French.

The material that was in the Auschwitz-Birkenau archive contained a bloody incrimination of the rulers of the Third Reich, and particularly the RSHA, its commanders and all those who planned and executed the extermination program.

All records of the prisoners and the activities performed there had been rushed to the Birkenau crematoria to be destroyed by fire.

Two issues weighed heavily on the burners of the archives and documents of Auschwitz-Birkenau: The well-known order of the Germans, on the one hand, and the unexpectedly rapid advance of the Red Army on the other. They found themselves in a terrible time constraint.

I shall explain the matter of German order: In bookkeeping there is a method of inventory-counting called Last In First Out (LIFO). This method is also used in the case of accumulating and preserving documents. The documents of the last prisoners who had come were at the top of the Auschwitz-Birkenau archive, and those who had arrived first were at the bottom. Since the Jews of Sopotzkyn were among the first transports to arrive, then according to the German order, the documents connected with those prisoners who had been received first were at the bottom of the pile.

The rapid and unexpected advance of the Red Army nipped in the bud the work of burning the documents. I am certain that if one more prisoner from Sopotzkyn had been left alive, and if he had children, they would have found the documents concerning their relatives among the documents transferred to Bad Arolsen. The fact that the German operators fled from Auschwitz-Birkenau, led to the unburned documents being brought to the Bad Arolsen Archives inside Germany.

When Dr. Susan Urban received my affirmative reply, that I wanted the material concerning Bluma Plaskovsky and Hanan Borovsky to be given to me, I received a further letter from her in English, the letter of an educated, sensitive and intelligent woman, whom I present to the readers of this book, which constitutes first-rate historic testimony to all human beings wherever they are.

At the Wannsee Conference in January 1942, the Nazis performed an inventory count of the Jews of Europe. As Germans, the execution of the extermination of the Jewish People, which constituted a danger to the security of the Third Reich, required a precise record of those who had been exterminated and those who were still prisoners, just as a commercial business would record the destruction of its unwanted inventory.

In her letter, Dr. Susan Urban reports to me that, according to the records of the S.S. officers at Birkenau, and of the RSHA, 2,050 Jews of Sopotzkyn arrived at Birkenau from the Grodno Ghetto on January 23, 1943. She reports that, according to the figures of the Nazi regime, upon their arrival 1,567 of them were killed, and the remainder, who were able to work, were given various occupations within the camp.

Dr. Urban explains to me the reason why Bluma Plaskovsky had the number 31119 tattooed on her left arm in blue ink, as was done to every prisoner who was sent to work. Dr. Mengele and his helpers were ordered by the camp commanders to collect two hundred women for work. The camp command decided to number the two hundred women who were selected as labor prisoners from 31100 to 31300. Bluma was the nineteenth – Bluma Plaskovsky, Birkenau prisoner 31119, of the holy community of Sopotzkyn – the number was stamped on her left arm, and remained there until she left us on August 25, 2016.

With her letter, Dr. Susan Urban also sent me a plan of the Auschwitz 2 Birkenau Extermination Camp, including that part which was called "Canada". In that part, according to my mother, the Nazis collected the belongings of the victims and the prisoners.

Among the prisoners from Sopotzkyn that were included among the 200 women (not all of them were from Sopotzkyn, due to the arrival of other transports on the same day), were also Bella Vinitzky, eventually Pollak, who moved after the war to San Diego, California, and Hassia, eventually Bornstein. The remainder died, were killed and murdered in the course of the hard labor.

Dr. Susan Urban explains further that, in the next part of her letter, she reveals to me very painful information, which she hopes will not shock me. Dr. Urban reports:

"Documents were found, and are attached herewith, evidencing that your mother took part in human experiments in the laboratories of the Waffen S.S. at Birkenau during a three-week period in the month of August 1944."

I I S .
International Tracing Service
Service International de Recherches
Internationaler Suchdienst

Mr Yitzhack Borowsky
Law Office
76 Ibn Givrol St.
Tel Aviv
Israel

Bad Arolsen, July 7, 2010

Inquiry 2329/SU

Dear Mr Borowsky,

regarding your questions about the circumstances of the "Arbeitskommando or Aussenkommando 105" in Auschwitz-Birkenau we want to share the information with you we found underneath.

Furthermore you asked for information about your father and other relatives which was handed over to the Humanitarian Department.

Other questions were linked with the administration and everyday life in Ghetto Grodno and the Transit Camp Kielbasin. A Ghetto named Sopotkyn was not found in our records and neither in other documentation.

Ghetto Grodno was established in two parts of the city, Ghetto "A" in the city's central part, where ca. 15.000 so-called "productive" Jews were herded together on an area which included less than half a square km. Ghetto "B" was erected in a Suburb named Slobodka, where around 10.000 so-called "non-productive" Jews were forced to live. The "Judenrat", established through German administration, was entitled to put the orders into action and also tried to enlist as many Jews as possible in the factories of so-called "war-needed supplies".

Commandant of Ghetto "A" was Kurt Wiese, Otto Strebelow was the commandant of Ghetto "B". Grodno was one meeting point for those active in Jewish Resistance in Bilaystok and Vilna, as Grodno was in-between these cities.

Liquidation of the Ghettos in Grodno started in November 1942, when Ghetto "A" was completely sealed off. Shootings began. The same period of time – in the beginning of November – Jews from other villages and cities were deported to the Kielbasin Transit Camp (Sammellager). From Kielbasin many Jews were deported to Auschwitz. Jews from Grodno were brought also there and then deported on to Auschwitz. Camp Commander was Karl Rinzler who was known for his brutality.

Deportations from Grodno started on November 15, 1942 and were directed to Auschwitz. Most transports were in their majority gassed upon arrival, only a small number of those deported were "selected" for work.

Following information from http://www.holocaustresearchproject.org/ghettos/grodno.html and the *Calendarium of Auschwitz*, edited by Danuta Czech (Reinbek, 2nd Edition, 2008), the prisoners number which your mother has to carry was given out on the transport which arrived in Auschwitz on January 23, 2010. 1.574 individuals were murdered after arrival in the gas chambers, only 426 people were "selected" and admitted into the camp. Your mother was one of those women who were only 191 individuals. The female prisoners' numbers ranged from 31000 to 31190.

These transports were called "RSHA transports by the Germans. The Auschwitz museum has records of these transports, testifying to the murders of the Jews of Grodno, Sokolka, Wolkowysk, and Pruzhany.

Going back to Grodno: On 13 March 1943 the German administration labelled Grodno as "Judenfrei" (Free of Jews).

The following website contains also important information about historical sources:
http://www.jewishgen.org/belarus/info_grodno_sources.htm
The underneath text in Italics is taken from this website and was compiled by Documentary Sources for the Study of the Grodno Gubernia compiled by Ellen Sadove Renck

1. *Vol. 6 of the Klarsfeld series: Documents Concerning the Murder of 29,000 Jews of Grodno by the Germans; 1941-1942. Ghetto and Deportations to Death Camps Cologne and Bielefeld Trails, Gathering Point before Transportation to Concentration Camps of Kelbasin, Treblinka and Auschwitz. Published in May 1989 by Jews from the town of Grodno, who survived the German occupation of 1941-1944 containing:*
verbatim translation of German record of The Court of Justice in Cologne in 1968 of two Gestapo officers in Grodno: Kurt Wiese (commander of Ghetto No. 1) and his superior, Heinz Errelis, commander of the two ghettos and the Kelbsin Camp;
excerpts from the Judgment by the Court of Justice in Bielefeld in 1967 of Gestapo officers in Bialystok uezd, primarily on death camp transports.
Apendices: published by the Beate Klarsfeld Foundation that provide a key to the original specific testimony in German

2. *USHMM: US HOLOCAUST MUSEUM MICROFILM RECORDS FOR GRODNO:*
   Aaron T. Kornblum,
   Reference Archivist, Archives Branch,
   United States Holocaust Memorial Museum, Archives Branch,
   100 Raoul Wallenberg Place, SW, Washington, DC, 20024.
   Tel: 202 488 6113. Fax: 202 479 9726.
   Email: akornblum@ushmm.org.
   website for more information: http://www.ushmm.org/access.htm
RG53.004M Grodno Oblast Archive records, 1940-1944 [microform]. mss. Selected Records from the Grodno Oblast Archive (mss.) 99 pages, seven rolls of microfilm.
RG10.052 01 Records relating to the Chaleff family of Grodno, Poland mss. 31 pages*
RG02.029 Nina Kaleska papers mss. 17 pages.
RG22.001 01 Records relating to the Soviet Union under Nazi Occupation, 19411945. mss.*
RG22.002M Selected records from the Extraordinary State Commission to Investigate GermanFascist Crimes Committed on Soviet Territory from the USSR, Archive of the October Revolution (mss.) [Towns in Grodno Guberniya that are described in the "Extraordinary State Commission to Investigate German Fascist Crimes Committee on Soviet Territory": Benyakoni, Berestovitskiy, Lida, Porechye, Porozovo, Radun, Rybnitsa,

Sobakintsy, Sopotskin, St. Dubova, Svisloch, Vasilishki, Volkovysk, Voronovo, and Zaboslot] 220 pages ($66.00). and 99 pages

RG15.070M Zespol podziemie prasa konspiracyjna = underground press, 1939-1966 (bulk 1940-1945) (mss.) 99 pages. Because of an agreement the United States Holocaust Memorial Museum has with the Jewish Historical Institute in Poland, which holds the original materials, the Museum Archives cannot duplicate entire rolls of this collection for researchers until the researchers first receive written permission from the JHI. After JHI's permission, the Museum Archives would be glad to duplicate microfilm rolls.

RG 53.002M The Sara Rosjanski Ross Donation Selected Records from the Belarus Central State Archives (mss.) 99 pages

3. Grodno Kahal records are in Minsk Historical Archives in Fond 2, Op. 3, Delo 699.

4. CONSCRIPTION INFORMATION:
    "The Provincial Grodno Records" is the title of a local newspaper kept in many libraries including the Russian National Library. Title: "Grodno Provincial Records" Lists of Jews eligible for conscription, missed when the Register Books were drawn up in 1804. Family lists and the 1810 supplemental list. 126 pages

5. Old Russian newspapers are available through Yale University, BLITZ, the St. Petersburg Russian Historical Archives, and also are available for purchase at http://www.nross.com/judaica/judaica3.htm

6. Card Catalog of Jewish Newspapers and Periodicals in the Russian National Library, St. Petersburg in Hebrew & Yiddish: The holdings of Jewish newspapers and periodicals cover the period from the early 1880s to the present. They include not only periodicals published in the Russian Empire and the former Soviet Union, but also in countries such as Poland, Romania and later Israel. The card file is divided into two parts: Hebrew and Yiddish. The newspaper section contains runs of Der Veg, Folkstime, Der Roiter Stern. All of the newspapers and journals can be ordered on microfilm.
    Yiddish: ca. 4,200 cards, 8 mf; Hebrew: ca. 1,500 cards, 3 mf Complete set, 11 mf,

7. Unpublished Materials for Belarus Towns in the Archives of Yad Vashem. That information can be obtained by sending an email to the Yad Vashem archivist.

Regarding the lives and "career" of those camp commanders we do not contain documentation; please turn to the Federal Archives/ Former Berlin Document Center, where the files on Nazi-party-members are stored.
See under:
http://www.bundesarchiv.de/benutzung/zeitbezug/nationalsozialismus/00299/index.html.de

The Außenkommando/ Arbeitskommando 105 you mention according to your mother's recollection was forced labour as "deconstruction work" outside Auschwitz-Birkenau.

We have to underline that we found evidence not in our collections but in the above named book by Danuta Czech, on page 963 in the German copy. (Calendarium of Auschwitz, edited by Danuta Czech, Reinbek, 2nd Edition, 2008)

A prisoners' commando was forced to destroy in 1944 and 1945 barracks in the former women's camp BI and BIII/ "Mexico". This commando was named "105-B-Baracken-Abbruchkommando BI und BII". The documentation is hold in Auschwitz Archives.

The commando was not forced to work outside the camp but I assume that recollections may vary and memory is shaped also by other circumstances. Some people recollect such atrocities with slight changes to historical facts – which is normal. Therefore I assume this is the Commando your mother was in, and as she was for sure in another barrack/block in Auschwitz-Birkenau she had to walk across whole Birkenau as you see on the underneath inserted map which shows that there was a footwalk. These barracks were not Polish houses but they probably seem to your mother as outside the camp as there is a birch forest around some parts. Details about this forced labour is not known by the ITS.

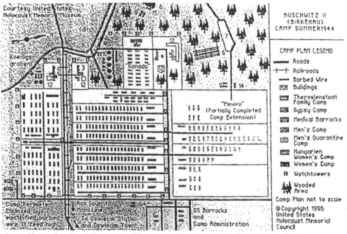

(http://isurvived.org/Pictures_iSurvived-3/AUSCHWITZ-2_Map.GIF)

As you mentioned the women who shared your mother's fate and were incarcerated the same time like your mother we found Manja Krakauer and Dora Cibula (she was written like this in the documents). The T/D-Case 334468 which is the ITS-correspondence with and about Mrs Cibula does not mention any connection to the Commando 105, but she was in Auschwitz the same time your mother was.

Another fact we found out was that your mother and Mrs Cibula were at the same time – the same date – in the so-called "SS-Hygiene Institute" in Auschwitz. They both were there between August 09 and August 25, 1944, both seemed to be there for examinations on August 19, 1944. Your mother was registered as Philly Plaskovska.

It is a list about those taken there for laboratory studies of urine, blood, stool, and saliva samples, as well as throat cultures taken from prisoners of KL Auschwitz. Nationalities are not stated. The report sheet by the SS contains the prisoner's numbers and the names. Medical "examinations" often led to medical experiments. It is a piece of information which is hard to bear and we do know that while reading this the past then is again present and it hurts. But we do guess that this information shall be given to you and it will perhaps shed light into your mother's fate as she probably does not recollect this examination (which is the case with many survivors).

The document with your mothers name from this "SS-Hygieneinstitut" is attached as a PDF as well. The description is what we have written above. The Document ID is on the footer so that you may quote it.

Please do take into consideration that the answer by my colleagues from the Humanitarian Department on possible documentation about your father will take few weeks.

With best regards,

Susanne Urban
(Head of Historical Research)

1 document attached.

A list of Jewish women written by SS officers containing names of prisoners under medical human experiments, which present Bluma's number on row 34.

Permitted to be exposed as evidences to courts where ever by the state of Germany.

Dr. Urban attached a photocopy of the records of the Jewish prisoners who were a part of the experiment, and I identified the prisoner number of my mother – 31119, her surname – Plaskovsky, but her first name, Bluma, had been hidden and replaced by the name Phyllis. Another name I could identify in the list was that of another good friend of my mother, whom I knew, Dorka Tzibola. Dorka was from another town. She and her sister Haika Tzibola, were also with Bluma in the Women's Commando 105, blue kerchiefs, and they were in the row of five women. The first name of Dorka Tzibola had also been changed to another name. They were from another place in Poland.

On the lists of the Jewish prisoners, among whom were Bluma and Dorka, as drawn up by the members of the Waffen S.S., which were sent to me, I placed a check sign to the right of the name and number of Bluma and Dorka. The records themselves contained details of the type of experiment they underwent, which concerned an injection of E-coli bacteria.

Dr. Susan Urban sent me the confirmation of the Archives, in the name of the Federal Republic of Germany, that under the authorization of the Federal Republic of Germany I may present the material sent by her in any court of law anywhere in the world.

I could not close my eyes for many days. I felt my heart bursting and tearing inside me, my throat choking with pain and compassion, while drum rolls pounded in my ears. Awful thoughts ran through my brain. Do I know everything? Is that all that happened? How, after three weeks of experiments with bacteria, does one return to Women's Commando 105? Did she return at all to Women's Commando 105? Was that the only experiment or were there others that were not recorded? Was no genetic physiological damage caused to her and her descendants as a result of these experiments conducted on human beings in the hygiene laboratories of the Waffen S.S.

On the one hand, I felt as if I had been hit on the head with a baseball bat. On the other hand, I admired her bravery and courage, and her ability to carefully select what she told me, her son, so that I should not be hurt, because she knew I would.

"Yitzchak", she said, "If the State of Israel catches Dr. Josef Mengele, I shall be the first to testify against him". Bluma gave no details, but the letter from Dr. Susan Urban is decisive corroborating evidence.

There is no need to explain why the Waffen S.S. officers defaced the names of the prisoners who had been used for human experiments in their laboratories. They could not have imagined that the archive records with the real names of the prisoners and the numbers that they had stamped on their left arms would be seized, and that one day they would be delivered to the descendants of the victims, on the instructions of the Chancellor of their state, Angela Merkel, a wise and loving woman.

The letter from Dr. Susan Urban, the director of the Archives at Bad Arolsen, the lists of women who had participated in the experiments in 1944 at the hygiene institute of the Waffen S.S., with the identity of Bluma and Dorka in the experiments, and the approval of the Federal Republic to display them to humanity are attached here along with the photograph of Bluma's arm, bearing the number 31119.

The German deceit after the fall of the Reich did not cease to operate, except for the integrity and decency of Dr. Susan Urban, of dear Mr. Thomas Flach, Director of the Reparations Office at Wiesbaden Darmstadt, who helped me greatly, of Sabina Weidner of the Hannover Reparations Office and of Dr. Dirk Langner, of Bonn, who turned out to be a welcoming and good-hearted man, who was of great assistance in the last period of Bluma's life with the Alzheimer's disease.

When Bluma signed the compromise arrangement with the Hannover office, the documents from Bad Arolsen were not in the possession of the Reparations Office. Dr. Langner, the physician in charge on behalf of the Federal Government of the reparations system and of liaison with the Claims Committee, told me that the material from Bad Arolsen justifies the reopening of the compromise agreement which Bluma had signed, after being so terrorized and lacking everything in 1956. Such a proceeding was opened, but even Dr. Langner, who supported me all the way, saw the helplessness of the Reparations Office and of the "Landes" courts (of the separate countries of the German Federation), which were forced to implement the cruel and tight-fisted BEG law, which had been written by the Nazi criminals who had forgotten the Hitler regime.

It was the bureau of the honorable Chancellor Mrs. Merkel which involved Dr. Langner in Bluma's affair so as to help me. The Prime Minister of Israel, Mr. Benyamin Netanyahu, whom I had approached a number of times in the years of my distress, has not taken the trouble to respond to this day. On the national aspect, Mr. Avigdor Lieberman was serving as Foreign Minister. I applied to his office saying that I had documents from the Federal Republic proving the Holocaust, which had been denied by the then President of Iran, Ahmadinejad, but that was of no interest to his office.

Post trauma was defined by world psychiatry, including senior German psychiatrists, in the 1980s, upon the return of U.S. soldiers from the battlefields of Vietnam. Studies were made of about one hundred and sixty thousand members of the U.S. military who returned from that war, and senior psychiatrists of that time defined the condition –

PTSD – in the American DSM [Diagnostic and Statistical Manual of Mental Diseases] and in the European ICD-10 [International Statistical Classification of Diseases and Related Health Problems] (manuals on human physical and mental diseases).

I imagined the American soldiers who fought in Vietnam, who underwent the horrors and terrible life dangers, which must never be taken lightly. But what is the similarity between the soldiers Steve from El Paso, Texas, or Harry from Chicago, or Alistair from Madison, Wisconsin, or Tom from Memphis, Tennessee. They all suffered mortal danger and horrific scenes on the battlefield, but each one of them had parents, brothers, friends, a home and a homeland. They still had hope.

Bluma's world, and that of hundreds of thousands who survived the extermination camps, had been erased. Not a living soul remained of her nuclear family, there was no property, no profession, no homeland to compensate, indemnify and see to her, no values, everything erased. The post trauma of the survivors of the extermination camps is described in the DSM and the ICD manuals, and rightly so, as the severest, and it also causes many changes in personality and characteristics. Bluma left Birkenau on the Death March, while her nose, her lungs and memory held the odor of the flesh of about one quarter of the members of her people who had been killed and burned there.

After I had been appointed Bluma's guardian, due to her Alzheimer's disease, I found among her things a note she had written to herself, in which she summarized, as was her habit, succinctly and pertinently, in a few words, her lessons as a "Guide to the Perplexed" for all human beings wherever they are:

"Suffering causes thought,

Thought leads to wisdom,

Wisdom creates energy,

And with energy it is possible to bear life."

A reader who is able to feel and interpret Beethoven's work, will understand that this message of Bluma is identical to the sounds given to us by the Fifth Symphony in its four movements. Beethoven described it in wonderful sound. Bluma described it succinctly, in a few simple words.

The note in her Hebrew handwriting is attached.

Brama wjazdowa do Brzezinki
Ворота ведущие в Бржезинку.

La porte cochère de Brzezinka (Birkenau)
The Gateway of Brzezinka (Birkenau)

Picture taken by the Red Army in January 1945 showing the three railroads coming from Hungary (left), Poland (center), and Czechoslovakia and Western Europe (right)

Please note the difference with previous picture, as rails were changed by Polish authorities thereby distorting historical evidence

Bluma's Barrack No. 25

Entrance to Barrack No. 25 in which
Bluma's Women Commando were kept

Looking into Barrack No. 25

Underground tunnel leading naked prisoners

to gas chambers

Ruins of crematorium next to Barrack No. 25

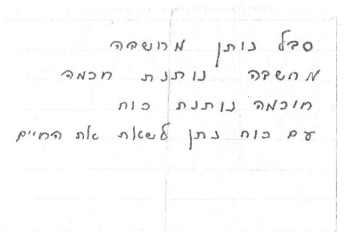

Bluma's life lesson: how to survive, written in her own handwriting in Hebrew

Dziedziniec egzekucyj na bloku 11-tym
Двор для казней в 11-ом бараке.

La cour d'exécutions de la 11-ème baraque
The Court of Executions of the 11-th Barrack

omando" na miejscu pracy
Командо« на месте работы.

Un „Komando" au trava
A „Komando" at work

Kozioł do chłosty
Le chevalet où l'on fouettait les prisonniers
Кобыла для порки.
The Whipping-horse

Krematorium (miejsce buntu w 1943 r.)
Le four crématoire (Le lieu de la révolte de 1943)
Крематорий (Место бунта в 1943 г.).
The Crematory (The Place of the Revolt of 1943)

Blok 11-ty — kary i śmierci
11-ый барак наказаний и смерти.
La 11-ème baraque de punition et de mort
The 11-th Barrack of Punishment and Death

Widok na blok 11-ty
Вид на 11-ый барак.
Une vue de la 11-ème baraque
A View of the 11-th Barrack

Evacuation from Birkenau and the Death March

Under the gloomy winter sky of October-November 1944, the last of the women who had succeeded in surviving the Women's Commando 105 straggled along. Apathetic, broken in body and soul, with the last of their strength they trudged the paths inside and outside the camp for another day of hard labor with the cold and hunger and the blows of the guards beating them mercilessly. One more day, and another. Flashes of last hope accompanied them, that they would survive the next selection of Dr. Mengele. They were broken souls walking in rows of five. They had no real hope to hold onto. There was no radio or newspapers, and the guards certainly did not speak to them or share with them any news of what was happening.

The prisoners of Women's Commando 105 with their blue kerchiefs were mostly Polish Jews In March and April 1944, they had been joined by Jewish women from Hungary and Czechoslovakia. They all knew only one thing; as a result of the war in which the German army had captured the countries where they lived, they were separated from the general population, were concentrated in ghettos and transferred to extermination camps. They were lucky to still be alive and that their captors were still interested in deriving some benefit from them.

At the end of November 1944, the women began to notice some unease among the German staff of the Gestapo and the S.S. operating the murder industry, and there was burning and destruction of evidence. The work forays were almost stopped. They were employed sometimes in work within the confines of the camp itself, in the region called "Canada" (see map), where the clothes and personal belongings of the murdered victims were collected and sorted. The energy of the camp operators was slowly replaced by apathy. But make no mistake, the crematoria still operated at full capacity, and the odor of burning human flesh filled the gloomy skies and did not cease penetrating the prisoners' nostrils day by day, moment by moment, night by night.

The second Belorussian front of the Red Army repulsed the Wehrmacht forces from Belorussia, and advanced into Poland. Birkenau is in the southeast of Poland. It was in close proximity to southern Belarus and Ukraine, where the Wehrmacht forces had been driven off earlier.

The Red Army, under the command of Marshals Georgy Constantin Zhukov and Konstantin Rokossovsky, were leading the largest land army in human history. This army was aiming to liberate Poland, Hungary and Czechoslovakia, and to enter the Berlin region in order to quell the Third Reich.

The Red Army, established by Leon Lev Trotsky who was Jewish, included about six hundred thousand Jewish combatants from the U.S.S.R. and many more Jews from Poland who had joined its ranks. Many Jews served in this huge army, some of whom were senior officers. My father's cousin, Elhanan Sereviansky, of blessed memory, was commander of an artillery regiment at the Battle of Stalingrad. May 9, 1945, is the victory day for the Russian people over Nazi Germany in the "Great War" as they so rightly call it.

The block commanders at Birkenau hinted to the prisoners that in the coming days they would be moving through Germany and that they must prepare for it. Of course, they did not give the reason why they would be going through Germany, but it was not difficult to interpret this decision. It concerned the results of the Wansee Conference, and the adherence to the extermination program on the one hand, and the rapid advance of the Red Army on the other.

Because of the Red Army's advance and the fact that it was close to the Birkenau camp, the Germans understood that it would be better if the Red Army did not discover what had been going on in that extermination camp. They were worried about that. Moreover, and more importantly, the work of exterminating the Jewish people, who were endangering the security of the Third Reich, was continuing without a break to the last moment, in accordance with the resolutions of the Wannsee Conference, to which they adhered. The conclusions of the Wannsee Conference were executed with resolve, so much so that the trains and engineering facilities operated tirelessly to conduct the extermination program at all costs to the very end. No European Jew would remain alive. The extermination would be performed to the last day of battle. Therefore, execution of the remaining Jews sentenced to extermination would take place inside Germany.

It was January 18, 1945, the same day when, two years earlier, they had been loaded on to the RSHA train from Ghetto Grodno for the inauguration of the Birkenau extermination camp. Now they departed from it with wrecked bodies, bruised, hungry and shivering with cold – into the unknown. While Birkenau – despite the fear of death, the hard labor, the beatings and punishments, so long as Dr. Mengele did not alter their fate by means of his fortnightly selections – was a kind of home, and a bunk to lay their hurting bodies and weeping and subdued souls, now they were going out to the unknown, in field conditions, in the cold, hunger and fear of death.

For about one week they plodded along in the cold and snow under the watchful eye of the Gestapo and S.S. guards, equipped with weapons and dogs, in the mud and snow of Poland in a north-westerly direction. In the evening their guards found abandoned train carriages and ruined houses where they could stay the night. In these conditions they lost even the poor food rations they had had in Birkenau, and they were forced to endeavor, with supreme effort, to gather potatoes, beetroots, carrots or other food they could obtain from the fields on their way. It even happened that they were forced to boil soup from the weeds they found in the fields.

In these marches of various groups on various routes, many women lost their lives or were shot by the S.S. guards, who had no desire to waste time with the weak and sick women. As was their habit, the women walked huddled in rows of five, the weaker ones being supported by the stronger ones, who walked at both ends of the rows, so that the evil eye of the guards would not discover those with difficulties.

On the pathways and roads, they often came under the hellish artillery fire of the Red Army, which had occupied most of Poland. A gigantic force of about six million soldiers from south and north was moving to take the Berlin region, from Dresden to Leipzig in the south to Kaliningrad in the north, with thousands of charging tanks and heavy fire from tens of thousands of cannons. But the Jews must be destroyed. Especially now that the Red Army had entered Birkenau and could see what had been taking place there.

Attached is another group of authentic pictures taken by the Red Army photographers upon entering Birkenau. There is no relationship between the current condition of the camp and as it was found in January 1945. The camp has been made over by the Poles.

After marching for about a week in the freezing snow and biting cold, with the hunger eating them body and soul, they reached a train station, and were loaded onto freight wagons going into Germany. On the way, the train stopped at the Magdeburg station. The train had come under heavy bombardment from airplanes, probably from the allies. Dozens of women had been killed outright, while others were wounded and bleeding. The wounded and the bleeding also ended their lives at the Magdeburg train station.

The women wearing the uniform of the Birkenau prisoners were taken by another train to a concentration camp north of Berlin, where the Red Army was not close by. They were placed as prisoners in the Ravensbruck women's camp. Here the destructive and cowardly Nazi brain could not do what had been done in the Polish extermination camps, while the Wehrmacht army had been in the U.S.S.R.

The beaten and defeated Wehrmacht, after the loss of Poland and of three million soldiers on the eastern front, regrouped anxiously inside Germany. At Ravensbruk there were no freely-operating mass extermination mechanisms, as there were at the extermination camps in Poland. Above them were the Allies' airplanes, seeing and photographing everything, so the Germans had no time for the planned extermination by gassing and burning bodies in the crematoria.

Now the soldiers of the Wehrmacht, the S.S. and the Gestapo understood that their defeat was approaching, therefore the plan changed and it was decided to transfer the prisoners to another women's camp, located south of Berlin, known as Melchov, near the present Berlin airport. Here, also, they understood that they would not be able to execute their plan to get rid of hundreds of thousands of men and women who had been smuggled into Germany for extermination. The free area to execute this task was shrinking in view of the encroaching fronts to the east and the west, under the closely scrutinizing eyes of the armies on both east and west.

When the Nazis who were in charge of the extermination of the Jewish people saw that the Red Army was concentrating its forces in the Berlin region, where Ravensbruck and Melchov were located, they decided to transfer the prisoners to a "safe haven" in the Elbe basin in the region of the city of Dresden, that had been totally destroyed. The plan was to drown hundreds of thousands of prisoners at the camp in the river Elbe. They had lost the method and organization of gassing and burning them in the crematoria as had previously been done outside Germany.

Bluma and her miserable comrades understood that their captors' end was near. All their wisdom and efforts were concentrated in safeguarding each other, supporting each other, to avoid collapsing, to hold on one more hour, one more minute.

They were led south again, both on foot and by train, to the Tauche camp near Dresden, a camp of Romani women, where they were housed. The plan was to take out a few hundred women each day and to drown them in the nearby Elbe river.

They stayed at Tauche for about three weeks, sleeping with fleas and lice, in the absence of any sanitary means. Until one day, the S.S. guards took Bluma and dozens more of her comrades in the direction of the Elbe River.

Every cloud has its silver lining. The U.S.S.R., under the murderous oppression of the Communist dictator, had built the strongest land army in the world, after millions of its soldiers had been killed in the battles with the Wehrmacht due to Stalin's crazy decisions. This army had been rehabilitated out of its own ruins, among others by genius commanders. It must not be forgotten in the history of the world, and especially in the history of our people and that of the Russian people, that almost 10% of its soldiers were Jews.

My father, Hanan Borowsky, of blessed memory, remained alive thanks to the British Army, which saved him from death when he lay in a pile of corpses, suffering from typhus and weighing 39 kg at the time of the liberation of the Bergen Belsen camp. Bluma's life was saved thanks to the Red Army soldiers, with the Jewish officers among them, near the city of Dresden. Not only shall I not forget that, but the whole of the Jewish people and its leaders must not forget it for all generations to come.

When Bluma and her comrades were being taken by the Fuhrer's S.S. guards in the direction of the river Elbe, they came under murderous artillery fire from the Red Army. The guards preferred to save their own souls rather than perform the task given to them, and they ran for their lives. Bluma and her comrades, in their Birkenau clothes, found themselves free of the electrified barbed wire fences, the Gestapo and S.S. guards and the hard labor, while the Red Army's cannons continued to fire thousands of shells on the region, and the women stood free in the fields but exposed to the cannon fire all around them. Indeed, fate is cruel and mocking – it is possible to be free even under artillery fire. Who would choose that?!

In the first few moments, with the shells exploding everywhere, they could not digest what was happening. When the firing died down a little, they began to understand that they must find a hiding place, supplies, clothing and protection from the cold. The date was close to April 1945, in the region of Dresden, in the State of Saxony.

The Rape Attempt in Riesa, the Surgery and the Mysterious Hospitalization

Bluma and her comrades gradually began to realize that the S.S. and Gestapo guards who had fled for their lives, had relinquished the right to hold them in the name of the Third Reich as prisoners without trial and to murder them, and that they were quite free. They awoke as from a dream. Red Army patrols were searching the area and the thunder of cannon could be heard from time to time. Bluma and her friends started out to find cover, food and clothing. Firstly, to preserve their lives, to free themselves from the dread, from the torturing hunger and their growling stomachs, and to endeavor at all costs to adapt and accustom themselves to breathing air without the stink of burning human flesh.

After two or three days they reached the town of Riesa, which serves as a center for the production of glass and porcelain. It lies between Dresden and Leipzig, in the State of Saxony, about 40 km north-west of Dresden, on the banks of the river Elbe.

At Riesa they found an abandoned house that had belonged to Germans and settled down there. The feeling in the vicinity was of German defeat. German soldiers were abandoning the front and fleeing for their lives, just as the women's guards had fled.

Bluma returned one evening from her daily search for supplies and for any kind of work that would enable them to purchase basic food. A German soldier who had escaped the battle attacked her in the yard of the house, and attempted to rape her. She struggled with him and he beat her fiercely, but she fought back with the last of her strength. Bluma told him explicitly that he was welcome to kill her, but that he would not get what he wanted. He continued to beat her, and threw her down on the ground, but she resisted and fought him with the remainder of her strength.

While they were still struggling in the yard of the house, two of her comrades returned and saw what was happening. The soldier understood that he was in trouble, and that since there were witnesses to the incident it would be better for him to discard his plan. In his despair and disappointment, and due to the blows he had received from Bluma, he drew his pistol and shot her in the stomach. It was an illegal hollow-point bullet which breaks into pieces inside the human body, and causes multiple wounds wherever it goes. The soldier fled and Bluma lay on the ground bleeding massively from the wound in her stomach, while her comrades did all they could to stop the bleeding and to call for help.

A sign from God in heaven saved Bluma. A Red Army patrol with motorbikes and a car passed nearby, and the women called them over to the house by waving to them. When the Russian soldiers saw how badly Bluma was bleeding, they dismantled the door of the house to serve as a stretcher, to which they tied her and took her to the nearby town of Oschatz, on the banks of the river Elbe, where there was a Wehrmacht field hospital.

On the way, with the women accompanying her together with the Red Army soldiers, one of the soldiers who had a little medical experience attempted to stop the bleeding. When they reached the hospital at Oschatz, they brought Bluma in on the door, with her lower abdomen bleeding from her serious wounds. There the field hospital commander, Dr. Doner, told them that he was very sorry, but medical treatment is never given to civilians who do not belong to the Wehrmacht.

It turned out that among the Red Army soldiers there were also two Jewish officers. No more than two seconds passed, before the Russian soldiers put their pistols to Dr. Doner's head and threatened him that if he did not operate on Bluma immediately, he and his staff would be executed on the spot.

Bluma underwent difficult abdominal surgery that lasted a number of hours, during which about eighty centimeters of the small intestine – the ileum – had to be removed. The function of this section of the digestive tract is, among other things, to absorb Vitamin B12, the lack of which might eventually cause the patient to contract Alzheimer's disease. The operation ended not only with an ileum that was eighty centimeters shorter, but also an 18 cm scar.

Bluma's comrades looked after her for a number of weeks within the Wehrmacht hospital at Oschatz in Saxony. Her recovery was difficult and she had a high fever, until it was discovered that she had developed an infection in the peritoneum. She was again taken in for surgery to deal with the infection, which resulted in another scar, six centimeters long.

This abdominal surgery on a twenty-year old girl, upon her return to freedom, is another serious event. Three and a half years earlier, at sixteen and a half, her whole world had collapsed, she had to discontinue her studies which she loved and at which she excelled, she had lost her father Isaac Plaskovsky and her elder brother Haim, who were murdered at the Treblinka camp, her home had been burned down, her home town had been destroyed and burned, and she had seen the bodies of neighbors, relatives, friends and family lying disfigured by the German air bombardment and artillery. In January 1943, on the platform at Birkenau, she had lost her mother and younger brother Zvi, after witnessing the atrocities committed by the S.S. officer Kurt Weise at Keilbasin and in the Grodno Ghetto. Add to that the horrors of the death camps of Birkenau, Ravensbruck, Melchov and Tauche. She apparently broke down, which led to a hospitalization the details of which we shall never know because she never told me about it. I learned of it only indirectly.

Since I was busy during Bluma's last years with my struggle with the authorities of Germany and the State of Israel, trying to improve the means of her maintenance, I tried with all my might to learn what had happened to her immediately after the second abdominal surgery, through the Saxony government, but to no avail. All I succeeded in discovering was that after the second operation at Oschatz, Bluma had been transferred to a sanatorium in Germany to recover. I do not know whether it was under the auspices of the Allied armies, and whether it also included supportive emotional treatment.

My dear father, Hanan, son of Yitzchak and Dvora Borowsky, of blessed memory, who had been searching for Bluma, arrived at this sanatorium in May or June of 1945. He and Bluma and two or three others out of the whole 2,050 Jews of Sopotzkyn had survived the most horrific events known to humanity.

Eventually, after I had matured and completed my education, and after Bluma had been widowed, in her last years before sliding into Alzheimer's disease, she began to share the horrors with me, grudgingly and not as one continuous narrative. I began connecting one fact to another, and all the data together, and managed to interpret the motives why my father Hanan, of blessed memory, who was fourteen years her senior, went in search of Bluma, to learn what had befallen her, whether she had survived and what he could do for her. It was because when she was a girl she had helped him to look after his first wife and their child in the Keilbasin trenches.

I repeatedly asked myself about the need which my father Hanan, of blessed memory, felt at the end of the war to search for Bluma who was fourteen years his junior. My father settled after the war in the city of Bremen in Germany. The distance between Bremen and Hannover is great. Bluma did not reveal the secret to me, but there could not have been any other reason.

The shortening of her intestine and the massive abdominal surgery she underwent placed a significant question mark over her ability to have children. At the time of my birth in October 1948 in Tel Aviv, just after the end of Israel's War of Independence, all her friends and acquaintances in Israel and the U.S. were anxious that she would not survive the birth. The very fact of my being able to write the story of her life is a sign that God in his heaven had planned to light her path, and to enable her to make a significant contribution to the establishment of a homeland for the Jewish people in the land of Zion and Jerusalem.

I had the opportunity in 1995 to travel to Germany with Tzofia, my wife, and my good friends, and on this trip we decided to focus on Berlin,

Dresden and Leipzig. While we were in the State of Saxony, I decided, with the consent of my wife and friends, to try and find the field hospital in the town of Oschatz. We arrived there in the afternoon. It was a day full of light and warmth in August, near the river Elbe, and I saw grandmothers and granddaughters licking ice-cream. I asked one of the grandmothers whether she had been living in the place in April 1945. Her face reddened, she picked up her granddaughters and left quickly. I approached another grandmother, more friendly than the first, and asked her, in a mixture of Yiddish and German, whether she knew the location of the Wehrmacht field hospital under the command of Dr. Doner. She indicated the place and I found it quickly. I had closed the circle.

Bluma and Hanan right after hospitalization

Life in Germany

Upon her release from the sanatorium where she had been for her second hospitalization and after she had met Hanan Borowsky, Bluma and her comrades travelled all over Germany by train, each one sunk into her own reflections and thoughts on how to continue on her way. She told me during our meetings in her kitchen of the journeys to Munich, Cologne, Frankfurt, Berlin and other places.

The purpose of these journeys was three-fold. The first was to find a place in the destroyed and ruined Germany where it would be possible to work and make a living and save some money. The second was to find any acquaintances and relatives who might have survived, and to inquire and know what was the fate of the others in the hell that just ended. The third goal was simply to travel on trains, to move about, seeing and watching in order to divert their afflicted souls from their gloomy and heavy thoughts.

Bluma told me that on one of these journeys she reached Berlin, where she found a place in the building of the Jewish community that had organized itself there. She stayed there a number of weeks, during which there was an incident where she slipped and nearly drowned in the river Spree, which circumvents Berlin and actually makes it into a peninsula. Passers-by helped her out.

In the end, Bluma decided to settle down in the city of Hannover, in a building which had been occupied and held by Jewish refugees who had survived the camps, on Hohe Street No. 20. That is where she lived. Eventually, while I was busy fighting for her income from the reparations, I found the building. Living in Hannover also reflected on the terms of her reparations, because the Reparations Office in Hannover was the worst and most strict of all the Reparations Offices in Germany.

Bluma found work at the home of rich Germans who owned a factory, and she was much loved by the couple. Eventually they begged her to stay with them, promising to look after her and enable her to continue with her studies that had been discontinued. But for her that was out of the question. The country was saturated with the blood of her family and her people, and was no place for her at all, no matter what the lure.

One day, walking in the center of Hannover, close to the bus station, Bluma noticed one of the S.S. women who had served in her block and had excelled in her cruelty to the prisoners. Bluma called the German police who detained the woman, but she never found out what developed in this matter.

Hanan decided to leave Bremen and moved to Hannover in the building where Bluma was living. He found work at a private German factory of precision mechanical instruments, and quickly did well there. He was a master craftsman in mechanics and metals, but because he had lost an eye at Bergen Belsen when he was wounded by the bayonet of an S.S. officer, precision mechanics work with only one eye was difficult for him. However, he did well at his work, and eventually the owner of the business asked him to stay on.

Bluma and Hanan slowly became a couple, he being 34 years old and she – 20, each of them with such a fragmented soul and body that the human mind could not digest. In the building at 20 Hohe Street in Hannover there were meetings among the survivors, and women and men became acquainted and became couples. [9]

Bella Vinitzky, Bluma's friend from Sopotzkyn, did not want to emigrate to Palestine. She and her Hungarian spouse, Berk Pollak, went to live in Stockholm, Sweden. From there they continued to San Diego in California, where Bella opened a successful women's clothing store. Bella was one of Bluma's closest friends.

---

9 Photograph of meetings of survivors in Hannover. Bluma's appearance and face leaves no doubt as to her emotional condition at the time. Is that what a 20-year-old girl looks like?

Not far from the city of Hannover, to the east, are the Herrenhäuser Gardens, which I had the opportunity of visiting. These gardens are no less beautiful than those at Versailles near Paris. There were often performances of opera and singing there, to which Hanan would sometimes take Bluma. He would also take her for walks in the gardens, where they had long heart-to-heart talks, and he, being an adult, who had entered the horrors as an adult, mature in spirit, devoted himself to Bluma and gave her enormous emotional support.

Bluma knew that the brothers and sisters of her mother Sheine Reisel and their children were living in the United States. She also knew that there were cousins from her father's family who were living there. She knew that the majority of them were in Chicago and the vicinity. Apart from her personal relationship with Hanan she exerted great efforts to make contact with her second-generation family, of whose existence in the U.S. she was aware, but of course she did not know their addresses.

One day, Bluma happened to meet a U.S. Army chaplain living in Chicago, Illinois. She told him that her mother's two brothers and their children were living in Chicago and that their family name was Horwitz. The chaplain decided to devote himself to this matter and a few days later he came back with the addresses of the uncles and cousins, Philip, Aida, Anni and Isidore Horwitz. They had opened a large Jewish bakery on Roosevelt Avenue in Chicago, which was known to the entire Jewish community.

Bluma made an enormous effort, and with the help of American soldiers, she sent letters in Yiddish to her relatives, but some of the cousins did not know that language, and she gradually began to learn English from the correspondence.

Bluma had her photo taken in 1946 by a photographer in Hannover, and on the back she wrote to her uncle in Chicago and to her first cousins, most of whom knew Yiddish. The photo is attached, showing both sides:

"Hannover March 12, 1946.

This is to remind you, my uncles and the Horwitz family

From me, the only living survivor from the Nazi hell.

Your niece and cousin

Bluma Plaskovsky" [10]

---

10 The photograph and her handwriting in Yiddish are shown here.

The cousins in Chicago referred her to her cousin Jack Horwitz of Brooklyn, New York, with whom she had met in the last summer before the war in his town of Yezori, Poland. Jack had managed to save his life and reached the United States in 1938. Jack and his wife Nancy, a smart and gracious woman, devoted themselves methodically to supporting Bluma and her fate until their death. Jack and Nancy had a factory which manufactured shoe decorations in Greenwich Village in Manhattan.

Jack connected Bluma with his twin brothers who had emigrated to the U.S. years earlier, Nathan and Irving Harvin. Irving was living in San Diego, California, and Nathan was living in Tijuana, Mexico. They owned a large business for the sale of clothes in Tijuana. Their elder brother, Saul Horwitz, was living with his family in Mexico City. They all began an intensive and warm relationship with Bluma, and did not cease helping her until they passed away.

The letter Bluma sent from Hannover to the Horwitz family in Chicago.

The relatives did not know of her relationship with Hanan, and suggested that she come to the U.S., where they would look after her. At a later stage, when she was already in Israel, she became acquainted with more branches of the family of her mother, Sheine Reisel, and her father, Isaac, in the U.S.

Bluma discovered that her mother's brother, Mendel Horwitz, was living in Los Angeles, California, near her aunt, Fannie Chester, who was also living in the vicinity, in Palos Verdes, South Los Angeles.

Uncle Mendel, Sheine Reisel's brother, had a huge business marketing tobacco, cigarettes and candy in Southern California, and it was expanded by his only son, dear Herbert Horwitz, who developed the business into an empire after the demise of his father. The wife of uncle Mendel Horwitz, Herbert's mother, did not give the letters that came from Bluma to her husband, who was blind. Herbert went to the community with his father, and read out to his blind father the letters from his niece. Herbert, whom I knew well, looked very much like Bluma, and was immensely good-hearted.

Fannie, the sister of my grandmother, Sheine Reisel, my mother's aunt, was the mother of Dr. Martin Chester and Anita Lyons, who was living in Silver Springs, Maryland, and was the editor of Bob Hope's TV programs.

On my first visit to the U.S. in 1966, I met Bluma's uncle in Chicago, Sam Horwitz, of blessed memory, and her Aunt Fannie, of blessed memory, in Los Angeles. They were charming people. Bluma had never met them.

Eventually, contact was made with more dear relatives from Wisconsin, Madison and Milwaukee: the Lipton (Lipchek) family, whose head, Isaac Lipchek, had come from Sopotzkyn. His dear children, who loved Bluma fiercely, Paul and Sam Lipton, Ethel Meir, Frances and Laurence Weinstein, Esther Lange, Ruthi Stein, Dr. Morris Finsky, the surgeon at the Southern Hospital in Chicago, who had been born in Sopotzkyn, all from Chicago and the vicinity, as well as her cousin Elaine Wayne. Bluma also found her cousin Beatrice (Bluma) Turetzky, who was living in Boston, Massachusetts. Beatrice had served as a nurse on a U.S. battleship in the Pacific War.

The family discovered by Bluma in the U.S. and Mexico, was very dear to her heart, because she was a "brand saved from the fire". The relatives enabled her to renew her contact with the world of good memories from the home of her parents in Sopotzkyn. Fate compensated Bluma with wonderful relatives, outstanding people, who supported her emotionally, and even financially as far as they could. The fact that there was a family in this cruel universe who were in the United States of America, who wanted her and could support her, contributed no end to her emotional strength and encouraged her. This family of Bluma and of my father whom I got to know, gave me, personally a real and precise measure of the quality of the human material that our people had lost in the Holocaust. The Nazis caused the Jewish people impossibly heavy damage, not only in numbers, but also in quality.

The only one of Hanan's family who survived without entering the death train of Sopotzkyn Jewry on January 18, 1943 to Birkenau was his elder sister, Esther Tolkovsky, of blessed memory, who emigrated to Palestine in 1925 in the year of Bluma's birth. Bluma, of course, never met her until she came to Israel.

Although the relationship between Bluma and Hanan continued to become closer, Hanan explained to her that if she wanted to be with him she would have to go to Palestine. It was his desire to live in the Land of Israel near his sister, Esther, and her family. After the horrors he had experienced he was not prepared to hear of any other country except that one. "I am not forcing you," he told her. "If you want to be with your family in the U.S. I shall not stop you and I shall accept it with understanding."

For Bluma it was a very painful decision to make on this point. Her relatives were insisting that she come to them to the U.S., and her German family in Hannover wanted to adopt her. She wanted Hanan to come with her to the States, where she would be together with the only people left to her on this earth, who were of her blood, and whom she could trust. She was torn apart.

Bluma never shared with me her considerations why she eventually chose to go with Hanan to the Land of Israel, but as I matured and understood the essence of life, my admiration of her for this decision grew stronger.

Bluma had encountered the horrors of humanity at a critical age in a person's life, between sixteen and a half and twenty. All the values she had absorbed up to that age had been destroyed and vanished. She was looking for a father figure and a provider, a partner on whom she could lean; she had not yet completed the process of entering and preparing for normal existence: she lacked a profession and her education that had been cut off in the middle.

She remembered Hanan from Sopotzkyn as the breadwinner for his family, his mother and his brothers and sisters, after the death of his father, and as one who was married and was a father of a child and who provided respectably for them and for his family. She had helped Hanan look after his daughter and his wife, Yochi, nee Umansky, in the Keilbasin trenches until they were murdered.

Bluma understood that Hanan had not enjoyed a "picnic" with the Nazis, after he had lost his mother, his daughter, his wife, his siblings. However, she understood, from what had happened to him and from what she saw in the Sopotzkyn Ghetto itself, that the S.S. officers were in need of him, due to his being a master craftsman in mechanics and metals. The S.S. officers' need of his professional talents, and his prominent charismatic conduct in company, made the period of the Holocaust easier for him, although it had been far from stress-free in its cruelty.

Hanan had also arrived on the train to Auschwitz from the Grodno Ghetto on January 23, 1943. Luckily for him, the Nazis were looking for professionals. When they understood that they had before them a master craftsman in mechanics and metals, they sent him to the Portland cement factory at Golschau near the town of Katowice in Upper Silesia. There he was employed in maintenance of the mechanical industrial equipment. He was there for about two years. Due to the conquest of Poland and Upper Silesia by the Red Army, he was transferred to the port of Altona near Hamburg, to the Wehrmacht's submarine dockyards. That was why, when the dockyards and the city of Hamburg were bombed, he was transferred to the Bergen Belsen camp, on the road from Hamburg to Hannover, near the town of Celle, the administrative capital of Lower Saxony.

Bluma's emotions and intelligence led her to the decision that it would be preferable for her to stay with Hanan and to go with him to Palestine. She would have a husband who was a wise, strong, experienced, reliable man, with a high level of morality, a father figure for her, a strong support, a professional who was a good provider, with a noble spirit, who was known to her from childhood, they were both from the same mental environment, united by the threads of fate.

It would be better for her to travel to the Land of Israel than to go to the United States. She had no desire to be a burden on her relatives whom she did not know, except for Jack Horwitz in New York. She also kept in mind the unforgettable picture of Fruma Horwitz, for whose welfare Bluma had been responsible as far as she could, at the risk of her own life and soul. Bluma understood that it would be preferable not to become a burden on anyone's shoulders.

When she arrived in Palestine on May 31, 1947, she worked at a printing house for a short time, where she met a professor of chemistry from the Weizmann Institute, who courted her before she married. She rejected his courtship politely, explaining that "the level of his education was not suited to hers". She did not share with me her deliberations on this subject. They are the result of my knowledge of those involved and their considerations.

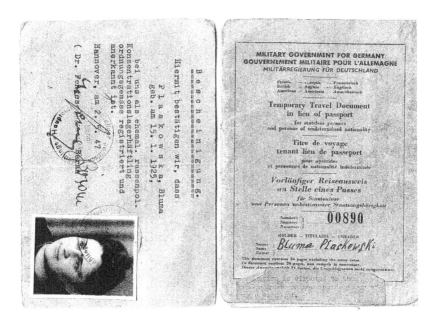

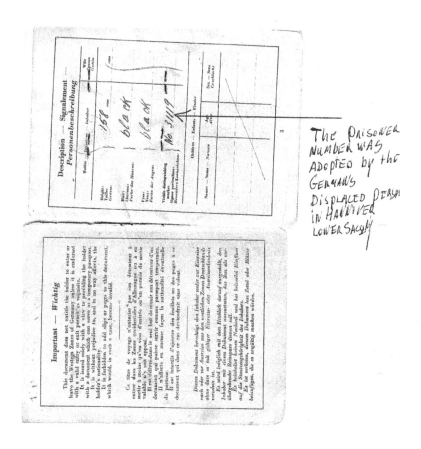

THE PRISONER NUMBER WAS ADOPTED by the GERMANS DISPLACED PERSON in HANNOVER LOWER SACSONY

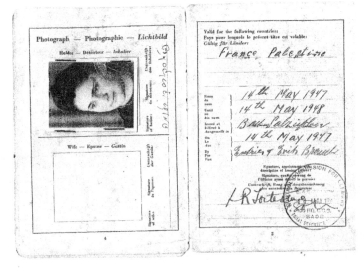

VISAS
SICHTVERMERKE

N.B. The name of the holder of this document should
be reproduced in each visa.

Le nom du détenteur du présent titre
devra être reproduit sur chaque visa.

Der Name des Inhabers dieses Ausweises
ist in jedem Sichtvermerk zu wiederholen.

6

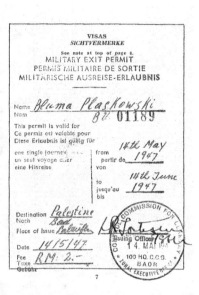

VISAS
SICHTVERMERKE

See note at top of page 6.

MILITARY EXIT PERMIT
PERMIS MILITAIRE DE SORTIE
MILITÄRISCHE AUSREISE-ERLAUBNIS

Name / Nom — *Bluma Plaskowski*

BV 01189

This permit is valid for
Ce permis est valable pour
Diese Erlaubnis ist gültig für

one single journey / from / partir de / von — *14th May 1947*
un seul voyage aller
eine Hinreise — to / jusqu'au / bis — *14th June 1947*

Destination / Nach — *Palestine*
Place of Issue — *Bad.*
Date — *14/5/47*
Fee / Taxe / Gebühr — *RM. 2.—*

Issuing Officer

14. MAI 1947
100 HQ. C.C.G.
BAOR

7

VISAS
SICHTVERMERKE

See note at top of page 6.

PLASKOWSKI, Bluma

BRITISH PASSPORT CONTROL
GERMANY

Date...
Visa for...
Signature...

8

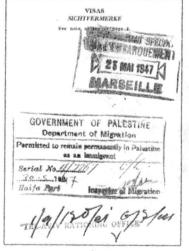

VISAS
SICHTVERMERKE

See note at top of page 6.

CONTRÔLE SPECIAL
DEBARQUEMENT
25 MAI 1947
MARSEILLE

GOVERNMENT OF PALESTINE
Department of Migration

Permitted to remain permanently in Palestine
as an immigrant

Serial No...
...1947
Haifa Port — Inspector of Migration

9

The Vessel Providence Enters Haifa Port on May 31, 1947

In the last week of May 1947, a French passenger ship named Providence sailed from Marseilles, France on the way to the port of Haifa, with a stop-over at Alexandria. Among the passengers on the Providence were also my mother, Bluma, and my father, Hanan.

The passengers on the Providence were an unusual lot. These were the remnants of the people of Israel – the brands saved from the fire of the Nazi extermination camps, whose entry into Palestine had been approved by the British Mandate. This human freight had been living as displaced persons on the bloody soil of Germany after the Holocaust in the DP camps in the states making up the Federal Germany, and had been collected group by group, and transferred via Holland to the French port of Marseilles. The souls of many of them had been consumed in the fires of hell, but their lungs still kept them alive.

The British Mandate grudgingly permitted entry into Palestine for the survivors of the extermination camps of the European Jewry who remained after the war with no family or property.

They endeavored to recover and to rehabilitate themselves after the most horrific atrocities in the history of mankind, that had been committed by the Nazi people, under the auspices of its state and its government, against another people which had lost its land and sovereignty thousands of years earlier. The majority of the Jewish people had been scattered in the cities, towns and villages of Poland, Russia, Lithuania, Ukraine, Hungary, Czechia, France, Holland, Romania, Bulgaria, Italy, Greece, Lybia, Tunisia, Algiers, Morocco and Iraq – the exiles of the Jewish people.

Similar to the other passengers on the Providence, Hanan and Bluma carried with them an intolerable emotional load. Terrible memories of horrors never before seen by human beings, the constant yearlong fear of death, 24 hours a day, the destruction of human values, the sharpening of survival mechanisms, endurance, coping with emotional and physical pain. The emotional and physical pains caused by hunger and cold and their overall accumulation, have a direct and everlasting implication on the personality carrying them.

All these components, including physical damage, were stamped on the passengers on the Providence, each according to whatever he had received from the Nazi oppressor.

The ship slowly approached from south to north in the direction of Haifa Port. Before it docked a boat reached it carrying Shlomo Dvorsky, the cousin of Hanan Borowsky, who had emigrated to Palestine before the Holocaust, and was the Secretary of the Seamen's Union in Haifa Port. Shlomo Dvorsky had been born in the town of Sopotzkyn, as were Bluma and Hanan, and they and another two or three were the only survivors from among its 2,050 Jews who were transported for extermination on January 18, 1943 on the train from the Grodno Ghetto for the inauguration of the largest slaughterhouse erected by humans for the extermination of humans.

Revival in Israel

Bluma and Hanan left Haifa port on May 31, 1947 and drove to the home of Hanan's sister, Esther Tolkovsky in Tel Aviv. They lived there a few months as friends, as they were not yet married.

Bluma found work in a printing house, and Hanan looked for a job in the field of metals, mechanics and metalwork. They married about six months after their arrival, on November 11, 1947, and rented a room on Yeshayahu Street in Tel Aviv without a kitchen. In the nearby building, Menachem Begin, who eventually became the Prime Minister, was hiding from the British.

Underneath the building on Yeshayahu Street there was an underground stash of weapons belonging to the "Hagana". The person in charge of the stash would often ask Hanan to fix a jammed weapon.

Bluma was 22 years old when she arrived in Palestine, and began to cope with the heat and difficult living conditions in the country. She prepared food on a "primus" stove which stood on the stairs of the building. Food products which were available and required cooling were kept in a box into which lumps of ice were inserted, that were bought from the ice distributor.

Bluma became pregnant and on October 10, 1948, at just about the end of the battles of Israel's War of Independence, after the State had been declared in May 1948, she delivered me after a difficult labor. Everyone who knew about her stomach surgery was concerned for her during the birth. My aunt Esther, my cousin Sarah and her friends in Israel and abroad were tense and anxious as to how the birth would go. Luckily, I emerged into the world.

One day, when my mother was preparing a meal for me in the kitchen in the stairwell, she was bitten by a scorpion, which was a regular part of the scenery in the sandy country at that time.

Hanan was accepted for work by the Electricity Company, at the nearby Reading Power Station. He was immediately appointed shift chief. But after a week, when he saw how bad was the work ethic in the place, he quit.

They lived on Yeshayahu Street for about two years, and then moved to another rented room at 25 Kalisher Street, Tel Aviv, near the building of the first Hebrew Gymnasium Herzliya. It was on the second floor, and it was accessed by an outside staircase, not from the inside stairwell.

On the floor where they lived there was a dear Haredi family, Haim and Shoshana Fried, of blessed memory. They had one daughter and four sons, who played with me as a child, and today they are all heads of Yeshivot in Israel. Haim and Shoshana Fried, of blessed memory, adored Bluma and Hanan, and life together on the second floor was a life of love and friendship between the two families. Many years after my parents left that house, Shoshana came to visit Bluma, because she could not say goodbye to her. Shoshana had a very elderly mother who lived with her, and Bluma would often help to look after the old lady.

In 1952, when I was 4 years old, Hanan's cousin Elhanan Sereviansky came to Israel. He had commanded an artillery battalion in the Red Army at the Battle of Stalingrad, and was in very bad shape. He was in pain all over his body from the shrapnel that had hit him on the battlefield, the pieces of which moved from time to time and it was necessary to remove them by surgery. He came without any family, since they had all been exterminated. He found a room near the Great Synagogue of Tel Aviv, on Allenby Street.

It was a time of rationing and shortages in Israel, and Elhanan engaged in selling goods that were illegal at the time, to make a minimum living. The Israeli police made every effort to get hold of the illegal goods and those who traded in them. I cannot forget how Bluma would go and help Elhanan to conceal and hide his wares in her home, at risk to herself, so that he could eke out an existence.

Elhanan Sereviansky moved to live in Kfar Malal in the Sharon. He became acquainted with Batya Ben Hillel, whose father had immigrated to Israel as a Zionist from San Diego, California, in 1913, before the First World War. Elhanan and Batya were married. My parents, together with Emanuel and myself, all travelled to Kfar Malal often, especially on Saturdays. We would bring home with us eggs, oranges and grapefruit, which were the main agricultural crops of the Elhanan's family. In those days, Kfar Malal was near the border with Jordan, before the Six Day War, and infiltrators would sometimes penetrate the region from Qalqilya.

On one of our visits to Kfar Malal we saw an elderly lady riding a donkey. The woman greeted us and Batya, whom she knew well. She looked at Bluma, and after we left she asked Batya who was the woman she had seen with her family. Of course, Batya told her.

The name of the lady on the donkey was Dvora (Vera) Scheinermann, and she was the mother of Arik Sharon. Batya's elder brother, Arik Ben Hillel, of blessed memory, was a friend of Ariel Sharon, who was one of the best of the sons of the State of Israel, and eventually became Prime Minister and Minister of Defense. He established the modern Israel Defense Army, and was one of its greatest field commanders. It was General Arik Sharon who vanquished the Egyptian army in the Six Day War at the battle of Um Katef, and who crossed the Suez Canal with his corps in the Yom Kippur War, which eventually led to the Egyptians' surrender.

Arik Ben Hillel, of blessed memory, was killed in the War of Independence, at the Battle of Kastel, while opening the road to Jerusalem.

Dvora Scheinermann asked Batya to let her know when Bluma was to come to visit again. She really wanted to speak with her. Bluma and Dvora met a number of times in Kfar Malal, when we came to visit there. Dvora would tell Batya that Bluma was a fascinating woman.

My brother Emanuel, four years younger, was born in December 1952. Bluma was then 26 years old. His birth reinforced our parents' need to find a better and more spacious place to live.

Bluma had three second cousins, two of whom were living in Israel, both born in Sopotzkyn. One was Yehuda Ayalti, one of those who established Kibbutz Ayelet HaShahar. The other was Zahava Pikovsky, who had been a partisan during the World War in the forests with her husband, Reuven, of blessed memory. The relationship with them was wonderful and close.

Yehuda Ayalti, with the aim of making things easier for Bluma, who could not afford home help, used to take me, in the summers of the last years of elementary school, to Kibbutz Ayelet HaShahar, and he would return me after two or three weeks. On the kibbutz I lived with the children my own age. Yehuda would arrive every few weeks in Tel Aviv on the kibbutz jeep, and would stay as a guest in our small house. We would often visit each other's homes. Zahava and Bluma were like sisters. Emanuel and I saw Zahava's children many times during our childhood and teenage years.

In the period when we lived on Kalisher Street, developments occurred of which I had no knowledge due to my young age (three to six). When I was six years old, we moved to an apartment which Bluma and Hanan purchased at 3 Shir Street, Tel Aviv. Bluma, who so wanted to have a home of her own, being the mother of two sons, was deceived by the State of Israel. She fell into an additional personal disaster which smote her at the time, and affected me, as well, in my later fifties. This economic disaster, was a direct result of the Nazi terror and the post trauma she suffered on the one hand, and the conduct of the State of Israel on the other, the nature of which I prefer to leave the reader to define. The Israeli governments did something appalling, which they could have corrected, even decades later, but they took no action. This affair will be discussed later.

When we lived on Shir Street, we used to go for walks on Saturdays with our parents along Dizengoff Street, which was not far from our home. At the center of the square was a pool of water about one meter deep. Bluma and Hanan met the contractor David Yellin and his wife near the pool, and were deep in conversation with him, while Emanuel my brother, and I played on the grass around the pool. Suddenly, my father Hanan, who always wore a suit and tie on Shabbat, jumped into the pool, and brought out my brother Emanuel, about eighteen months old. We had not noticed that he was drowning.

This incident deeply shocked Bluma and Hanan, and reinforced the post trauma. I began to sense that Bluma and Hanan were focusing more on Emanuel, because they felt guilty that such a thing had occurred. Ever since then I sensed that the most attention, especially Bluma's, was being given to Emanuel.

On Friday evenings, we would go to the home of my aunt Esther, my father's sister, and these were interesting and happy family gatherings. Bluma loved my aunt very much, who was twenty years older. My aunt Esther, of blessed memory, showered enormous attention on me, both in my childhood and later on.

On the floor above us on Shir Street lived Leah and Arye Reich, two Holocaust survivors from western Poland. They had no children. Bluma and Leah became good friends, and Leah greatly helped my mother raise me. Leah would take me to the movies and on walks, and enabled my mother to devote more time to Emanuel who, she felt, "required protection".

The Sinai War broke out while we were living on Shir Street in Tel Aviv. In that campaign, the IDF, together with British and French forces conquered the Sinai Peninsula but had to evacuate it under pressure from President Eisenhower. The State of Israel was then very young and the sirens' wailing and the need to go down into bomb shelters did not contribute much to Bluma's condition, who was depressed and sad.

Our mother Bluma was a housewife all our lives, ever since we were born. She was always very quiet and sad. Our home was as clean as a museum, always tidy, bedclothes and clothes were orderly, starched and ironed like soldiers on parade before the Queen. When we left the house we were well-groomed and dressed in the best of taste. But I found it difficult to bring friends home because the atmosphere there was not happy, which children do not like.

Regarding studies and health, both of her children and of herself, Bluma was very strict, and motivated that her children should be educated, smart and independent.

She found it very difficult to get on with me in my childhood. Contrary to Emanuel, I had the ability to stand up to her, and there were quite a few confrontations between her and me. When she saw she was unable to enforce her will on me, she would wait for my father and would complain to him about my stubbornness on certain issues.

In my childhood and teenage years, the arguments with her often turned into outbursts, which usually ended in my feeling guilty for having dared to hurt her and distressing her after everything she had gone through. Not once I burst into tears after such events.

I loved playing football. I loved the company of other children and horse-play, but it was never negative. She was always concerned that nothing would ever come of me. "Look how Emanuel studies well and is obedient. You are a 'julik' – a prankster", she would say.

After Emanuel travelled to Santa Barbara, and especially after my father's death, a closer relationship developed between my mother and me. She saw that I had achieved something in my life, that many people appreciated me, that she was received with love and esteem by Tzofia and my children, and our relationship became closer and deeper.

However, although our relationship improved, still one of the qualities which she had developed at Birkenau – suspicion – did not enable her to present all the paperwork and her rights and those of my father to the Reparations authorities. It was very difficult to win her trust, and the only ones who enjoyed such trust were her relatives in the U.S.

Bluma was an excellent cook. The meals she prepared for us were delicacies. She knew how to make gourmet dishes, both for the warm summer days and for the cold season.

The brother of Yehuda from Kibbutz Ayelet HaShahar, the author Hanan Ayalti, who lived in Manhattan and was also Bluma's second cousin, born in Sopotzkyn, was the editor of the largest Yiddish newspaper in the world, "Forverst". When Hanan Ayalti would come to Tel Aviv from New York, he loved to eat the salt herring with fried tomatoes and onion which she made. Whenever he came she would make it for him, and she derived great pleasure from his enjoyment of the delicacies she prepared, which of course were what she remembered from her parents' home in Sopotzkyn.

Around her relatives from Sopotzkyn and her cousins from the U.S. I sensed that she was celebrating and opening up, while in daily life she was very rational, and did not express her feelings.

The mothers of my friends used to kiss and hug their children. I do not remember Bluma ever hugging or kissing me. She always told me to see reality, and not to follow illusions. But Emanuel she kept under her wing. He was the obedient and disciplined child who required protection. I was the "naughty" one, in her opinion. I never enjoyed any indulgence from her in my childhood.

I noticed that my classmates enjoyed celebrations, birthdays and Jewish festivals. We did not have any of these. Bluma did not celebrate, nor did she bloom, as did other mothers, at the approach of a festival or event. The only thing that made her happy was visits of relatives from the U.S. to our home. Another source of happiness for her was academic achievements. Apart from these, a heavy depression always emanated from her look and her eyes.

Bluma was always anxious in managing the household. Everything was calculated, and food that was still edible must not be wasted or not utilized. "Yitzhak", she would say to me, "You see this piece of pie, people would dream of something like that for weeks."

In my childhood I noticed that she would place blind faith in people with authority, policemen, army officers, lawyers, doctors and medical professors. I did not understand that phenomenon in my youth, but as I became older I understood its source – the post trauma. On the other hand, my father, who had entered the Holocaust as a person with a well-formed personality at age 31, would always say to me: "Yitzhak, I know many professors who are only half human." Life has taught me that my father was right, and that the awe Bluma felt towards people in positions of power and authority derived from her fear of them that had seeped into her personality during the long period of survival.

Any attempt raised within the family regarding economic development, to try and attain greater economic achievements, encountered her objection, which was accompanied by trembling and perspiration. She never agreed to risk even 5% of what already existed in order to attain a higher profit or income.

A distant relative of Bluma's, born in Sopotzkyn, Ya'acov Ben-Yehuda, re-established his home in a new city built in Israel – Ashdod, about forty kilometers south of Tel Aviv. That was in 1956. One evening, Ya'acov visited us and told my father that there were plots for sale in Ashdod at a ridiculously low price. He suggested that my father take a small loan from the bank, if he did not have liquid assets at that time, purchase an area on which at least ten apartment houses could be built at a basement price.

When Bluma heard of this she suffered an attack of anxiety. She implored my father to not even think of entering into such a transaction, which might endanger the loss of their modest savings or for which a small loan would have to be taken from the bank.

Eventually, there were many suggestions that I also made, which if she had accepted them would have alleviated her situation as well as mine for the future. Any attempt to pay a small price in exchange for a greater potential profit, including for her, always resulted in an anxiety attack and absolute refusal to cooperate. This anxiety was reinforced subsequently, when Hanan passed away, when she lost him as a breadwinner, and when her cousins also passed away.

In the days when we grew up as children and youths in our parents' home there were no dishwashers or laundry dryers. Bluma would wash the dishes after the meal, dry them and put them back in their places. She used to hang the laundered clothes on the roof of the building to dry. The house was like a museum on display. Nothing must disturb its order.

In 1959, when she received reparations from Lower Saxony, she went, together with my father, to look for a larger apartment for us to move in to. Bluma knew how to choose apartments, and in my youth many would come to get her advice regarding the purchase of a residence for themselves, and as to what are the most important elements in selecting one.

We walked for whole days in the area of North Tel Aviv, which was entirely covered with sand and orange groves at that time. On one of the sand hills, Bluma found her last apartment, where she lived from 1960 to 2008, about fifty years, until I, her firstborn, was forced to uproot her, on April 7, 2008, from that beloved apartment at 6 Epstein Street, Tel Aviv.

Her well-lit and well-ventilated apartment, in a quiet but central place in Tel Aviv, helped her in her difficult distress. It gave her a sense of having been uplifted from the depths of her fate. The neighbors and other residents loved her very much. She saw to it that the room which was our bedroom on Epstein Street was decorated with light and joyous colors, and when her relatives from the U.S. visited, she loved to play host to them. When her cousin from Mexico, Nathan Horwitz, of blessed memory, his wife and twin daughters came on a lengthy visit, she rented a neighboring apartment on the same floor.

Bluma and my father made their home a second home for Johnny, Mayer and Gigi. From the balcony facing north a large, well-kept garden could be seen, the likes of which there are not many in Tel Aviv.

In the years of her widowhood, and especially in the last ten years before she slid into the Alzheimer's disease, she used to sit on the balcony and watch the little children playing in the garden. She followed their development from the balcony, and whenever she noticed any change or achievement in any child she would watch them with loving eyes. She would dissolve with pleasure. She would even share with whoever was with her on the balcony her joy at the development and antics of the child she was watching.

In the same building lived an attorney, and judges and respected people from the generation of those who established the State of Israel. There were quite a few who knew her and appreciated her from the depth of their hearts.

While I was studying at university, Bluma met my good friend, attorney Shimon Elsner, of blessed memory, who had grown up with his mother, who was a Holocaust survivor, in one room in a remote neighborhood of Tel Aviv, to whom life had not been good. She asked me to invite him for lunch with us, when we were both studying for our exams, because she suspected that Shimon did not have enough to eat.

As she grew older, she suffered from many sicknesses. She would visit the doctor in good time. She would go deep into the details of her condition and would comply with all of the doctor's orders. Every week or two, both alone with her and also in front of the family, I repeatedly asked her to enable me to review all the documents and her correspondence with the Reparations

Office, but she refused. I explained to her that it could only be for her good. She replied, "Yitzhak, I don't want you to have anything to do with them. You don't know who they are."

Together with many people who had survived the Nazi hell, Bluma had applied to a legal firm in Tel Aviv, which was lacking in experience and understanding of the legal and medical material. Bluma, Hanan and hundreds of thousands were in existential distress. They had no homes or the wherewithal to buy one. Most of them had no parents or relatives who could help and support them. They had all been murdered. They were not healthy, and the signs of the damage to body and soul began slowly to emerge, and that made it difficult for them to conduct their work and a normal lifestyle compared to others of their age. Even during the period when the law firm was handling their affair, new diseases emerged and revealed themselves. The lawyers did not know how to instruct them, and she was afraid that what she had complained of was all there was, and that it was forbidden to report any further injury or illness.

The few law firms that undertook to handle the filing of these claims, most of whom spoke German, had no knowledge of damages and medicine, and they had no previous experience with the legal procedure. On the other hand, their clients, the Holocaust survivors, were broken in body and spirit, crying for help, not one of whom had completed a high school education. Those who applied to lawyers in Germany attained much better results than those miserable ones who placed their fate in the hands of the Israeli attorneys. And of course, the government gave no assistance in consulting and instructing these poor people.

The limited number of legal firms handling these claims were doing nobody any favors. Thousands had applied to them, and the lawyers were seeking only to compromise with the Reparations Offices, and were not interested in investigating the truth in the courts. All they wanted was to get their remuneration as quickly as possible, while the good of the client was far from their minds.

"Yitzhak", Bluma told me, "I came to the law firm, and dozens of people were waiting for their turn on benches. Clerks employed by the firm would receive you, give you empty pages and tell you to sign at the bottom of the page. In view of the long queue outside they would ask you briefly and quickly what happened to you, they would have you sign a legal fees agreement and a power of attorney, and send the claim off to Germany."

"After a few months you would be invited again to the office, and the clerks would tell you that the medical committee of the Reparations Office wants medical documents. After you send them, another invitation would come referring you to a doctor appointed by the Reparations Office in Israel, whose responsibility is to verify your complaints, and to forward his opinion to the Reparations Office."

What can a woman of 29 understand about the implications of all the atrocities, the beatings on the head, the hunger and cold on the present and future condition of her health? Is everything revealed to her and to the eyes of hundreds of thousands like her? Did the State of Israel think of providing medical advice, by means of its own Ministry of Health, to the survivors of the extermination camps before they submit their claims to the Reparations Office? Did the health funds give any medical advice to the hundreds and thousands groaning under the pressure of the emotional and economic distress, who were raising small children without housing, in the period of rationing and difficulties in making a living on the one hand, and the security events on the other?

Would it not be preferable to "restrain oneself a little more under the distress, to see whether the claimant was aware and understood the extent of his damage?

"Yitzhak, I described on the paper the clerks gave me what had happened to me in the Sopotzkyn Ghetto, Keilbasin, the Grodno Ghetto, Birkenau, the Death March, the Ravensbruck, Molcho and Tauche camps, my stomach wounds from the shooting after the attempted rape."

Eventually, when I was Bluma's guardian, I found among her papers medical certificates showing that when her story was written on the page which she had signed when it was a blank paper, in the law firm in Tel Aviv, the spinal damage was already there. While waiting for the replies from the Lower Saxony Reparations Office in Hannover, serious damage to the retinas due to head beatings had already been discovered, and there were problems with bowel movements and constipation as a direct result of the stomach surgery and the shortening of her intestine,. Where did all this damage come from? Why was it not included in her claim? Why was no request made to withdraw her claim and resubmit it? She paid the price in her quality of life, and afterwards I did, in the quality of my life.

Indeed, to memorialize the Holocaust one day each year is an important thing, but to look after the brands saved from the fire from among your own people, and the concept that the better and more comfortable is their situation, the stronger the State will also be, never occurred to anyone. The State of Israel and the heads of its government established the "Yad VaShem" memorial to perpetuate the memory of the Holocaust. On the national anniversary of the Holocaust, ministers of the government of Israel and a significant number of the Members of the Knesset remind us each year of their cousins and distant relatives who were exterminated by the Nazi oppressor. But when in their vicinity sit first generation survivors of the extermination camps who were actually there, on whom they impose the judicial presumption that they had been persecuted by the *people of the specific German State (Land) as opposed to the German Federation,* that is an eternal disgrace to both the State and the people of Israel. It is the greatest ignominy, shame and disgrace that the leaders of the people have imposed on the very individuals who were the most damaged and sensitive in the history of humanity and of the people of Israel, and all without Knesset approval.

The Reparations Agreement (the Luxembourg Agreement) – Damage to the Individual and the Public

In order to understand the further chain of events in Bluma's life, in the shadow of the severe post trauma that was exacerbated, we shall halt the flow of the story, and turn to an external matter over which Bluma and hundreds of thousands of others had no control. This matter had serious implications for the survivors of the extermination camps, both for individuals and for the State, regarding rehabilitation of the survivors of the camps. It was a perversion of justice, and the vilest injustice committed by the governments of Israel over the years.

The Federal Republic of West Germany was of the opinion that those whom it was obligated to compensate were the displaced Jews who were currently on the soil of the countries and cities of the Federal Republic of Germany. These included the following: Bavaria, Baden Württemburg, Rhineland-Palatinate, Hessen, North Rhine-Westphalia, Lower Saxony, Bremen, Hamburg and Schleswig Holstein. The government of the Republic of West Germany was located in Bonn. Concerning the other German states who participated in the Holocaust (Saxony, Thuringia, Prussia), about 17,000,000 Germans under the control of communist East Germany, the West German Republic took no responsibility.

Who is a person who escaped the Holocaust, and who is a survivor? Many Jews, especially in Russia, Ukraine and the Baltic States, as well as a few hundred thousand Polish Jews, fled into Russia. Although their lives were difficult, they retained their family frameworks, and they were spared the terror of the S.S. and the Gestapo, the denial of freedom, the hard labor, the torture and the atrocities that occurred inside the extermination camps. These Jews were saved from the Holocaust. They escaped the Holocaust. Although some bore the scars of bodily injury, and some suffered emotional damage, they lived as free persons inside Russia.

The Federal Republic, under pressure from the Allies, was prepared to pay reparations for the displaced persons who were living on the soil of the Federal Republic of Germany, after its surrender in April 1945. About half a million displaced Jews were living then in West Germany. Who were these Jews? They were the survivors of the extermination camps, like Bluma, who had been transported at gun point into Germany in order to complete the final solution of the Jewish problem, inter alia by drowning some of them in the River Elbe. The Jews of Germany had already been exterminated at the beginning of the war in the extermination camps within Germany.

The majority of the displaced Jews who were on the soil of the West German Federation were young people who had undergone the horrors, the majority from Poland, Hungary and Czechia. The Jews of France had returned to their homes. It was mainly the Polish Jews who had nowhere to return. Their homes had been wiped off the face of the earth, and for the majority not a single soul remained in the countries they had come from – they had all been exterminated. The Jews of Czechia had also lost their property due to the actions of the Soviet government, as had the Jews of Hungary.

On September 10, 1952, the Reparations Agreement was signed between the Government of Israel and the Federal Republic of Germany, known as the Luxembourg Agreement. It was signed after talks had been held between Prime Minister David Ben Gurion, of blessed memory, and Chancellor Conrad Adenauer. The Agreement was intended to arrange payment of reparations for damage to body and property committed by the Nazi regime of the Third Reich (National Socialism as it is known in Germany), only to survivors of the extermination camps brought into West Germany on the

Death Marches, or those who had already been in the extermination camps on the soil of the Federal Republic of Germany before the Death Marches, the majority being Jews from West Poland and Czechoslovakia, Hungary, France, Belgium and Greece. For those who escaped into Russia, who had never been imprisoned by the Nazi regime but had fled from it, there were no reparations.

I shall commence the further description of the affair ahead of the agreement with the bitter, appalling and shocking information that every Jew in Israel and the world must know, that every student in the Israeli education system, must digest and assimilate:

The government of Israel consented and agreed to expropriate the property rights of 500,000 displaced Jews, survivors of the camps, who remained in the West German Federal Republic after the German surrender. That is to say: it waived in their name, but without their authorization – contrary to the rules of any human law – their right to compensation for the bodily and emotional damage caused by Nazi Germany to each and every one of them.

Chancellor Adenauer stipulated that the West German Federal Government at that time could pay each of the 500,000 displaced persons who had survived the extermination camps the sum of 6,000 marks in goods and services. The Chancellor asked: "How do you want to receive the reparations?" One way was for each of the above displaced persons, whom we shall call as they were known by the Israeli Supreme Court, the "Deprived Group", to file a claim against the West German Federal Republic. Obviously, if that had been done, even the quota of 6,000 marks per person would never have been fulfilled, and payment of reparations for individual claims would have been postponed for years.

Another way was for the State of Israel to immediately receive payment in goods and services in the scope of three billion marks. Should the Israeli government decide to accept that payment, the Germans insisted and demanded that all members of the "Deprived Group" should lose their right to sue the West German Federal Republic, by way of an undertaking by the government of Israel to the Germans. Germany would not agree to pay the

Israeli government and then be subject to claims from members of the Deprived Group. Moreover, to the extent Israel should choose payment to the government, Germany would demand a further undertaking, in addition to exempting them from responsibility for the fate of the Deprived Group. That undertaking would be for the government of Israel to enact a law for the compensation of survivors of the extermination camps – i.e. the Deprived Group, whereby it undertakes to Germany that Israel will compensate them out of its own means in its own country.

Without considering the economic aspects of Adenauer's two proposals, and without the approval of the Knesset, the Government of Israel sent the letter known as Appendix 1A to the Reparations Agreement, signed by the Minister of Foreign Affairs, Moshe Sharett, of blessed memory, advising them that it had decided to take the reparations for itself, and that the payment made would exempt the West German Federal Republic from compensating the members of the "Deprived Group" who had survived the extermination camps, as distinct from those who had escaped the Holocaust – 500,000 persons, who would enter the boundaries of the State of Israel by October 1, 1953. The Government of Israel undertook to the West German Federal Republic to enact its own reparations law on this matter.

This critical information did not spring from the imagination of the writer of these lines. These things were said expressly by the honorable Judge Shlomo Friedlander, quoting from the letter of the Minister of Foreign Affairs, Moshe Sharett, of blessed memory (Appendix 1A) in Nazi Persecution Invalids File No. 676/09, Reuven Kovent et al v. the Competent Authority under the Nazi Persecution Invalids Law 1957:

"The citizens of Israel will not retain personal rights regarding such bodily injuries, as granted to the Jews of the Diaspora in the agreement with the Claims Committee, in consideration for the collective undertaking made by West Germany vis-à-vis the State of Israel."

In paragraph 11 of Case No. 676/09, the honorable judge further held that, when issuing the letter Appendix 1A in the name of the government:

"The question [the exemption for Germany – Y.B.] was not discussed

at the government session and no preliminary examination was made in that connection, whether financial or otherwise. Accordingly, it is not a legal arrangement as held by the Respondents, because it was never brought to the Knesset for ratification."

In High Court of Justice [HCJ] Case No. 207/60, Friedlander v. the Competent Authority for the Purpose of the Nazi Persecution Invalids Law, et al, Supreme Court Judgments 14, p. 2890, Judge Dr. Yoel Zussman, eventually Presiding Judge of the State of Israel Supreme Court, said:

"**If the argument of the Applicant's counsel is correct, it would be a matter for the legislator to answer, and he should give some thought to the fact that an Israeli legislation and a treaty of the Government of Israel (the Luxembourg Agreement – Y.B) has deprived its citizens who had survived the Nazis of the compensation they would have received from the German government. The consequence is that a Jew would gain from not being a citizen of Israel, because the arrangement made by the Israeli government does not hold for him, and the German government is beneficial to him.**"

The Vice President of the Supreme Court, the honorable Judge Shlomo Levine, held in HCJ File 5263/94, p. 844:

"**There is a basis for the Appellants' argument that in order to achieve the said goal the State prejudiced the members of the Deprived Group. This is a violation of their property rights which, as of 1992, has become a constitutional right. This violation caused unjustified discrimination between the members of the Deprived Group who arrived in Israel by October 31, 1953, and acquired Israeli citizenship, and those who remained abroad and did not receive Israeli citizenship, whose rights to claim higher amounts from Germany were not prejudiced. At the same time, it has always been acceptable to us that where the authorities expropriate a property right of the individual in order to finance public needs, it is the individual's right to receive appropriate compensation for the damage done to him, and the argument that such compensation imposes on the authority a financial burden that it cannot comply with is no argument. The situation of the members of the Deprived Group**

should be no different from a person whose land has been expropriated for public needs according to the expropriation laws. The case of the Deprived Group is identical to that of a person who, due to the enactment of a law, is deprived of his right to exploit a more useful alternative from his point of view by filing a claim to the government of Germany. It is sufficient at this stage to hold that the entire issue was not given due consideration which, by law, should have been done."

In this HCJ No. 5263/94, Hirschson v. Ministry of Finance, the honorable Supreme Court Judge Dalia Dorner (who eventually headed the State Committee concerning the Nazi Persecution Invalids Law), gave her interpretation of the term "property rights":

"The term "property rights" in the Basic Law: Human Dignity and Liberty covers rights having economic value, and not only those of them that are protected."

What is expropriation of property rights? When the State, by legislation or order or undertaking, deprives a citizen of personal property right. For instance: John Smith of Arizona was driving his car in Mexico City, and was hit by a vehicle of the Mexican Army. By what right and under what authority may the U.S.A. negate the right of the citizen John Smith to claim compensation from Mexico for the bodily injury he was caused by the Mexican Army? No regime has the right to expropriate property rights, except by imposing a tax or a criminal penalty under a judgment rendered in a court of law.

A person's right to compensation for bodily injury is a property right. Depriving him of this right by law and/or international undertaking in an agreement between states is an expropriation of the property right. These things are not my own private thoughts. They are rooted in the judgments of the courts of Israel (see HCJ file 5263/94, MK Avraham Hirschson v. Minister of Finance, Judgments 49 (5), p. 846).

As the years passed since the liberation in 1945, Bluma's medical problems gradually appeared. First it emerged that the beatings she had received on her head from the guards at Birkenau on the one hand, and the blows of the wooden ram used in the work of demolishing the buildings on the other, caused damage to her retinas which worsened with time. At a relatively young age, due to this damage, she lost her eyesight in her right eye, as a result of the serious damage to her retina. Was this the whole extent of the damage?

It further turned out, when she was only thirty years old, that Bluma suffered from extensive damage to her spine in the cervical and lumbar areas. She also had digestive problems resulting from her abdominal surgery and the shortening of her intestine.

But worst of all were her nightmares, the worrying thoughts and the terrible sense of depression, due to the memories, difficulties and terror that had been stamped on her soul, and she told nobody of them. Bluma wanted to go to work outside her home to help support the family and to assist in establishing it economically. However, my father would not allow her to go out to work, nor did he agree to her going to the markets and places crowded with people in order to obtain foodstuffs at a cheaper price.

These were young people who already bore significant physical and emotional scars, who could not contribute to the workforce like other people of similar age who were free of such damage.

Until 1980, the condition of post trauma was not known or defined in medicine. When the survivors of the extermination camps immigrated to Israel many of them were hospitalized immediately in mental hospitals, and unfortunately, some who are still living are there to this day. They never saw a home or family, and were hospitalized permanently.

In the 1950s, about three years after declaration of the State, a program of rationing was initiated in the country, in view of the shortage of basic products and the lack of foreign currency reserves, and the as yet undeveloped economy. The funds that reached the government served mainly to enhance the armaments and strength of the Israel Defense Forces.

On the other hand, Israel had undertaken to the West German Federal Republic to enact a law concerning the 500,000 deprived persons, whose right of claim vis-à-vis West Germany it had expropriated. It received the funds for itself and for its needs, but was slow to enact this law as it had undertaken against receipt of the reparations.

The survivors of the extermination camps wandered around the places where they lived in Israel looking for a day's work to make a living for themselves and their children. From time to time there were bloody incidents with terrorists and infiltrators, and the difficulties of existence grew and intensified. Bluma had two small children, with no ability to work for health reasons, and even if she could work, she would not have been able to pay someone to look after the children. The situation was becoming desperate. Hanan was injured in the metal workshop a number of times by metal splinters which flew from the lathe into his good eye, and he also began to have severe problems with his spine. Bluma and Hanan had no home of their own, and they were forced to rent a place to live.

During this time the only ray of light for Bluma was her cousin Jack Horwitz and his wife Nancy, who sent her a modest financial help for many years. The only ray of light for Hanan, of blessed memory, was his cousin Harry James Plaus of Milwaukee, Wisconsin, the owner of a company named "Spic & Span", who sent him machinery to open his own metal workshop.

Due to the government of Israel's breach of its undertaking to Germany, and its failure to enact the Israeli reparations law for the 500,000 deprived persons whom the State of Israel had robbed of their property rights, while hundreds of thousands of them had no means of making a livelihood, desperate, hungry and depressed, a great cry arose in Israel against both the government of Israel and the West German Federal Republic: "What kind of arrangement have you made? You have abandoned us. You are not fulfilling your undertakings. Where is the Reparations Law of the Israel Knesset? You promised the Chancellor." In those days, the Allied armed forces were still present on German soil. Dr. Nahum Goldman, president of the World Jewish Congress, undertook to deal with this affair with all his might. He met many times with Chancellor Adenauer, with Prime Minister Ben Gurion, with U.S. President Eisenhower and with the British Prime Minister. At the end of the day, he succeeded in bringing about a certain change. It must not be forgotten that this was already 1953, eight years after the end of the war. With the help of the Marshall plan, in which the contribution by U.S. Jewry was much higher than their proportion in the taxes of the U.S. population, West Germany was gradually recovering from its wounds.

Chancellor Adenauer decided to make things a little easier. From the legal aspect, Germany had complied with all its undertakings under the Reparations Agreement, and had paid the government of Israel three billion marks in goods and services. Germany agreed to help the government of Israel, which was not able to pay the reparations. The Federal Republic would undertake to pay out of its budget, under a legal mechanism within the German Federation, additional amounts to aid the 500,000 deprived persons, whose property rights vis-à-vis Germany for payment of personal compensation had been expropriated by their own government, without ratification by the Knesset, as in Appendix 1A to the Luxembourg Agreement.

I discovered, as I studied the material in Germany and in Israel, that in 2013, in Issue 18 of the German magazine "Der Spiegel", there was an article that dealt with the Ministry of Justice personnel of the Chancellor's government who sat in the Rosenburg Palace in Bonn. It was they who applied and planned the "Consent for Additional Assistance" by the Federal Republic to Prime Minister Ben Gurion and to Dr. Nahum Goldman, regarding assistance to the government of Israel in the matter of those deprived 500,000. It emerges that the majority of the personnel in Adenauer's Ministry of Justice in Bonn had been Ministry of Justice personnel in the Third Reich, and among them were murderers. With these people the State of Israel made a new arrangement which is essentially another crime against the State, based on German-Israeli cooperation who had been deprived by their own government. The survivors of the extermination camps who had immigrated to Israel actually became Holocaust victims only in those States of the Federal Republic where they had been registered as displaced persons, not in all of Germany, since East Germany was "exempt" due to that irresponsibility, and still is to this day. When I was handling Bluma's affairs in Israel and in Germany, which had been unified twenty years earlier, the ministers of the government of Israel and the heads of its government had forgotten that the citizens of East Germany never participated at all in the burden of paying the reparations, and raised not even a finger in that context. This subject never occurred to them. They were busy with self-enrichment and self-gratification in the merry days of Netanyahu's rule.

Tür an Tür

The original publication in Der Spiegel

[Article in Der Spiegel]

Current Affairs

DOOR NEXT TO DOOR
A long time after World War II
The Federal Ministry of Justice was still under the control of Nazi jurists

For officials in the Federal Ministry of Justice, which is called the "B.M.J." for short, "Rosenburg" in the suburb of Kessenich outside Bonn was more than a place of employment from 1950 onwards. The picturesque castle, surrounded by forests and green lawns, offered the possibility of long strolls at lunchtime, carnival like celebrations in the spring and garden parties in the summer, and fruit picking in autumn.

"All this", writes a ministry official in 1977, after the government ministry moved to a concrete castle in Bad Godesberg, "created a fertile social ambience, which it was not possible to recreate". The work colleagues at the "Rose Castle" [Rosenburg] "had a high sense of belonging together".

The results of recent research has shown an additional reason for this feeling of camaraderie at the Justice Ministry, which went beyond the frolicking around and the picking of apples. The Justice Ministry was full of longstanding, die-hard Nazis who, after the fall of the "Third Reich", returned to their posts and positions of honor and sat door next to door at Rosenburg.

This is the conclusion reached by an independent commission of historians that was appointed by the Justice Minister, Sabine Leutheusser-Schnarrenberger, which has shed light on the Nazi past of employees of the Ministry of Justice[11]. This is the first time that there are numbers that corroborate these longtime suspicions. In 1950, 47 per cent of all senior officials at the Ministry of Justice were former members of the Nazi party, and nine years later the percentage was still 45. Amongst them, in a very prominent position as advisor to the minister was Heinrich Ebersberg, the head of a department, Hans-Eberhard Rotberg, and a section chief, Eduard Dreher.

---

11 Manfred Görtemaker, Christoph Safferling (publication) "The Rosenburg. The Federal Ministry of Justice and the Nazi past – a stocktaking" published by Vondenhoeck & Ruprecht, Gottingen, 376 pages. Price €49.99

The accepted assumption that the number of former Nazis in the German authorities had dwindled with the passage of time did not meet the test of the results of an investigation of the upper echelons of the Justice Ministry by the commission of historians. In 1966, 60 per cent of the heads of departments and 66 per cent of the managers of sub-departments had been members of the Nazi party in the past. In addition to that, there were a small number of public servants who had indeed not been party members, but who participated in the execution of death sentences that were imposed by the People's Courts.

Members of the brown party (the color of their uniforms) intentionally sabotaged a reform of the German courts. In the chapter published by the commission of historians, many examples are given of the continuation of Nazi norms. Thus, for example, upon the establishment of the republic in Bonn, it was theoretically possible to start a criminal investigation against young boys from twelve years upwards if this was necessary "for the protection of the people".

From 1939 it was possible to apply the Penal Law for Adults also in relation to majors, if and when this was required "according to the sensible logic of the people by virtue of especially condemnable intentions of the offender or due to the gravity of the offense he has committed". Up until 1943 a total of 61 majors had already been sentenced to death in reliance on this section. Only ten years later was the appendix containing Nazi ideology removed from the laws regarding the arraignment and trial of juveniles.

Some of the economic laws even served for this after 1945 – literally, "for the overall good of the nation and the Reich". In conformity with the Shares Law of 1937 the board of directors managed the business of the shares company under independent responsibility – according to "the Fuhrer's principles", the general meeting of the shareholders was, to a very large extent, powerless and without authority. The amendment to the Shares Law in 1965 did little to change this substantially.

The historian Manfred Görtemaker, one of the two heads of the independent commission of historians, regards the information in the personal files of the officials "as being pure dynamite". Also, when the Frankfurt lawyer, Professor Joachim Rükert, an expert on legal history, alludes to the fact: that some of the laws were often given a different interpretation after World War II, sometimes by the very same people.

This chameleon like ability of some of the lawyers to adapt themselves led to a number of absurd situations at Rosenburg. Thus, for example, the attorney, former Nazi Georg Petersen, who in 1938, in the course of the "Aryanization", even grabbed a share of the profits from the confiscation of property of German Jews, was nonetheless in charge, twelve years later, at the Ministry of Justice of the department whose field of authority included "the law for recognition of the freedom to marry of persons who had been persecuted due to racial or political reasons".

Der Spiegel   18 / 2013

This BEG law, which was drafted by lawyers, some of whom were Nazis who served Hitler, was also used, unfortunately and regretfully, by the Israeli Knesset as the basis for enacting its Nazi Persecutions Victims Law in 1957.

The article in Der Spiegel, with its notarized translation, relies on the findings of the examination committee of the Ministry of Justice in Berlin concerning the Ministry of Justice that served Chancellor Adenauer in Bonn. The significance of the findings is, in essence, that those who drafted, planned and implemented the BEG law (Bundesentschädigungsgesetz = the German Federal Compensation Law) concerning those of the "Deprived Group" who chose to apply to the State where they were registered as displaced persons, were Nazis. In clear language, for the prevention of doubt. The State of Israel referred Bluma, Birkenau Prisoner No. 31119, in order to establish her future property rights, to the Nazi planners and executors.

One of them was Andreas Bremer, Director of the Lower Saxony Reparations Office in Hannover, to which Bluma belonged, who in 1992 sent her a threatening letter.

I find it appropriate to present this in the documents themselves, as attachments, translated and notarized by my colleague, the honorable notary and attorney Michael Ossip. The documents bear his notarization stamp. They include a photocopy of the Der Spiegel article in German, the cover page of that magazine of 2013 and the notarized translation of the article from German to Hebrew.

The significance of this affair of "opening the faucet" by means of the BEG Law to those of the "Deprived Group" who chose to do so will be expanded on later, with all its implications on tens of thousands of people, their relatives, the second generation and the State. The article, the cover page and the translation of the article "Door Next to Door" is attached here.

The 1952 offer to the government of Israel of 6,000 marks for each of the five hundred thousand displaced persons, left it to the Israeli government to decide to whom to transfer the payment – to itself as the government or to the Displaced Persons who would file claims against the West German Federal Republic. Should the government choose the first option – to itself as a government – i.e. three billion marks, we demand exemption from liability for their personal claims. We shall not pay twice.

They knew that the ceiling of 6,000 marks per person would not be in their favor in a German court of law if personal claims were filed. They also knew that payments of personal claims would take a long time after the claims were filed. They were right. The State of Israel which had just been established was in dire need of finances. It was almost obvious to the Germans that the decision of the Israeli government would be to receive the money or its equivalent to its own pocket on optimum terms from the aspect of the German Treasury. But they did not expect the government of Israel to easily give up on the honor and future of the survivors of the extermination camps, since if they had not immigrated to Israel the State of Israel would not have been established.

The Vice-President of the Israeli Supreme Court, Dr. Shlomo Levine, said in HCJ judgment 5263/94 on page 840: "There is a weighty argument that in signing this document the government of Israel made a grave mistake, both in assessing the said risk, and when it turned out in retrospect that the scope of the claims by the citizens of Israel, the filing of which was blocked by the document (Appendix 1A – Y.B.), was tens of times greater than the estimates made upon signature thereof." The honorable Vice-President Shlomo Levine was mistaken. The honorable Judge Friedlander, in Petition Committee File 676/09 put it more correctly: No calculations were made at all. But regarding the other matter Shlomo Levine was right. The government of Israel had sold its people's birthright for a mess of pottage.

The government of Israel had never been in the extermination camps. It was in need of the money quickly. This fatal error could have been corrected over the years, as Germany recovered, especially after the unification of both parts of the country. Now the reader may ask, What is the connection between Bluma's story and this external event? Why have I delved into the depths of these general issues? They certainly are connected and they have implications not only on Bluma but on hundreds of thousands of survivors, their children and the Treasury of the State of Israel.

It may be that with the establishment of the State, the financial difficulties were so great that it was forced to accept for itself the "basement price" offer. My criticism and anger are aimed at the criminal negligence of the subsequent governments, especially after the definition of post trauma in medicine in 1980. This concerns the Likud governments and especially the governments headed by Prime Minister Netanyahu, while in Germany there was a Chancellor who was (and is) a scientist and a woman of integrity. With her it would have been possible to settle easily the terrible distortions that had been created. In Bluma's HCJ file No. 8766/11, the Supreme Court judges called for a discussion of this issue with the German government, but that did not interest Netanyahu and his Minister of Justice. This was the recommendation of the honorable Judge Elyakim Rubinstein in HCJ file 8766/11 Bluma Borowsky v. The State of Israel:

The criminals of the Ministry of Justice in the Rosenburg Palace in

Bonn decided to continue to hold close to their heart the exemption from responsibility they had received from the government of Israel in Jerusalem, seeking to be released from its financial liabilities. What was the legal solution they created? The comprehensive prohibition against personal compensation claims by the five hundred thousand survivors is cancelled. However, the right to claim is against a German Federation State, where the plaintiff could prove that he was registered as a DP after the war. There neither is nor will be a claim by any of the five hundred thousand survivors against Federal Germany. In each of the German Federation States where there were Jewish DPs, the law had established reparations offices, to which all who desire it may submit a claim. This gift given by the Israeli government to the German people is a valuable one. The claim is only against an internal German state, where the claimant must prove that, according to documents of the military government over Germany, he was a DP in that internal state.

The significance of the BEG law, that was adapted for the renewal of the claims by the survivors of the extermination camps who arrived in Israel and had been Displaced Persons in the German states, is as follows:

1. The claimant has the right to sue only the state in Federal Germany in which he is able to prove his registration as a DP pursuant to a document of the military government in Germany.

2. In all the states of Federal Germany where there were DPs, such as Bavaria, Hessen, Rhineland-Palatinate, North Rhine-Westphalia, Lower Saxony, etc., a reparations office was established for the "renewal of benefits", in which there was a medical section and a financial section, and it was subject to the Ministry of Finance in the particular Federation state. For instance, in Bavaria – the government of Bavaria and its Ministry of Finance.

3. Whenever a certain disease or disability is recognized by the Reparations Office as having been caused by the Nazi oppression, a level of invalidity is set, according to which the claimant will be paid the monthly compensation in the form of "renta" – an allowance from the Federation state in which it was recognized – not compensation from Germany, as has

been assimilated erroneously in the consciousness of the public and many judges in Israel.

4. The levels of invalidity consist of five groups of loss of work capacity.

5. The allowance is based on a low salary level in the German civil service. However, if the claimant can prove that he had lived on a high level of income, it is gradually improved somewhat.

6. Claims to the Federation states may be filed only up to 1969. After that date the statute of limitations applies absolutely. This decision was fatal for Bluma, and for thousands more, and for the State of Israel itself.

7. It was also possible to file claims concerning exacerbation after recognition of a disease even after 1969. If the claimant passed the age of 68 any exacerbation was attributed 66% to age and 33% to Nazi oppression, under Section 35 of the BEG Law.

8. The Treasury of the relevant Federation state would receive into its budget, from the Federal Republic, by way of subrogation, a reimbursement of the extent of its liability recognized by its Reparations Office, out of the Federal Republic's budget – then in Bonn, and today in Berlin. In this way, as in every normal civil service, the Reparations Offices in the Federation states sought to prove that they were being frugal and limiting their recognition of disability in order to save on expenses for the Federal Treasury which was supporting them.

We shall now assimilate and summarize this development created by the BEG Law with absolute consent and cooperation between the governments of Germany and Israel. We shall see how Bluma's road and that of others led to the rehabilitation of the survivors of the extermination camps in the re-established State of Israel.

The significance emerging from the BEG Law of 1953 itself, and from a publication of the Federal German Ministry of Finance confirming and ratifying it, is that all survivors of the extermination camps who were displaced against their will on the soil of Germany after World War II were entitled to exercise their property rights regarding emotional and physical injuries only in the German Federation state in which they lived, and not against the

Federal German Government, which had replaced the Third Reich. The rest of the German people did not participate in the Holocaust!

This statement completely contradicts the reasoning of the Israeli Supreme Court in File 8766/11 that the above "arrangement" is a normative procedure between two countries, and that it prevails over the allegation of discrimination against the survivors of the extermination camps. It does not prevail, it is the discrimination itself.

The shocking, serious, major significance of the Luxembourg Agreement and the letter Appendix 1A is that Bluma Plaskovsky, Dora Tzibola and any other Holocaust survivor who, in his/her distress, sought compensation from the Nazi oppressor, was totally prevented from doing so. The agreement between the West German Federal Republic and the State of Israel followed the "judicial doctrine" of the German legal scholar Jahring, which was adopted into Israeli contract laws – good faith agreement.

The main points are as follows:

1. On September 10, 1952, under the Luxembourg Agreement and Appendix 1A thereto, the Israeli government creates what the Israel Supreme Court called the "Deprived Group", i.e. 500,000 survivors of the extermination camps who were Displaced Persons on the soil of the West German states. The real survivors of the extermination camps have no personal remedy due to their country's consent to receive compensation from the German oppressors in exchange for its undertaking to their government. The survivors of the camps who arrived in Israel up to October 1, 1953 are the "Deprived Group" due to the expropriation of their property rights.

2. The government of Israel undertakes to the West German Federal Republic to enact a law of compensation for victims of Nazi persecution in exchange for receiving the negligible and ridiculous compensation from the German government.

3. The government of Israel and the Knesset, controlled by the government, breach their undertaking and do not enact the Israel compensation law, as they had undertaken to the Germans, in favor of a third party – their citizens who had survived the camps and who were living among them in

Israel. This law was first enacted in 1957, only after the amendment to the BEG Law, which enabled claims to be filed in the Federation states.

4. In Israel a loud cry is raised by the survivors of the camps, who are suffering from emotional problems which at the time are unknown to medicine at all, and other diseases which are discovered from time to time. They have no property and have difficulty in working. Those who have families are suffering serious hardships.

5. Dr. Nahum Goldman, President of the World Jewish Congress, who is a person with a great heart, but lacking all legal knowledge and who has no legal backing, causes a unilateral change in the position of the Federal Republic which was gradually emerging from its ruins. The Federal Republic agrees to enable the members of the Deprived Group to claim reparations only in the West German Federation state where they can prove their registration as a DP. The West German Federal Republic remains exempt from responsibility, and the other Federal states in which a claimant from the Deprived Group was not a DP are also exempt from responsibility for that particular person.

6. The members of the Deprived Group in Israel have the right to file claims until 1969, since the German judicial personnel in the Rosenburg Palace in Bonn believe that 16 years are more than enough to file a claim, and that it is reasonable to assume that health problems that may be discovered or may develop later could find expression in that period of time.

The Israeli government was in heaven when it was advised in 1955 that the West German Federal Republic – the Nazis in Bonn – were prepared to ease its burden. It would be an improvement on the Luxembourg Agreement, although they were under no legal obligation to do so. "We understand in Bonn the distress of the Israeli government which is unable to pay compensation as it had undertaken to us. The claim of the Deprived Group or any of them who wishes to do so, will be filed only in the Federation state in which he/she can prove registration as a DP prior to emigration to Israel."

And what does the State of Israel do? It is in no hurry to enact the Israeli Nazi Oppression Invalids Law as it had undertaken to do, despite the alleviation it had just been granted. The Israeli government refrained on purpose, and did not rush to enact the law as it had promised. It was interested in having a larger number from the Deprived Group file their claims in the German Federation states under the principles of the BEG Laws. The more people who file such claims, the smaller will be the burden on the State's shoulders.

Accordingly, it purposely delayed the enactment of the law until April 1957, about five years after its undertaking under the Luxembourg Agreement and four years after the German Nazi Persecution Invalids Law. This intentional foot-dragging was intended to lessen as far as possible the number of members of the Deprived Group that it would have to support.

The honorable Supreme Court Judge Dalia Dorner committed a material error in HCJ File 5263/94 when she stated in Paragraph 2 of her opinion that:

"The Law enacted following the reparations agreement with Germany denied from the Holocaust survivors, citizens of Israel, reparations which they were entitled to receive from Germany. Instead of such reparations, the law entitled them to compensation significantly lower than the amount they would have been entitled to receive under German law if it were not for the Law, thus the Law violated the property right of those entitled to reparations under German law."

These words by the honorable Judge Dorner are basically mistaken. It was not the Nazi Persecutions Invalids Law 5717-1957 that caused the expropriation of the property rights of the Deprived Group. That was caused by the Luxembourg Agreement and Appendix 1A thereto, which constituted a grant of exemption from liability to the West German government regarding the Deprived Group, and the Israeli government's acceptance of responsibility for payment of compensation under the Israeli Law, as stated by the honorable Vice-President of the Supreme Court, Shlomo Levine.

The late opening of the way for the members of the Deprived Group in 1952 to file claims in the Federation states in which they had to prove their being DPs reduced the scope of liability of the Israeli government and dumped a disaster on the majority of the Group who, due to their immediate distress, sued the Federation state in which they had been DPs.

The Israeli government used the Israeli Nazi Persecution Invalids Law to compensate many Holocaust survivors who had not been under the guards of the S.S. and the Gestapo, those who had fled from the Nazis and those with completely different criteria, for whom the past 25 years had been good, both for them and their families, in a way and a manner that has no similarity with those who, due to the severity of their injury and damage, jumped onto the distorted wagon of compensation from the DP Federation state. The extent of the diseases and conditions recognized by Israel was greatly expanded for those entitled by the Authority for the rights of Holocaust survivors (the Treasury under Israeli law) compared with the scope of diseases recognized under the BEG Law.

In the course of the High Court of Justice deliberations on the file I submitted concerning the rights of our late mother, HCJ 8766/11, we also filed an appeal for disclosure, without names, of the levels of invalidity and amounts of compensation paid by the Israeli authority executing the Nazi Persecution Invalids Law of Israel, without names and without identification. The panel refused, and they had good reason. They did not want to provide me with any evidence.

Those who escaped the Holocaust but had not been in the camps received, and still do, compensation that was higher, sometimes by hundreds of percent, than that received by those who had survived the camps. There were some among them whose suffering had lasted no more than one or five months, and who had not been under the S.S. and Gestapo guards.

If the day comes in the history of our people when the World Jewish Congress and the UN Committee for Human Rights, together with the Court of Justice of the European Union, will initiate an investigation of the allowances paid in the German Federal states, and the levels of invalidity from 1990 to date, for what diseases that had been recognized and what conditions of hospitalization and nursing in old age, the reader's hair will stand on end and even completely fall out, and they jaw dropping will drop in horror..

See how those who had never been in the Holocaust, or who had suffered only slightly, are entitled in Israel to a higher allowance that is twice as much or more than those who had been for long periods in the concentration camps.

I would remind you that the 500,000 members of the Deprived Group who were in Israel up to October 1, 1953 have become much less. From them should be deducted those who, in the window of time beginning 1955, filed their claims in the Federal states of West Germany under the BEG Law. These were usually the most severe cases. Those who waited for the Nazi Persecution Invalids Law 5717-1957 were usually those whose economic, family and personal situation was better or those who were able to wait before making their choice.

When the Nazi Persecution Invalids Law was enacted in 1957, the majority of the severe cases of the Deprived Group were already included in the reparations mechanism of the Federation states who recognized the presence as DP of each claimant therein.

The Israeli Nazi Persecution Invalids Law of 1957 directed, in Section 3A-B, that whoever had filed a claim for reparations is obligated to notify the competent authority in writing within three months after filing the claim in the Federal Republic of Germany. Seriously???

The Israeli Knesset enacted a law that was signed by the President of the State, the Prime Minister and the Minister of Justice, as required under Israeli law, while establishing a deception. There neither is nor can be a claim to the Federal Republic of Germany, nor to the Democratic Republic of Germany, which was and remains exempt from liability, and the "opening of the faucet" did not rectify its exemption from liability.

In Section 3B(b), the duty of whoever had "filed a claim to the Federal Republic of Germany and whose claim had been approved there" to notify the competent authority thereof – was cancelled.

Federal Ministry
of Finance

Compensation for
National Socialist Injustice

Indemnification Provisions

Compensation provisions in the occupation zones

As far as compensation law governing personal injury cases and damage to property not covered by restitution is concerned, Land laws were adopted in the American occupation zone as early as 1946. They provided for provisional payments for healthcare, vocational training, self-employment, remedies for distress situations and pensions for victims and their dependants. On 26 April 1949, the Act on the Treatment of Victims of National Socialist Persecution in the Area of Social Security (Compensation Act) was adopted for the entire American occupation zone by the Southern German Länder Council. This was promulgated by Land laws in Bavaria, Bremen, Baden-Württemberg and Hesse in August 1949. In line with Article 125 of the Basic Law, these Land laws became federal law when the Federal Republic of Germany was established and the Basic Law entered into force. Corresponding laws were enacted in the Länder of the British and French occupation zones and in West Berlin. With the exception of Länder in the British occupation zone, these laws governed the same types of damage as the Compensation Act.

1.3 Luxembourg Agreement, Hague Protocols and Settlement Convention

Just as the Länder and municipalities had done prior to its establishment, the Federal Republic of Germany continued to treat moral and financial compensation for the wrongs committed by the National Socialist regime as a priority. The German Government decided as early as on 26 July 1951 that victims of pseudo-medical experiments should be compensated. Over the course of the year, great efforts were made both in the Länder and at federal level to introduce nation-wide compensation rules. At a special meeting of the German Bundestag on 27 October 1951, Federal Chancellor Adenauer declared that Germany was responsible for the atrocities committed by the National Socialist regime and offered to enter into negotiations with the state of Israel and the Jewish Claims Conference (JCC). This "Conference on Jewish Material Claims Against Germany" had been founded by 23 Jewish organisations on the previous day with the aim of enforcing compensation claims against Germany. Talks with representatives of Israel and the JCC were taken up in The Hague on 21 March 1952.

As a result of these talks, the Hague Protocols was initialled on 8 September 1952 and an agreement with the state of Israel was signed in Luxembourg on 10 September. In this "Luxembourg Agreement", Germany committed itself to paying DM3 billion to the state of Israel and DM450 million to the JCC. Germany made a large part of its payments to Israel in the form of deliveries of goods. In return, Israel waived compensation for Jewish victims of persecution who were resident in Israel in 1952.

According to the second protocol to the agreement, the DM450 million fund for the JCC was intended for the support and integration of Jewish victims of persecution living outside Israel. In the first protocol, the German Government committed itself to establishing a legislative programme for Germany-wide restitution and compensation rules, and the basic principles of this legislation were defined.

Principles for uniform restitution and compensation legislation were also set down in the Settlement Convention concluded in 1952 with the three Western occupying powers (Federal Law Gazette II 1954, p. 57, 181, 194).

The Final Federal Compensation Act considerably extended the deadline (originally 1 April 1958, cf. I.5) as follows:

> The deadline was annulled in cases of claims for immediate assistance and for mitigation of hardship (section 189 subsection (1) of the Federal Compensation Act)

> The original legal position was restored in the case of failure to submit applications prior to the deadline through no fault of the applicant (section 189 subsection (3) of the Federal Compensation Act)

> The deadline for subsequent registration of claims was extended to 31 December 1965 (section 189a subsection (1) of the Federal Compensation Act)

> The subsequent registration of facts that had come to light after 31 December 1964 within one year (section 189a subsection (2) of the Federal Compensation Act) was introduced

Nevertheless, Article VIII (1) of the Final Federal Compensation Act provides that even in cases of the original legal position being restored, no claims can be made after the 31 December 1969 deadline. In other words, claims for compensation payments under the Federal Compensation Act can no longer be submitted today.

However, payments for damage to health can be adapted in cases where the victim's condition deteriorates.

Furthermore, initial decisions can be revised through secondary procedures if they have been proved wrong according to the current interpretation of the law.

The compensation and restitution acts were complemented by laws on compensation for public sector employees and in the sphere of insurance and pension law.

1.7 General Act Regulating Compensation for War-Induced Losses

The payments provided for in the compensation laws are reserved for those who were victims of typical National Socialist injustice – those persecuted for reasons of race, religion or political conviction. For other injustice leading to loss of life, damage to limb or health, or deprivation of liberty, compensation is granted under the General Act Regulating Compensation for War-Induced Losses of 5 November 1957 (Federal Law Gazette I, p.1747). Pensions and one-off compensation payments could – and, in exceptional cases, still can – be paid under section 5 of this Act in conjunction with the general legal provisions.

1.8 First comprehensive agreements with European states

From 1959 to 1964, comprehensive agreements were concluded with Austria, Belgium, Britain, Denmark, France, Greece, Italy, Luxembourg, the Netherlands, Norway, Sweden and Switzerland for the benefit of nationals of these countries who had suffered National Socialist persecution. The Federal Republic of Germany made available a total of €496.46 million (DM971 million) on the basis of these agreements. It fell to the governments of the countries concerned to distribute this financing amongst the victims. The comprehensive agreements have now been closed.

II. Provisions based on the Federal Compensation Act

2.1 Federal Compensation Act

The Additional Federal Compensation Act of 18 September 1953 (Federal Law Gazette I, p. 1387) was the first law to codify compensation for National Socialist injustice at national level, although it was only intended as temporary legislation. Prior to its introduction, only the compensation laws of the individual *Länder* applied, which were based on the compensation provisions in the occupation zones of the Western powers. The **Federal Compensation Act** of 29 June 1956 (Federal Law Gazette I, p. 562) entered into force with retroactive effect from 1 October 1953. It is a comprehensive piece of legislation that covers all aspects of compensation for National Socialist injustice. It is implemented by the compensation authorities of the *Länder* (section 184 of the Federal Compensation Act). Disputes are settled by the ordinary courts (section 208 of the Federal Compensation Act). The structure created by the Federal Compensation Act was also used as a basis for extralegal provisions that were subsequently introduced. The purpose of the Act is to compensate those subjected to oppression by the National Socialist regime.

a. Victims of persecution as defined in section 1 of the Federal Compensation Act

Only victims of persecution by the National Socialist regime are eligible for compensation. Section 1 of the Federal Compensation Act defines victims of persecution as those who suffered damage to life, limb or health, depreciation of freedom, property or assets in their business or professional career as a result of National Socialist oppression (as defined in section 2 of the Federal Compensation Act) due to their political opposition to National Socialism or for reasons of race, religion or ideology. Those who suffered oppression as a result of being involved in artistic or academic pursuits of which the Nazi regime disapproved, or because they were close to a victim of persecution, are themselves treated as victims of persecution. Under the Federal Compensation Act, surviving dependants and close relatives who, as such, were adversely affected by National Socialist oppression are also considered to be victims of persecution.

When applying the Federal Compensation Act, it became necessary to define the reasons for persecution more precisely. For example, in cases of persecution for reasons of political opposition, distinctions were

The Death of Hanan and its Implications

In October 1977 Hanan was rushed to Beilinson Hospital by the family doctor. Bluma and I were also called there. We were told that unfortunately, Hanan had been diagnosed with an aggressive lymphatic cancer, and that they would try everything possible, but the prognosis was that it was terminal. Hanan was 66.

Emanuel had already been in the U.S. for two months, and Bluma and Hanan decided together not to tell him that his father was so ill, although Hanan himself did not know what the diagnosis really was and for a few weeks he was quite sure that it was just an inflammation.

Bluma and I were distraught with the pain of the disaster that had fallen on her and us. She devoted herself body and soul to looking after Hanan. There was no oncologist with whom she did not consult. We sought every spark of hope. Bluma accompanied Hanan in his hospitalization, the lengthy chemotherapy and radiation treatments at the Beilinson Hospital. I went with Hanan many times for the radiation, and he would complain to me that he felt that the radiation machine was not directed correctly at the radiation field marked by the oncologists.

He was right. In the middle of May 1978, it turned out that there had been a malfunction in the radiation treatment and that the radiation had burned his esophagus. He could not eat at all. We would sit him on the balcony, and Bluma would sit days and nights for about three weeks in order to drip a little water onto his mouth with a teaspoon to keep him from dehydrating. This was the period of the Shavuot festival with its heavy heat and dry east winds. He would sit on the comfortable chair and never complained, while not a gram of food came into his mouth. After about three weeks there was a little improvement and he succeeded in eating a little.

Summer was at its peak and Hanan came and went for treatments at the Beilinson Hospital. One day, around Rosh HaShana, I went to visit him, and Bluma was not at home, because she had gone out shopping. He told me: "Yitzhak, I feel I have a lump at the top of my spine, just where it joins my head". Despite this, I saw that the color of his face and his weight had improved to some extent, and I cheered him up.

I visited him two or three days before Rosh HaShana, in September 1978. He was siting opposite Bluma at the dining table, and he said to her in Yiddish: "Blumkeleh, I feel that you will be without me on Rosh HaShana". Tears streamed from his eyes, and she sat like a stone.

On Friday, September 29, 1978, at 6:30 a.m., Bluma called me at my home in Holon, to tell me that Hanan had been twisting and turning in bed, chocking. I reached my parents' home within a quarter of an hour, and Bluma's house help, Mrs. Simha Trager, who had been with her for forty years, helped me take Hanan downstairs on a chair. A Magen David ambulance came and rushed him to Emergency. All the doctors of the oncological department came to Emergency, but they told me that unfortunately, his death was a matter of minutes.

Hanan was taken into an isolated room in the oncology department, and Bluma asked me to return home and call her cousins Irving Harvin of San Diego, and Herbert Horwitz, to tell Emanuel to be on his way to Israel from Santa Barbara in California, because the death of Hanan our father was imminent. I drove to my parents' home in Tel Aviv, and succeeded in contacting Bluma's dear cousin Irwin Horwitz. He found Emanuel, and told him to leave immediately for Israel.

I returned to the hospital, and entered Hanan's room, where he was lying dead on his back. Bluma was sitting there frozen, like a stone, with a heavy head, Hanan covered with a white sheet. I asked her when he had died, and she said that it was about half an hour ago: "He took hold of the side bars of the bed", she said, "tried to sit up, then collapsed and died."

I lifted the sheet from the face of my beloved father, a wise, charismatic, noble-hearted man; I kissed his forehead, stroked his face and hands, and said goodbye.

The eve of Rosh HaShana that year fell on October 1, 1978, a Sunday evening. According to the Jewish religion, Rosh HaShana is celebrated for two successive days. That year it started on Sunday evening, and continued on Monday and Tuesday.

I asked my mother whether she preferred to wait from that Friday until Wednesday before burying him, because of the festival, or whether we should have the funeral on Sunday morning, which was the eve of Rosh HaShana.

Emanuel was to land on Sunday evening. Bluma said to me: "Yitzhak, we shall lay Father to eternal rest on Wednesday, and you, his two sons, shall walk after him on his last journey. It cannot be otherwise."

Emanuel arrived on Sunday, October 1, 1978, the eve of Rosh HaShana, and on Wednesday, October 4, 1978, Hanan Borowsky, of blessed memory, was laid to eternal rest. Hundreds attended his funeral. Bluma remained a 54-year-old widow, who had lost her husband and breadwinner.

Emanuel was studying in the U.S., and was in need of financial assistance in his studies, because he was forbidden to work in that status. I was married and the father of a two-year-old boy. My wife, Tzofia, was about to give birth any day, and we were both at the beginning of our careers.

At that time, I had been working for about three years in the Tel Aviv District Attorney's office, and had appeared at many trials in the Tel Aviv District Court. I worked with attorneys who were eventually appointed senior judges.

During the seven-day mourning period many came to comfort us, among them judges in the Tel Aviv District Court before whom I had appeared. "Yitzhak", they said when I returned to work after the mourning period, "your mother is a most impressive woman and has an amazing personality. What is her education? What did she study? From where comes her ability to express herself in such rich Hebrew?"

I replied to the honorable judges and attorneys in the language of the national poet, Bialik: "There was a small town in east Poland named Sopotz-kyn, with a "Tarbut" school and Zionist youth movements, all of whose Jews were exterminated. My mother opened and closed the Birkenau extermina-tion camp, and remained alone in the world. That is where she completed her education."

Emanuel stayed in Israel until the thirtieth day after the death of our father, and while he was here, without the knowledge of either of us, out of the fear and distress which fell on her upon the death of her husband and breadwinner, the post trauma anxieties that were buried inside her broke out, and led her to do something, which was seriously detrimental to her subsequent life and mine, that I discovered only after I had been appointed her guardian in 2006.

In the same building where Bluma's apartment was, in the north of Tel Aviv, lived a well-known Israeli attorney, whose firm also handled claims for reparations from Germany. This attorney, a tall and impressive person, was already at an advanced age, and he would come home every day for a midday rest. When he returned to his office at around 16:00 p.m. he would sometimes stop near the elevator and speak to Bluma for a few minutes. He liked to talk to her and to ask her advice concerning a second spouse with whom he had bound his fate.

I did not know that Bluma had asked him, without sharing it with me, and as a consequence of the Nazi terrorization that never left her soul to her last days, to have his office send a letter in her name to Hanan's Reparations Office to tell them that he had died, and that they should cease to send his handsome allowance which they had been receiving each month while he was alive.

Why did she do that without sharing it with me? Due to the Nazi terror which remained within her almost to her last day. She shivered with fear and anxiety at the thought that if she did not tell Hanan's Reparations Office in the state of Hessen of his demise, the Reparations Office of that state in Darmstadt would advise the director of her Reparations Office in Hannover, Andreas Bremer, the "villain", as she so rightly called him. Bremer would punish her, as the Nazis had punished her and the other millions, and would also deprive her of her own allowance from the Hannover office of the state of Lower Saxony. The post trauma and the irresponsible politicians of the State of Israel are responsible for that.

Moreover, when I was appointed her guardian, I discovered that at the same time, when Emanuel and I were with her on the thirtieth day after my father's death, she had requested her attorney neighbor to write to Andreas Bremer that she had lost her husband's allowance, that her economic situation was serious, and she asked the Reparations Office in Hannover for financial assistance.

All this information was unknown to me until I gradually began to receive the documents, in my capacity as her guardian from the end of 2006, and the pain and sadness of it all hit me in the face.

At that time I did not know of the "callous ingenious arrangement" made by the State of Israel for settling the filing of claims in the German Federation states according to the country in which the Displaced Person was registered. That affair I exposed when I was battling the German states to rectify the wrong caused to Bluma, and to enable me to finance her anticipated hospitalization due to her Alzheimer's disease and due to Emanuel's absence from Israel and the situation in which he found himself in 2006. Moreover, a dear and experienced judge gave me a warrant under which I was able to summons the Government of Germany to the Israeli court, since she also believed that the Germans "were paying reparations to individuals". She was also totally mistaken. When the warrant she issued was served on them, they were amazed at the very fact that it had been issued.

Bluma did not understand that the "villain" Bremer had no authority to punish her for not reporting on time to Hanan's Reparations Office of his demise. Such a thing would not have happened anyway.

However the greatest blow I received when, for the first time in 2006, by virtue of my authority as guardian, the agreement and judgment reached me concerning the reparations arrangement of my dear father Hanan with the Reparations Office in Darmstadt, Hessen. Bluma had never shown it to me, and my father Hanan had never spoken to me about it, except for these words in the hospital: "Yitzhak, you are responsible."

When I opened the reparations agreement and the judgement between Hanan and the state of Hessen, I was amazed to see that it included the fantastic provision that, in the event of Hanan's death, Bluma would be entitled to 60% of his monthly allowance which was quite handsome – about 800 euro a month. If she had collected these amounts since his death in September 1978 until it was discovered, her economic situation would have been immeasurably better, and I would have been released from undergoing what I did in order to enable her to return to her Maker with the respect due to her, to which she was entitled both from her country and certainly from her son.

I do not bear even a milligram of a grudge in my heart against Bluma. This affair that I discovered in 2006 was part of her post trauma that she bore in her soul, which twisted the whole of her life, in which the terror and fear of the dictator and ruler, which control the victim, all become part of his behavior. The American author Jack London, described this very well in his book "Call of the Wild", where he told of the behavior of dogs which had been trained under conditions of terror to drag sleds in the Arctic.

In 1978 Hanan had gone, Emanuel was abroad and in need of economic support. In the years 1978-1980, the cousins Irving Harvey, Nathan Horwitz and Herbert Horwitz were still alive. They supported Bluma, who had lost Hanan's reparations allowance, which had been intended for her from the Federation state of Hessen. But their support did not last very long – they died one by one.

Each day Bluma would call me and my wife a number of times. She was lonely and miserable. Emanuel invited her to the U.S., and took her around with the relatives for about a month and a half. When she returned home, wandering around alone between the walls, the memories began floating up. Expensive trips abroad with relatives always come to an end. Although I had two little children to look after, Bluma would come to us from time to time, and we visited her. She loved her grandchildren, Avinoam and Hanny, very much, and would take them for walks and to play, and when Avinoam grew up he helped her a lot.

Opposite Bluma's apartment lived Miriam and Shmuel Brilliant, a childless couple. Miriam loved Bluma and our family very much. Never a day passed that she didn't come to visit us. To the left of Bluma's apartment lived Mrs. Ahuva Weinberg, who was a sick widow. In the apartment on the right lived Mrs. Lamdan, who was also not well. We never knew or heard anything, neither from Bluma nor from her neighbor Miriam and her husband Shmuel, who admired my parents and our family.

Eventually, after I had been appointed guardian, information reached me from the dear neighbor on the fourth floor, Mrs. Paulina Elad, of blessed memory, who helped me with testimony on Bluma with regard to the reparations due to her many years of acquaintance with Bluma, that in the first years after the death of Hanan, my mother eked out her existence by cooking and looking after her neighbors, for pay, but Emanuel and I knew nothing of this.

The only thing that had made Bluma happy was when her relatives and their children used to come to visit from the U.S. or Mexico. She was so excited when someone came to visit. She and Hanan had accommodated John and Gigi Meir in their home for about three months before they married. Bluma's home had been a second home for Johnny Meir.

Bluma loved her cousins, Ethel Meir, Frances and Laurence Weinstein and their children, Esther Lange, Sarah Kahan, Paul and Sam Lipton. Bluma was very happy when Joan and Dan Weinstein and their children came to visit her, and she would always say that these are real people who lift up her heart.

Six years after Hanan's demise, some of the U.S. cousins who had helped Bluma as far as they could also passed away. One day, she turned to me and said, "Yizhak, a woman introduced me to a widower, older than me, and he is interested that we should live together. What do you think?" I immediately replied that I was in favor, and I am sure that my father, Hanan, if he could be asked for an opinion, would have supported such a move. She told me that marriage was out of the question, and that she would draw up an agreement with him, and it would alleviate the loneliness of both of them, and they would manage a joint household. At first she hesitated and even decided against, but eventually it came to pass.

Emanuel visited Israel in 1982. He had met a lady, a new immigrant from Romania, who was working as a teacher. Without our knowing anything about it he had invited her to Los Angeles where he was living at that time, and a few weeks later he phoned Bluma and told her that he had married her, and that she would be staying in the U.S. He came to us for Pesach with that lady, and Bluma whispered in my ear: "Yitzhak, tell your brother to give her some money and to divorce her immediately upon his return. She gives me the shudders."

A few days after their return to the U.S. he called Bluma and explained to her that he could not live with that woman under the same roof for even one more second. Bluma told him not to wait even one hour and to divorce her. He did so and then a blow fell on Bluma and on me. Emanuel blamed us that we had pressured him to marry her, which had never happened. He cut off all contact with Bluma and myself. Bluma was so devastated, she did not know what to do with herself. We did not know where he was living because he had moved somewhere else. Bluma suffered six years of emotional torture due to her son Emanuel's breaking off all contact with her.

Eventually, Bluma asked her cousin Herbert Horwitz, of blessed memory, who was living in Beverley Hills, to try and locate Emanuel. Herbert made a great effort, and he found him. Bluma asked me if I were willing to travel with her to Emanuel's home with no prior notice. I agreed after some difficult deliberation, and in April 1988 I travelled with Bluma to the U.S. for the first time. On the way we stopped in New York, and from there we went on to Los Angeles. Herbert Horwitz was waiting for us at the airport. He took us to Emanuel's home in North Hollywood, Los Angeles. We knocked on the door. When Emanuel opened it he was shocked, and almost collapsed. Herbert left us and returned to his home.

The visit to Emanuel's home was a nightmare for Bluma and myself. I shall not go into detail, but he threw at his mother some very harsh statements, with the majority of which I could not agree. Among other things, Emanuel accused Bluma of having created a hell for him. At that point I suggested to Bluma to leave and go somewhere else, although Emanuel actually did try to be hospitable. In the end Bluma extracted a promise from him that he would maintain contact, and would not consider disappearing and cutting off contact with us ever again.

At the end of the difficult visit to Los Angeles I hired a car. I travelled with Bluma to Las Vegas in Nevada, and we stayed at a hotel there. In Las Vegas we were received by Bluma's dear cousin, Sam Lipton, who was living there on a pension from his job at the U.S. Department of Agriculture, researching proteins. Sam was a wonderful person, with a constant smile on his face, a good heart and unlimited love bubbling up.

Sam invited us to the Jubilee show and spent some time with us at all the hotels and casinos in the town. He helped to raise Bluma's spirits after her difficult visit to Los Angeles.

We returned to Israel, and Bluma and her new partner, Moshe, came to visit us, and we visited them. Bluma often came to our home in Holon by bus, and once she slipped and fell on the steps of the bus.

In 1992, Bluma asked me to come with her to the office of an attorney in Tel Aviv who had been "recommended" to her. He dealt with claims concerning exacerbation of health conditions which were due to recognized Nazi persecutions. "Yitzhak", she told me, "I filed a claim concerning the deteriorating condition of my nerves, because I have reached the age of 68, and under the German Reparations Law, 66% of any decline occurring after that age would be considered to be due to age and not because of the persecutions". In 1992 I was already 44 years old, an attorney with 20 years' experience.

"What have you attached to support your claim for deterioration?" I asked.

"I brought the opinion of the neurologist, Dr. Goldenberg," she replied.

"Who sent you to that neurologist?" I asked.

"I asked a few people."

I did not ask her why she had not turned to me, why she had not shown me her file in the Hannover Reparations Office.

"Why do I have to go to the attorney's office?" I asked.

"Because they called me, and told me that a reply had come from the director of the Hannover Reparations Office, Mr. Andreas Bremer himself," she replied.

"So why are you asking me to accompany you?" I asked.

"The clerk told me that a very difficult reply had arrived," she replied.

I felt my heart shuddering inside me. I understood that Bluma was concerned that due to her request concerning deterioration they would deny her allowance from Hannover. I went there with her, and I shall not forget that event my whole life.

The elderly secretary of the attorney, who was absent from the office, took out a letter that had arrived from Hannover, from the director of the Reparations Office, Andreas Bremer, which said: "Your application for deterioration of health is denied. If you dare to send a claim for deterioration again I shall deny your allowance altogether, because in 1965 you went on recuperation for two days at the expense of the Office, but without their approval." No more, no less. Under Section 35 of the BEG Laws, she was permitted to file for deterioration after age 68, subject to loss of 66% of the level of the deterioration.

I was 44 years old, with well-established life experience. Before me stood my mother Bluma, red with perspiration, shivering with fear. I brought her a glass of water and tried to explain to her logically that the letter was a low threat lacking in substance, and that legally, even a German Nazi judge would not accept that denial or the threat.

"Mother," I said, "we shall file an appeal and we shall win."

"Yitzhak," she replied, "I don't want to, do not dare to mess with them. You do not know these animals. Don't dare to mess with them."

I understood that nothing would help at that time, and I left her alone.

A few days passed. I expected her to calm down and I again said to her, "Mother, you must not accept this. We must appeal. You have a son who is an attorney who was born free, did not undergo the terror, and he is not afraid of them. Justice is on our side, and the very fact that Andreas Bremer is threatening you now, in 1992, from my point of view will not be ignored."

"Yitzhak, leave me alone", she replied. "I don't want to have anything to do with them, and do not want you to deal with them. I got by with much less, and I shall manage with what I have."

I felt I was going mad. What deep terror had Bluma undergone and how had she not got free of it?

At the stage in which I served as her guardian, it became clear to me why she referred to Andreas Bremer, Director of the Hannover Reparations Office, as the "villain", and why, at a certain time at the beginning of the 21st century, he was removed from office based on complaints against him, while he died a short time later. It was for good reason she called him "villain", but she also could not understand the reason for it. I believe I was able to solve that riddle.

On the left-hand side of the road leading from Hannover to Hamburg, near Celle the Administrative capital of Lower Saxony, lies the Bergen Belsen extermination camp, surrounded by forests. My father Hanan was in this camp at the end of the war, and here he lost his left eye from a bayonet that penetrated his eye when a Nazi beat a Jewish prisoner with his rifle. Her Majesty's army saved his life from typhus which he contracted subsequently.

Upon liberation, Bergen Belsen was turned into a Displaced Persons camp by the British and US armies, who were close by. Tens of thousands of Jews who had fled into Russia and never saw Germany the entire war, understood that this was a good time to profit from the situation and to obtain compensation. They arrived in their thousands to the Bergen Belsen DP camp, and planted themselves there as having been led from the extermination camps before prisoner numbers had been stamped on their arms, since those who were designated to die did not get a number. By means of false testimony that some of them gave about each other, they were registered as extermination camp DPs who had participated in the death marches into Germany. Germany was unable to deny it, due to the burning of the majority of its archives.

For the Germans everything was counted and calculated. Andreas Bremer, director of the Hannover Reparations Office of Lower Saxony, whose office handled the DPs of Bergen Belsen and of Saxony, calculated that the number of DPs from Bergen Belsen who were suing his office was much higher than the figures that had been in the S.S. and Gestapo lists showing the actual numbers of DPs who were there. Bremer understood that some of the claimants were only pretending to be DPs. His displeasure at this ruse was expressed by a most strict and brutal attitude, to which thousands fell victim, who would otherwise have been entitled to much higher levels of invalidity and allowances. One of these victims was Bluma. In 2006, when I first saw Bluma's reparations agreement I was shocked.

Expansion of Bluma's Family and Deterioration of her Health

In the 1980s and 1990s, Bluma became close to her grandchildren Avinoam and Hanny. She came to visit them often, with and without Moshe. She had them stay with her. Avinoam, who has many technical talents, would help her, and she was amazed by him. From to time she would even describe some points of her history in front of Hanny. Hanny would joke and say "I have a grandmother with stories about camping." Grandmother and Hanny developed strong ties of love.

Bluma's health condition deteriorated due to problems with her damaged spine, the main part of which was caused by the hard labor in the Women's Commando 105 in Birkenau. She found it difficult to walk long distances, and was forced to sit every few hundred meters. In her youth she would walk every morning about half a mile to the sea to bathe, but in the 90s she could no longer do that.

Bluma was sent for many X-rays of the neck and lumbar parts of her spine. She was examined by an orthopedic surgeon and asked me to accompany her. When she gave him her X-rays, he said, "Mrs. Borowsky, you have growths on a number of vertebrae".

Bluma kicked me under the table. While the doctor continued to scan the X-rays, she whispered in my ears: "Yitzhak, he does not know what he is talking about." When we left the orthopedist and were on our way home, she said: "Yitzhak, I have no growths. But you should know that, even if I do, I shall get out of it."

I repeated to her the need to confront the Germans because they had done her a great wrong. She never received any help or advice from medical and legal entities in the 50s, nor in later years. In 1989 she underwent surgery for problems arising from her intestines and constipation. All those years she would lie awake half the night, and the only real sleep she managed to get was in the morning hours until 07:00 a.m. There were many, countless nights when she would awake out of nightmares, soaked in perspiration, due to the horrors rising up from her subconscious, and she could not find peace for her soul.

Bluma would walk slowly every evening a certain distance, as long as she could. As time passed the distance grew shorter, and she would sometimes sit on the public benches she passed on her way.

Before she met Moshe, Bluma used to rent out one of her rooms. Eventually, she rented a room for three consecutive seasons to Mimi Berger of Los Angeles, a Jewish woman born in Czechia, who was the first air hostess on El Al, who brought to Israel the first President of the State, Chaim Weizmann, in 1948. Bluma had a wonderful relationship with Mimi Berger and her husband, who was a pilot on pension from United Airlines. They also hosted us on our visit to Los Angeles in 1988.

After we returned from the U.S. in 1988, Bluma asked me if I could make the effort to go to Emanuel so that he would not remain alone on Yom Kippur and Sukkot. I asked Tzofia for her consent, and indeed in the years 1992, 1993 and 1994 I would go to him to California, after he had moved from Los Angeles to San Francisco. Each time I went there for two or three weeks, and would take a trip around northern California and Oregon.

In 1996 Emanuel notified us that he was about to marry a Jewish woman from Boston. My wife and I had the opportunity to meet her in the summer of 1995.

The wedding was set for October, and the bride's parents invited Bluma and myself to the wedding. They rented rooms in a charming motel on the shores of the Atlantic Ocean in the town of Swampscott in one of the bays north of Boston. I joined Bluma, and we landed at the Kennedy airport.

From there we were flown by a small propeller plane above the forests of New England, which were at the peak of their fall colors in October. We arrived at the small town north of Boston, where the motel was located. I stayed there with Bluma for about seven days before and after the wedding. We got to know the bride's parents, her sister and brother, who was a senior oncologist. I spoke with her father in Yiddish. There in Swampscott Massachusetts, in the Captain Jack motel, I stayed with Bluma for a whole week, and she was able to see the high and low tides of the Atlantic Ocean and the white hills of New Hampshire.

Since Emanuel had divorced his first wife, he had established himself well. For years he had done well in his work as senior software engineer in leading companies like Sun Micro Systems, Perkin Elmer and others. He had saved handsome sums, and even boasted to me quite a bit that he could stop working already, at age 44.

We did not know his new wife, and we are doubtful whether he knew her. Her parents hosted Bluma and me royally, and organized the wedding in the Boston Yacht Club in the town of Marblehead Massachusetts. It is the custom in the U.S. that one or two evenings before the wedding the bride would meet with her female friends for a whole day.

Bluma, Emanuel and I travelled to the White Hills in the State of New Hampshire to be together. We sat and explained to Emanuel that this was his second marriage, and in view of the bride's descriptions of her success in selling medications and medical appliances in California, he had no obligation to put into their joint account all the money he had saved in recent years. We explained to him that he could deposit the majority of his capital with us in trust, and we would protect his interests, so that he should not be damaged as he had been in his first marriage, if this second one was also unsuccessful.

We said all this in view of the lesson we had learned from his breaking contact with us between 1982 and 1988, following his first unsuccessful marriage. He complained to us of his terrible experience with his first wife. He felt as if he were imprisoned. Bluma repeatedly told him, "It is preferable to be alone than with a spouse with whom you are unhappy. Ten years with a beloved spouse are better than thirty with an offensive one. In such case – loneliness is happiness."

This conversation between Bluma, Emanuel and myself in the White Hills of New Hampshire at the beginning of October 1996 reverberates in my ears to this day. Inside me I knew that Emanuel, despite his extraordinary talents in mathematics, computer engineering, languages, history and botany, had no resistance to women. That was why he had been led to the wedding with his first wife, of which we had no knowledge, and into which we had not pushed him. His anger at his disappointment he took out on Bluma, on me and indirectly – on my wife. Bluma was concerned, as was I, that due to our not being acquainted with the new bride, who was marrying for the first time at age 40, he might be caught in pressures he would not be able to withstand.

Emanuel bought a home in San Ramon in California, and moved to live there with his wife. They had a son. Bluma travelled to Emanuel at San Ramon, and stayed there for about two months. She returned shocked at his wife's behavior, and could not calm down.

In 2000 Bluma's condition worsened terribly. Her ability to move about and walk declined. The orthopedists and neuro-surgeons who treated her explained to me that her spine was ruined. The condition of the vertebrae and discs of her cervical spine resulted in cervical myelophathy, which put all her limbs at risk of paralysis due to pressure on the spinal cord.

Bluma decided to undergo surgery privately, although she had medical insurance, and she allotted an enormous sum (for her) out of her remaining savings. She decided to place her fate for this surgery in the hands of a senior neurosurgeon she trusted who worked at the Assuta Hospital in Tel Aviv, a few streets away from her home.

The operation was performed on November 6, 2000, by entering from the front of her neck, and lasted about three and a half hours. I accompanied her to the hospital. She was moved to the recovery room after the surgery, and the surgeon Dr. Ashkenazi reported to me that all had gone well. He said that she would remain in the hospital for another four days for observation.

About two hours after being taken from the recovery room to the regular ward, she sat up in bed and said, "Yitzhak, take me home".

I replied, "Are you out of your mind?"

She said, "Yitzhak, now I need to rest in bed for three days, and perhaps once a day a doctor will come in for inspection, but not for treatment. I live nearby. What does it matter where I lie in bed. At least there I do not take up the place of another person who perhaps needs a hospital bed urgently."

I said, "Alright, I shall ask Dr. Ashkenazi for his opinion."

Dr. Ashkenazi heard what I had to say and couldn't believe his ears. "Mrs. Borowsky, you have just had major surgery, and going home is a great risk for you, even though you live nearby. There is no doctor or nurse at home."

"Dr. Ashkenazi," she answered with a smile on her lips, "if God forbid anything happens, my son will bring me straight to you. If I remain here, not only do I occupy a bed which might be needed by another patient, but you might also be in another room. If anything happens, my son will bring me directly to you."

The neurologist Dr. Ashkenazi stood there openmouthed. "Alright, Mrs. Borowsky, go home, and if anything unexpected happens, come here immediately."

There was nothing unexpected. Bluma could still walk with difficulty for another few years, until the next operation in 2003, after which she hardly could walk.

In 2001 Bluma asked me to take her to Emanuel in San Ramon, California. She was not happy with what might be happening there. We arrived at Emanuel's home and understood that the situation there was like a carriage hurtling down a steep slope, and that his wife's conduct was destructive. We had no idea how destructive. When we were about to return to Israel, Bluma stumbled against a plant pot that stood at the door of Emanuel's home. We notified Lufthansa, with whom we were to return. They suggested that Bluma remain there for another two days. Bluma refused, and finally we flew on that same day to Frankfurt, where we had to wait for about ten hours until the flight back to Tel Aviv.

When the Germans in Frankfurt noticed the number tattooed on Bluma's left arm, a group of young people who worked at the airport got together and said that, since she had been a victim of the persecutions, they would give her and me one of the air crew's rooms free of charge to stay there over the waiting hours. They also brought us trays with fruit, chocolate and cakes, and towels, and were very respectful to her. Their behavior astonished me, but it didn't take very long before I met the clerks in the Hannover Reparations Office a few years later, except for one lady, Sabena Weidner.

Miriam Brilliant, who would visit Bluma's home every evening, passed away. After her demise, her husband Shmuel began to suffer terrible loneliness. He began to visit Bluma and Moshe every evening before they went to bed. They would sit for about two hours together every evening. Shmuel admired my mother, Bluma, and my wife. I was a person he could trust. He was born in Romania, was a very acute person, an importer of medications for operating theaters. He was always interested in when my wife and I would visit Bluma, and asked us to visit him at his apartment as well, which was opposite Bluma's apartment.

For years, ever since the death of his wife Miriam, Shmuel Brilliant would sit with Bluma and Moshe in their apartment to alleviate his loneliness. In his later years he developed total dependence on them, and if Bluma and Moshe were not at home in the evening, he would stand in the street and wait for them. Shmuel contracted Parkinson's disease, and as it progressed he also began to suffer cognitive damage. He died in 2002.

From 1993 onwards, after I again attempted to persuade Bluma to sue the Germans, she began to tell me details of the horrors she underwent place by place, but not in chronological order. She told me of the hard labor, the hunger, the fear, the cold, the beatings and the worry of Dr. Mengele's periodic selections. Bluma told me that whoever lost his nerve did not survive, and that the comradeship, the sharing, the companionship and the restraint among the tortured souls were the foundations stones of survival, as were personal cleanliness and the suppression of the will which beats in the heart of every free and healthy person.

In the years 2003 and 2006 Bluma suffered a number of falls due to loss of balance. One day, Moshe called and told me that "Mother had fallen in her home on the floor, when she picked up the phone to talk to you, and I cannot lift her." I went immediately from my home in Holon, and took her in an ambulance to the Emergency at the Ichilov hospital, where they diagnosed a fracture of the hip. I was advised that the next day, Friday, she would undergo surgery.

In preparation for the operation she had to fast. But the next day they said that they were very sorry but the operating theaters were overloaded and there were more urgent cases. The surgery was postponed to Friday afternoon. Bluma continued to fast. On Friday afternoon they said that they would have to postpone the operation to Saturday evening, because only then would one of the operating rooms be free. Finally the surgery took place on Sunday morning.

I remembered that Bluma had told me that the Red Army managed to get her into surgery within half an hour in the German Wehrmacht military hospital. Here in her home town, in her homeland, the doctors see the number on her arm and postpone an operation for a woman with an open fracture of the hip for over sixty hours, while she was fasting, which caused a disruption in the supply of electrolytes to the brain.

I understood quickly that the policy was that people over 80 must allowed to leave this life. Immediately after the operation, Bluma entered a condition of delirium. I couldn't believe my ears. The painkillers caused her to hallucinate and to say things that had nothing to do with her past at all, but were pure delirium.

At the end of the hospitalization in the orthopedic department, Bluma was sent for rehabilitation. She stayed there for about three weeks, performing all the exercises like a disciplined soldier. She ended the rehabilitation period with "honors", and walked rather slowly on her own two feet, but she required a walker for support for a few weeks. Bluma returned home and resumed her life, and Moshe helped her with the shopping.

A few months later, an ultrasound of her pelvis showed something suspicious which required examination in the gynecology department of the nearby Ichilov hospital. I went there with Bluma and it turned out that she would require two days hospitalization. The department director, Dr. Lessin, saw the number on Bluma's arm and asked all the doctors and nurses in the department to gather in the conference room there and brought Bluma in. He asked Bluma to describe to the department staff the nature of the number on her arm and to give a short history of herself. They sat for about forty minutes and when they came out I saw some of the young female doctors had tears streaming down their faces.

Bluma returned home, continued with her life, occasionally telling of the horrors she had experienced. One day, when I was with her in the kitchen, she told me of the S.S. officer who had hit a pregnant Jewish woman in the stomach with a hoe, killing her on the spot. Days passed and the horrors rose up and were described by her aloud to me faster and faster.

Bluma was becoming slower. Her speech, which was not rapid, but slow, became even slower. She could hardly function in the kitchen, so she suggested to Moshe to go to a nearby institution where readymade meals could be bought for the elderly, where he could eat if he wanted.

Moshe began to report to me in the middle of 2004 that Bluma was not herself. She would often become angry with him for no reason, would snap at her devoted house help, Simcha Trager, who had been cleaning her home for forty years. She was restless, would wander around the house like a sleepwalker, and from time to time would mumble things connected with the Holocaust, which he could not understand. Moshe was not a young man himself. He was 85 years old.

Not long afterwards he asked to talk with me. He said he did not know what was happening to my mother, but he could no longer live with her under the same roof. She was bad-tempered and angry, suspicious of her housekeeper Simcha, who would help her every Friday, that she had "taken" things and had done damage to the house. He intended to leave and to go and live in a home for the elderly in October 2005.

I spoke with my wife, Tzofia, who was the Deputy Principal of the Holon high school, and told her that we must move to live near my mother in

Tel Aviv, because Moshe would be leaving soon, and I could not leave her abandoned, alone and solitary. All the neighbors with whom she had been friendly had died, and she remained in the building with neighbors the majority of whom were young, who had rented apartments and who did not know her.

Bluma asked me to come with my wife to live with her. I understood that she was very afraid to be alone. Tzofia made it clear that moving to Tel Aviv would make things very difficult for her, since at the end of the school day there was very heavy traffic from Holon to Tel Aviv. In the end Tzofia agreed, because she understood that Bluma was deteriorating and her condition was bad. We rented an apartment in Tel Aviv in August 2004 not far from Bluma's home, and we rented out our home in Holon.

When Moshe left in October 2005, there was another decline in Bluma's health. I would visit her twice a day, I did her shopping for her and I almost stopped working. She was busy with blaming and complaining about Moshe and Simcha the house-help that they had done damage to the house. She began to suspect that they had stolen from her. Occasionally she would say strange things that I understood to be connected with her bitter fate, but I could not understand their meaning.

Around the middle of 2006, Bluma began to say, "Yitzhak, this is not my home. I want you to take me to my home." I would take her in the car so that she could see where her home was. We would drive around the streets and come back. She would calm down a little, and then it began again. She would repeat on a daily basis, "This is not my home, it is the Hekdesh", referring to the wayside inn in Sopotzkyn where Jews could stay.

"Yitzhak, what work is arranged for me tomorrow?" she would ask me.

"Yitzhak, take me to my mother and father."

Again and again she would say, "This is not my home". I would come and drive around the streets with her to enable her to point out her home. At that stage I had no idea that with a person in such a cognitive state one must not argue, one must just flow with him. Twice or three times a week I took her out to a café to be among people and to eat the ice cream she had always loved.

At home she would be busy all day, taking out kerchiefs, towels and pieces of fabric. She would fill them with different items which a person usually takes with him on a journey, like soap, a comb or toothbrush. She would put down the little packages she had prepared and every few hours would move them from place to place. This went on for years, as long as the Philippine caregiver was in her house.

In previous years, when we grew up in Bluma's home, her closets where she stored bed linen and clothes were all perfectly tidy. Everything was ironed, folded and was pleasantly fragrant. It was forbidden to touch or go near. Exemplary neatness. A sparkling home. There was a sense that you were in a museum, not a home in which people live. It was forbidden to go near the closets she had tidied.

Suddenly the house had become untidy. There were packages in sheets and lengths of fabric in which she had packed objects as if she was about to take a hurried journey. Nothing remained of the exemplary order that had been in the house. When she forgot where she had put something or other, she would open the packages which she had packed, and the confusion and muddle would worsen. She collected all her handbags and shoulder bags and concentrated them on one table. I had the feeling that she was preparing for an emergency departure. The old horrors had returned. She had to be ready "to take to the road". With her broken leg she would climb a ladder to reach the hiding places at the top of the wardrobe to hide clothes. In those days I felt that my heart was bleeding. I understood that all her past had burst out with enormous force.

These phenomena worsened, as I saw her sitting at the table with all her handbags lying on it, and she was ready to take to the road, saying "This is not my home".

In this period Emanuel came to visit and slept in a room in her home. One day, when I came to her while he was sleeping, she turned to me and asked: "Who is that man?" I was appalled.

After he returned to the U.S., she again said, "This is not my home". My wife and I came to drive her around in the car to calm her, and then she turned to my wife and said of me: "That is an S.S. officer".

I invited two psychiatrists to obtain an accurate diagnosis. One of them stated that this was the onset of Alzheimer's disease, with symptoms of paranoia. And no wonder. The content of the paranoid symptoms consisted of memories of the Holocaust.

I applied to the Tel Aviv Family Court and was appointed Bluma's guardian in September 2006. I knew that she was receiving an allowance from the Hannover Reparations Office.

I knew that I must find a foreign caregiver, and to keep Bluma at home as long as I could. By the end of a week I had to recruit a replacement caregiver. From the experience I gathered, I understood that keeping an Alzheimer's patient, whose movement was restricted, at home could not last long, and that in the end I would have to find her an institutional arrangement.

How would I cope with this problem, while I learned that my brother Emanuel and his second wife were seeking divorce, after she had used up all his money, the value of his home in San Ramon, and his special-needs son, Noah, remained in Emanuel's custody? Emanuel saved his divorced wife and himself by declaring bankruptcy in the U.S. under Chapter 11 of the Bankruptcy Law. He was left a pauper.

At that time, I had to hospitalize Bluma. So what should I do – sell all her property and her home to finance her hospitalization? I was not prepared to have her cared for on a low standard, that would not be respectful of her. On the other hand, if I should use up her meager property, I would not be able to help Emanuel and myself to recuperate, since I was hardly working at all and my health condition was, as Bluma would put it, "not of the best." I decided to start an all-out war to improve Bluma's income, which appeared to me to be absolutely unreasonable. This knowledge had been growing inside me, based on the hundreds of cases that were known to me, where people with much lower levels of invalidity had received much higher allowances. But mostly it appeared to me that, in view of the harm that had been caused to her by the Nazi persecution and terror, her reparations agreement had no basis in reality.

The Consequences of the Terrorization Suffered by Bluma and How her Post-Trauma Affected Her, my Brother and Myself

In my description of Bluma's story I related, not necessarily in the right sequence, and placed strong focus on a number of events in which the post-trauma from which she suffered affected the course of her life in a way which an ordinary person would not have encountered.

Upon her arrival in Palestine at the age of 22, bearing in her soul the terrible post-trauma, the most fundamental effect was significant damage to her capacity to work. She tried and began working in a printing house, but apparently the horrific nightmares, lack of sleep and the shortage of regular and vital nutrition to her body in its final maturation period, hindered her ability to work and persist at any job beyond two or three hours which, of course, has no place on the labor market. As she grew older, this little ability was also reduced, so she preferred housework, and in her spare time she saw to the needs of the home. Hanan would help her upon his return from work. On Shabbat it was he who took the reins into his hands.

In 1955, when the damage caused by the Luxembourg Agreement had been successfully mitigated, Bluma did not consult with any doctors before filing her claim at the attorney's office in Tel Aviv. She had no knowledge of medicine, and certainly nobody in the world at that time had ever diagnosed or even knew what post-trauma was.

Moreover, Bluma knew that due to her being shot in the stomach with a hollow point bullet she had undergone surgery which shortened her ileum (small intestine) by 80 cm, as well as a second operation to deal with the inflammation on the right-hand side of her stomach, which caused additional damage to the ileocecal valve. How could she not have said that at the attorney's office? How could the Reparations Office in Hannover and the doctors there not understand that? How could the irresponsible doctors of the State of Israel who headed the Foreign Reparations Unit not know that?

When Bluma applied to the attorney's office I was 8 years old, and Emanuel was 4. The economic distress was acute. Hanan and Bluma were in need of all the help they could get. After she had completed the empty forms and signed them, the clerk at the Reparations Office asked what had happened to her, and she said: "Stomach injury". The attorney's office in Israel filed the claim for damages, with the stomach injury being an event and not a disorder. Much later she understood that she had made a mistake, and asked a German-speaking neighbor to help her to rectify it, but she was refused.

While the Reparations Office in Hannover was investigating the claim, medical tests revealed damage to her lumbar vertebra and her retinas.

A person free of post-trauma would have immediately reported that he possessed medical evidence of additional injuries and would not have waived their inclusion as damage caused as a direct consequence of the persecutions.

That is not the case with a person suffering from post-trauma. He has been terrorized by the Germans, and if he dares to ask, to wish or to rectify he will be punished. He fears that the claim he filed concerning the "stomach injury" will also be rejected. She said to me: "Don't mess with them, Yitzchak."

While I was examining the paperwork, when she became sick with Alzheimer's, by virtue of my function as guardian, my heart burst inside me. What suffering she could have saved herself all those years, if the invalidity percentages had not been robbed of her, whether by the Reparations Office or by the irresponsibility of the State of Israel, not only under the exemption it granted in 1952, but by a lack of regular advice and handling. If only another 45% invalidity for the shortened intestine, retinas and spinal defects had been granted to her, she could have been economically independent when

Hanan died. She could have released me from looking after her financially, and from sacrificing my work and another eleven years of my life for her, at a time when I also had to look after my children and provide for my old age.

Failure to include 100% post-trauma invalidity was not her fault, or that of the German Reparations Offices. The condition was first diagnosed only upon the return of the U.S. soldiers from Vietnam in the 1980s – 12 years after 1969, the year in which the German Reparations Law became obsolete. Those responsible for the loss were the Israeli governments who served from 1980 onwards, who could not understand that it was necessary to reopen negotiations with the Germans, <u>since all survivors of the extermination camps and ghettos who applied to the reparations offices in the German Federation states received no compensation for post-trauma and emotional damage beyond the 25% granted to them by the BEG Reparations Law.</u>

Although in my childhood, due to my resistance, I often had conflicts with her, when I grew older and more mature no trace of anger or hate towards her arose in my mind or in my feelings for the terrible errors she had made as a result of her post-trauma, which affected my brother and especially myself during the days of her terrible illness. I came to understand that, only because of her wisdom and restraint, which were able to withstand the test of survival, the hardest test of all, did she succeed in saving herself, raising a glorious family, and enabling the State of Israel to exist, which I hope will eventually be under another management, with better quality and morals.

In 1993, when she received the mean, threatening letter from the director of the Hannover Reparations Office, the low-down and wily Mr. Bremer, after she had appealed due to the worsening of her emotional condition, I was again appalled by the fear and dread that consumed her as she entered the attorneys' office in Tel Aviv.

I have described in detail the loss of Hanan's rights, which he left her in his great wisdom, but which she gave up.

The post-trauma which remained untreated, if it could have been treated at all, worsened and resulted in an effective gain for the German oppressor of at least a million dollars only from her, over the years.

"Thanks to" the governments of Israel, Bluma's case was not the only one. There are many more thousands like her. It was the light cases of post-trauma which actually did succeed in settling their rights, both at the German Reparations Offices and in Israel.

When I opened my parents' reparations agreements, which I had never seen, since to my regret they also remained a "deep secret", my world fell apart. I found both Bluma's reparations agreement and that of my father, Hanan, including two judgments in his case. They were both in German. I obtained their translation from German to Hebrew. When their contents were revealed to me, my whole body shuddered in sorrow, pain and insult. I felt guilty that I had not asked to see them more insistently in previous years, when I asked but she evaded me and refused.

All those years people came to our home who had also received reparations. I listened from time to time to conversations and facts that they told, and I understood that what was happening regarding Bluma's reparations was simply incomprehensible. I understood that people whose injuries were much more minor than Bluma's received regular allowances and accumulated handsome savings.

What did I discover about Bluma? She had been receiving reparations at the lowest possible level, at the rate of between 25%-39%. The BEG Law, under which she had been permitted to sue the state of Lower Saxony, stated that every DP who had been on German soil should be considered to have suffered 25% emotional harm with no proof of damage. The law did not determine any emotional diagnosis, which was also unknown then, but created the legal assumption that whoever had been in an extermination camp or ghetto would have suffered emotional disability which was then defined as – "vegetativen Störungen".

This assumption is basically correct, but remained in total darkness, and this time it was not the fault of the Germans. In actual fact, this assumption created for the German Federal Government savings of tens of billions of dollars in the future, and led to the loss of enormous sums for individuals who sued there and were living in Israel, for the Israeli Treasury and its financial system, mainly in the form of foreign currency reserves that would have been deposited in its banks.

I shall subsequently present the information to the readers, layer on layer, and at the end of the day the true factual and legal picture will stand revealed to all.

Bluma's reparations agreement granted 25% emotional invalidity under the law for nervous disturbances – that was the diagnosis. However, to my amazement, I found in the agreement the following provision: "10% invalidity on account of persecution due to stomach injury."

Is stomach injury a disability? Has anyone lost his mind? One of the greatest experts in the world in civil wrongs law, the late Jewish American Judge Benjamin Cardozo, would have wondered whether someone had gone mad. Stomach injury is an incident, isn't it? The question should be, what are the physical results of the stomach injury incident, as the question will always be – what are the physical results of any injury.

Where is the expression of the removal of part of the small intestine and the two abdominal scars? Was she not shot in Risa with a hollow-nosed bullet, and did she not undergo two abdominal operations which left her with an ileum shorter by 80 cm and two leaking scars, and peritoneal adhesions and constant digestive problems? Why, from the day on which the clerks in the Tel Aviv attorney's office wrote on their pages "stomach injury" until the end of the process in the Hannover Reparations Office, did nobody add injuries to the eyes and spinal column, which were discovered while waiting for the process in the Hannover Reparations Office to be completed? Why were the deceiving German doctors in the Hannover Reparations Office so eager to grab the opportunity?

How did the Ministry of Health operate in 1995-1996, when it was aware of the fact that hundreds of thousands, among them Bluma, due to their distress and the omissions of the Israeli governments, were crying out for immediate help? Why did the Ministries of Justice, Health and Finance not appoint units to examine and assist these people, for whom the very contact with the Germans aroused shuddering fear?

In 1955, when the Israeli government enabled the 500,000 Deprived Group to file claims in the various German Federation States, a department/unit was set up in the Israeli Ministry of Finance called the "Foreign Reparations Unit" (not necessarily from Germany). The aim of this unit, the personnel of which also included doctors, under the conclusion between the governments, was to assist the Reparations Offices in the German Federation States to obtain medical material from the claimants' health funds for the purpose of recognizing or not recognizing diseases caused by the persecutions and the exacerbation thereof.

The Israeli Treasury, on the other hand, had a strategic goal in maintaining this unit. The unit collected information on all those claimants who were citizens of Israel whose claims were approved by the German Federation states. This information enabled the government to avoid its obligation under the initial Reparations Agreement to compensate those victims in Israel under the law enacted in 1957, i.e. Israel's Nazi Persecution Invalids Law 5617 – 1957. This law was enacted for the first time five years after receipt of reparations from West Germany by the Israeli government and four years after the German BEG Law.

By means of collecting the information on who had received what, the State of Israel unlawfully avoided paying them real and correct compensation, and sold their honor, their birthright, that of their children, as well as its own birthright for a mess of potage.

The goal of the Foreign Reparations Unit in the Treasury was to monitor and collect information on those of the "Deprived" who receive reparations from the German Federation states where they were a Displaced Person. The name of the unit from the legal aspect was correct. The German government, which adhered to the eternal exemption that it had received from the "Wise Men of Gotham" in Jerusalem, insisted that its "opening of the faucet", despite the Reparations Agreement, would involve no liability whatsoever by Federal Germany for those claimants from Israel in the Federation states in which they had proved their registration as DPs.

I read Bluma's agreement with the Hannover Reparations Office in Lower

Saxony, and ask myself, day and night, aloud and in the dark of the night in 2006, fifty years after she had signed the compromise agreement, where is the shortening of her intestine, where are the consequent chronic digestion problems? Where are the scars?

Fifty years of loss of at least 60% invalidity which subtracted hundreds of thousands of euro from her welfare over the years. That concerns only the direct invalidity created by the shot in the stomach in Risa and the surgery on the soil of Saxony. What about the damage to her eyes and to her spinal column which she had never claimed until the end of the recognition process in 1955 in the Hannover Reparations Office?

The central question I ask myself is: Negligent, conceited, irresponsible politicians, Knesset members and Directors General of Government Ministries, you have committed a crime against the precious population thanks to whom the right of the Jewish People to establish its national home in the Land of Israel was recognized – the survivors of the extermination camps, the ghettos and the forced labor camps. You expropriated from them their property rights in 1952, you prevented them from filing claims against the Federal Republic. Why, in 1954 onwards, when the BEG Law unilaterally made it possible to file claims in the West German Federation states, did you not assist these people to file their claims from the legal and medical aspects? You left their fate in the hands of attorneys who aspired only to accept as many claimants as possible as clients and to complete their cases in compromises, by means of clerks who had no expertise or knowledge of the material, in order to collect their fees quickly and efficiently?

How did the Director of the Hannover Reparations Office, Andreas Bremer, not see that a stomach injury, as a compromise agreement with a recognized invalid due to persecutions, is a definition known in law to be void ab initio and of no legal validity?

How is it that, in the Treasury, where the authorities of the State of Israel were in communication with the Reparations Offices, years come and go, and nobody sees that Bluma had signed an agreement that was not legally valid – a stomach injury is not a disability, it is an incident. Nobody in the

Foreign Reparations Unit cared. After all, it should also be in the Treasury's interests that its citizens' pockets and the financial system should be fuller. Is that not so?

I turn over the papers in the drawer and see the documents that dealt with the application concerning the worsening of her condition in 1992, even before Section 35 of the BEG Law took effect, whereby after the age of 68 any deterioration is granted 33%, and my world collapses.

I find the letter from Mr. Andreas Bremer, the Director of the Hannover Reparations Office, as a decision in the application concerning the decline in her condition, in which he writes, "If you dare to apply once more for deterioration in your health, I shall deny your allowance, because in 1962 (thirty years earlier) we approved for you two days of recuperation with no proof."

Mr. Andreas Bremer, Director of the Hannover Reparations Office, was a smart and experienced man, who had contacts with the greatest of Germany's psychiatrists, who knew well that people such as Bluma were suffering from severe terrorization. Together with his knowledge, he was a lowlife. By virtue of his position to "make good again [Wiedergutmachung]", he took advantage of his experience, knowing full well that the compromise agreement between Bluma and his office was invalid. He threatened her in order to prevent the possibility that someone would give her the correct counsel to appeal to court to cancel the agreement, by means of terrorizing her, saying "if you dare to apply again I shall cancel your allowance".

Mr. Andreas Bremer knew two more facts. He knew that in 1978, after the demise of her husband Hanan, Bluma had written to his Reparations Office two letters through an attorney who had drafted them in German for her, in which Bluma explained to her office in Lower Saxony in Germany, which was "making good again", that she had lost her husband and his income, that she was in economic distress, and requested them, if it was possible, to improve her allowance a little for social reasons.

The other fact he knew from 1978, due to the flow of data between the Reparations Offices in the various Federation states, but I knew it only from 2006, after I had been appointed Bluma's guardian, and that was that the late

Hanan had an agreement with the Reparations Office of Darmstadt in the Federation state of Hessen, whereby in the case of his demise, 60% of his allowance from the state of Hessen, which was high, would be paid to Bluma his widow for the rest of her life, without binding the cause of his death to his recognized diseases. Additionally, such payment would be regardless of the fact that the Lower Saxony Reparations Office had received approval for two days of recuperation thirty years earlier.

Mr. Bremer knew that it was illegal to deny the terrorized Bluma the allowance to which she was entitled after Hanan's death from the Hessen Reparations Office, which had been at least 600 dollars a month for fifteen years up to 1992, when he sent her the threatening letter.

When I saw Hanan's agreement in 2006 for the first time, my hands shook again, and my soul took a serious blow. I understood that from 1978, when he had died, up to 2006, she had lost twenty-eight years of widow's compensation from the state of Hessen, which amounted to a principal sum of 260,000 U.S. dollars.

I was shocked. I knew what to expect in connection with the development of Alzheimer's disease. I sent a letter to the Director of the Darmstadt Reparations Office, Thomas Flach, and demanded that they pay Bluma her widow's allowance that had been due to her since 1978 from the Darmstadt Reparations Office, which had moved to Weissbaden. I complained to them: How did it happen that the allowance had not been paid? Why did you not advise her that she was entitled to it?

The Reparations Office sent me proof, black on white, that in 1978 Bluma had advised them that Hanan had died and that they should not send her the allowance after his death. The Reparations Office of the state of Hessen sent her letters, which I had never seen, and were shown to me in 2006, in which they requested her to cooperate with them so that they could pay her the allowance as Hanan's widow, which was due to her from the Hessen Reparations Office. They wrote to her that the claim must be filed within one year after her husband's death, and that she must answer the questions in the files. These I had not seen in 1978. She had never shown them to me.

In 1978 I had already been an attorney for three years. I could have died of shame. I sent a letter to the Director of the Reparations Office, apologizing for having been so abusive to his office. I explained to him in detail what had been revealed to me.

Bluma suffered a wave of anxiety upon the death of Hanan concerning the loss of her source of income, so she believed mistakenly, and requested the help of her Reparations Office in Hannover. She wanted to prove, in order to receive the help she requested from Hannover, that she had "behaved well" and had reported to the Reparations Office in Hessen of the death of her husband, so that they should cease to pay his allowance, 60% of which would be due to her after his death.

Her dread of the Nazis that had penetrated her soul, and of which she could not rid herself all her life, disqualified her from dealing with her affairs vis-à-vis the Reparations Offices in Germany, because fear and dread confound all logic. The fact that she did not share with me was a consequence of her fear that she would be dragging her son to a bottomless pit with the Nazis, as had happened to her, and she wanted to protect me. She could not understand that her son Yitzchak was not afraid of anyone, and that he had not been in a years-long college of terror.

I understood that Bluma was worried that she would be punished by Andreas Bremer if she did not prove [to him] that she had advised the Hessen Reparations Office of Hanan's death, and that she was also worried, because she was ignorant of the law, that if she should file her widow's claim within a year in the state of Hessen, the Hannover Reparations Office would stop her allowance. That was in 1978.

In 2006 I learned from my own experience that all the things she had told me of the Director of the Hannover Reparations Office, Andreas Bremer, and how evil he was, were correct. The evidence for that is – the threatening letter he sent her in 1992, knowing that her compromise agreement with his office, concerning the stomach injury, was completely invalid. He also knew in 1993 that that year was the 13th anniversary of the diagnosis of PTSD – Post-trauma Stress Disorder, and that there were dozens of cases in his office which had won higher invalidity percentages on the background of hardships that could not be compared to those suffered by Bluma.

Eventually it became clear to me that disabilities such as those that resulted from the shooting of Bluma in Risa in April 1945 should have been awarded 40% and not 10% as she received. But it was not Bluma's fault. It was the fault of the terrorization and its consequences, and the lowlife Andreas Bremer who, due to thousands of complaints, was removed from his position, and who died a short time later.

Accordingly, honored readers, here is living proof as to how terrorization and severe post-trauma thwart the ability of the victim to exercise his rights. "If I do not notify Hessen of the death of my husband and if I claim there, that lowlife Andreas Bremer will rob me of my allowance in Hannover. I, Bluma daughter of Isaac and Sheine Reisel of Sopotzkyn, who have been widowed at the age of 54, and have been left with almost no means of a livelihood, have no government and no state. My government, because I am suffering from severe post-trauma, has put the fate of my rights, which it had expropriated in 1952, in the hands of the Nazi oppressor and their successor, Mr. Andreas Bremer. The main thing is that the governments of Israel are exempt from paying me and those like me. The government officials, ministers and prime ministers received their handsome fees on time, and abandoned all the severe cases who required instruction, direction and treatment, both for their own sakes and for the sake of the Treasury of Israel."

Emanuel was at that time in the middle of divorce proceedings in California after all his property had been lost, and my head was occupied with the manner and means I could obtain for Bluma. Her mistakes did not make me angry for one moment. One may not be angry with a sufferer of severe post-trauma, as our scholars say, "Do not judge your friend until you are in his place."

My goal was to increase Bluma's income from any source I could find, including replacing the allowance from Hannover with a current allowance under the Nazi Persecutions Victims Law, 1956, and in 2008 I filed a claim in that regard to the Israeli authority under that law, on the recommendation of one of the supervisors there, and that claim was denied. "Your mother is receiving from Germany", they told me. They were guarding the Treasury that had been rescued under the BEG Law. From Germany nobody received and never will, but from a Federation state they do receive – in 2008 half the amount paid by the Israeli Treasury to the Persecutions Victims that it had registered, who had not suffered even 5% of the torment and torture experienced by Bluma.

I wanted to give my mother the best treatment, to maneuver the retention of her maintenance and to see to it that if Emanuel could not rehabilitate himself I would be able to help him.

I applied to the director of the Hessen Reparations Office, Mr. Thomas Flach, a dear and good-hearted man, and asked him what to do. My widowed mother's post-trauma had "released" the state of Hessen and its reparations office from paying an allowance totaling 260,000 dollars. I wanted to see to it that she would depart this world in the most beautiful and respectable manner and with good treatment.

Mr. Flach who, as director of his office was duty-bound to speak with me in German, said, "Mr. Borovsky, under the law, the claim of your mother, Bluma, for widow's allowance due to your father's death, became obsolete in 1979. If I deviate from the rules and approve her collection of the differences, an investigation will be initiated against me on suspicion of my taking a bribe from you." I asked, "My friend, Mr. Flach, how can you help me?" He said, "Wait a few weeks, and I shall try as hard as I can to find some solution."

A few weeks later, in a telephone conversation, Mr. Thomas Flach, director of the Darmstadt Reparations Office in Weissbaden, Hessen, told me: "Mr. Borovsky, I cannot agree that your mother and you will be in this situation when she has Alzheimer's disease." I shall never forget what he said in German: "Diese Situation will ich nicht erlauben [I shall not permit her to be in this situation.]"

I travelled to Mr. Flach, and I met a pleasant German in his fifties, smiling, good-hearted and very intelligent. A few more weeks passed and he sent me a registered letter inviting me to enter into a compromise agreement with the Hessen Reparations Office, whereby Bluma would receive a social pension from the state of Hessen in the amount of 1,050 euro per month with a retroactive amount equivalent to five years of payments."

Seven months later, after I learned in July 2010 that Bluma had undergone human experiments in the laboratories of the Waffen S.S. at Birkenau, I called the office of the Kanzler, who answered me ten days later, and appointed another dear German, Dr. Dirk Langner, who was in charge of the whole payments organization located in Bonn, to inquire into the matter.

Dr. Langner recommended to me to file a petition to cancel the agreement drawn up by Bluma in 1955 with Hannover, which I did, but that claim is again not against the German Federal government, which had been made exempt from its liability for my mother and the other 500,000 victims of the extermination camps, but to the administrative court of Lower Saxony. It was not successful, because there they got up on their hind legs, when they understood that Bluma had been entitled from 1955 to 100% invalidity due to post-trauma and 40% due to the damage to her small intestine and the leaking scars.

In the end, we reached a compromise agreement, whereby the state of Hessen agreed, by means of the honorable Mr. Flach and Dr. Dirk Langner to add to Bluma retroactive payment for five additional years, on condition that I, as guardian would have no additional claims against the Reparations Authority. Against the Federal Republic I could do nothing. Bluma's, Emanuel's and my State, had exempted the Federal Republic from liability. German executives with a conscience helped me to the best of their ability, while the Israeli Treasury rejected me, and generously distributed allowances to people with much lighter invalidity.

The missing money that had led me to legal battles, both with the states of Lower Saxony and Hessen and with the Israeli government, the authorities and the High Court of Justice in file HJC 8766/11, the deliberations of which lasted three years, disrupted my life, affected my work critically and forced me to confront serious hardships including emotional difficulties.

Alongside the aspect of the memory of the Holocaust on which the State of Israel places emphasis on the Holocaust Memorial Day and in the Yad Vashem institute, the State of Israel's handling of the affair up to the minute of writing this book, is base, horrific and beneath all contempt. These battles affected me in preparing myself and my family for old age, and due to the terrible pain caused by the facts and information which were revealed to me.

In the court case in the Israel Supreme Court, the Presiding Judge, the honorable Judge Elyakim Rubinstein, said that "the Representative of the Petitioner, Bluma, is well versed in this affair" (HJC file 8766/11).

In Bluma's case, I asked the Supreme Court why Alzheimer's patients who had survived the camps, who were hospitalized in institutions and receive allowances from the Reparations Offices of the German Federal Republic, such as Bluma, were charged V.A.T. on their nursing hospitalization, while the survivors of the extermination camps and others, including those who had never seen Germany but had been recognized under the Israel Nazi Persecutions Victims Law, were not charged V.A.T. on their hospitalization.

Even tourists visiting Israel, who are hospitalized during their visit, are exempt from paying V.A.T. under the law, but Bluma, thanks to whom, and others like her, the Jewish State was established, was charged V.A.T. in the amount of approximately NIS 300,000 in the course of her hospitalization. Others who receive allowances from the Israel Treasury, are exempt from payment of V.A.T. on their hospitalization. Bluma Plaskovsky, Birkenau Prisoner no. 31119, is a second-class Jewish Holocaust survivor. Other Holocaust survivors and those who escaped the camps who receive allowances in Israel are first-class.

Supreme Court case HJC 8766/11, Bluma's petition against the State of Israel, was attended by the Arab Justice Salim Joubran, who was the Vice-President of the Supreme Court. I shall never forget his reaction when he heard that survivors of the extermination camps who receive reparations from the German Federation states and are hospitalized in Israel are charged V.A.T. on their hospitalization, while those who receive allowance from the Israel Treasury are not charged V.A.T. The honorable Justice Salim Joubran, and in front of a room full of people, asked the representatives of the State of Israel in the room, "Are you out of your mind? How does such a thing happen?" These words I shall never forget.

At the time of writing this book, the Nationality Law was enacted under the auspices of the present Prime Minister, Benyamin Netanyahu. In Bluma's Supreme Court case No. HJC 8766/11, the panel of the judges in the Supreme Court recommended to the Prime Minister to rectify the distortions, and to rectify various issues with the government of the Chancellor – in Berlin. Of course, the Prime Minister did nothing. In Germany there are other interests. The new Nationality Law did not correct the eternal facts which remain in full effect to this moment, which are:

1. In the State of Israel there are First-Class and Second-Class Holocaust survivors. First-Class survivors are those who are supported by the Israeli Treasury. Now I discovered that for the past two years, after the majority of the recipients of reparations from the Federation states were no longer with us, the Israeli Treasury had begun to compensate those who still remained by paying them the difference between what was paid by the Israeli Treasury and the discriminating amount paid by the Federation countries.

2. Second-Class Holocaust survivors are those who had been forced in 1954-1955 to apply to the Reparations Offices under the BEG Law which had been enacted in 1953 due to the State of Israel's violation of its undertakings to Federal Germany in favor of the 500,000 members of the Deprived Group.

3. Second-Class Holocaust survivors who contract Alzheimer's disease or other conditions requiring nursing in their old age do not benefit from any support from their state and pay V.A.T. on their hospitalization. All their property, including the old-age allowance they receive from the National Insurance Institute is subject to collection. First-Class Holocaust survivors do not pay V.A.T. on their hospitalization, they retain most of their National Insurance allowance, and other types of income do not participate in financing their hospitalization.

4. In the days of Benyamin Netanyahu, the Israeli Authority in the Treasury recognizes Alzheimer's disease for Holocaust survivors who have become nursing patients as entitling to an additional partial allowance, while Second-Class Holocaust survivors who are registered in the Federation states are not entitled to that. Germany does not recognize Alzheimer's as a consequence of the persecutions.

Hurrah for the new Nationality Law! Jews of the U.S., Canada, Britain, France, Argentina, Australia – do not remain silent. <u>Due to corrupt and avaricious politicians and the lack of a constitution, we shall lose our third Home.</u>

It turned out that just about the date of the judgment in Supreme Court File No. HJC 8766/11 in Bluma's case on January 27, 2014, Prime Minister Netanyahu was in contact with Germany on the matter of the submarines. What interest did he have in raising and reopening with the honorable Chancellor what the High Court of Justice had recommended to him?

Post-trauma, Significance, Shame and Damage Caused by the State of Israel to Itself, the Survivors of the Extermination Camps and of the Ghettos

Terrible and difficult diseases lurk in wait for a person throughout his life. They are classified as deadly, they cut his life short, they are the serious malign diseases, diseases of the blood vessels which cut a person down by means of damage to the brain, the heart and life functions such as the lungs, the liver, kidneys and pancreas. These are diseases which usually do not last very long until they become terminal. To these we must add the serious dementias, some of which are also fatal.

Post-trauma, especially in the most severe cases, is distinguished from the traditional deadly diseases by killing a person's soul over many long years, impairing his function and even changing his personality. Eventually, medical research showed that post-trauma even causes the deadly Alzheimer's disease to break out and kill its victim. This has been proven in a study made of about one hundred and sixty thousand American soldiers who returned from Vietnam, when it emerged that a significantly larger number among them than in the regular population developed Alzheimer's dementia. For women with Alzheimer's who had survived the extermination camps, there the ratio is also five times that of the regular population.

Post-trauma or Post-trauma Stress Disorder (PTSD) was defined in psychiatry by the World Health Organization (ICD-10 DSM).

The diagnosis refers to survivors of the extermination camps as suffering the highest severity of the disease, and even more so – those who had been exposed to the traumas of terrorization, fear and immediate risk to life for a long period.

Bluma was in Birkenau for two whole years, from the day it opened until it was closed down. The Jews of Hungary were in Birkenau, some for six months and some for four months. The age at which Bluma was under the traumas was the critical age in human life, the personality formation age. She experienced the traumas hour by hour, day by day, night by night, and there is nothing worse that can be described.

Bluma was given no treatment for the simple reason that the disease was defined only 35 years after the end of the horrors and the methods of treatment were formalized only then. The only treatment Bluma received was in the form of pills for sleep disorders, headaches and dizziness from which she suffered chronically.

When Bluma sent her claim for deterioration in her medical condition in 1992, the Director of the Hannover office, Andreas Bremer, sent the medical aspect to the German doctor in charge in the state of Baden Würtemberg, Dr. George Beutzel, who replied to Mr. Bremer's question as to whether a deterioration had occurred: "Mrs. Borovwky is suffering from a disease known as PTSD – post-trauma. In your agreement with her you did not classify her condition correctly, but a certain deterioration should be recognized for her under the BEG Law."

Mr. Bremer concealed this letter from the Israeli attorney, and instead sent Bluma, the post-trauma patient, a letter threatening that if she dared to apply to him again he would suspend payments of her allowance altogether.

After I had spent tens of thousands of shekels in fighting this decision, I appeared on October 13, 2020 in the court in Hannover, Lower Saxony, and the court denied my claim. The supreme administrative court of Lower Saxony in its capital Celle accepted the appeal, and set Bluma's invalidity for post-trauma, including the "stomach injury", on account of Nazi persecution, at only 39%-49%, as of 1992.

The help she received from the Israeli government in 1953, and from the Nazi lawyers in the Rosenburg Palace in Bonn, for release and alleviation of the reparations for the survivors of the extermination camps and ghettos by the Israeli Treasury was expressed in the following:

1. Not one of those who applied to the Reparations Offices in the German Federation states received compensation for the principal condition of post-trauma except indirectly – only 25% for emotional invalidity, which is not defined as post-trauma.

The reason for that is simple and obvious. Post-trauma was first defined only in 1980, eleven years after the lapse of the last date for filing claims in the Reparations Offices.

2. It can be said almost with certainty that the survivors of the extermination camps suffered from post-trauma, at a severity of between 75% and 100%, except for isolated cases which were at a lower level. The majority range between 75% and 100%. Even the authors of the ICD-10, the psychiatry book of the World Health Organization, classify the extermination camps survivors as the worst cases of PTSD.

3. If a State committee of inquiry is set up in the State of Israel, the fact that I am arguing will be proven: that the Authority for the Holocaust Survivors' Rights in the Ministry of Finance, which is in charge of the Nazi Persecutions Invalids Law 1957, recognizes people who had not been under the horrific conditions of the extermination camps and ghettos as suffering from post-trauma at 50%-100%. For some of them, the events of their lives and history did not attain even 1% of the sufferings of the actual survivors of the extermination camps and the ghettos. The leaders of the Jewish people all over the world are obligated, in order to memorialize the Holocaust and the results thereof, to direct that an inquiry be made into this affair.

4. When post-trauma was defined in 1980, the governments of Israel, "slept" and were unable to understand that hundreds of thousands of survivors had each been deprived of invalidity at tens of percent on account of their principal disease which was not known at the time. The governments did not lift a finger, did not plan anything and did not formulate any strategy to rectify

this affair in talks and negotiations with the German chancellors, among them worthy personages, especially the Chancellor Mrs. Angela Markel.

5. Upon the unification in 1989 between West Germany and East Germany, whose citizens had been full participants in the Holocaust, the latter were granted full exemption, and no negotiation was conducted between the Israeli governments and Germany for additional compensation from the new sector, which accepted a part of the guilt but not of the reparations.

6. The extent of the diseases and conditions which were recognized by the BEG Law as consequences of the persecutions up to 1969, and those recognized by the Israeli Treasury are completely different. Under German law, post-trauma, osteoporosis, heart disease and hypertension are not recognized. The Authority for the Rights of Holocaust Survivors in the Israeli Treasury does recognize them.

7. It was found that sufferers from post-trauma or Alzheimer's, who belong to the Israeli Treasury, are awarded 100% invalidity, entitling them to an allowance of NIS 9,000 a month, or State-subsided hospitalization with no V.A.T. thereon, and without being forced to participate with their own additional means.

8. On the other hand, those in Israel who claimed from the German Inner States do not get a single penny for post-trauma and Alzheimer's, and they pay from their own pockets for hospitalization, including V.A.T., and are also robbed of their old-age allowance.

9. When a son or daughter of a survivor goes to battle to rectify the financial situation in the German state, he gets the shock of his life. The State of Israel caused that, apart from the Federation state in which the Reparations Office is located, where the claimant had proved that he had been registered as a DP after the war, all the rest of Germany is exempt from liability.

10. He also learns that the scope of diseases recognized by the Israeli Treasury for hospitalization and geriatric nursing is much greater better than for those who had been the worst victims of the Holocaust – the survivors of the extermination camps and the ghettos, whose levels of invalidity and the extent of the diseases recognized for them are immeasurably limited, and

the hospitalization and geriatric nursing expenses imposed on them and their families by their State are much higher. That is a clear and humiliating discrimination of the severe victims of the Holocaust, the actual survivors of the extermination camps.

Bluma is Hospitalized with Alzheimer's Disease

After about three years during which I kept Bluma at her home with a Philippine caregiver, while my whole life had changed – no weekends, no holidays, shopping, looking after her and replacing the caregiver on weekends – the caregiver announced that she wanted to go to the Philippines for two months and then to return. I agreed, and the manpower company sent Bluma another, older caregiver. But a few days later, there was a general decline in her condition because she was found to have contracted cellulitis, and the new caregiver could not look after her. I hospitalized Bluma at the Ichilov Hospital, as I understood that a solitary caregiver, no matter how good and devoted, could not cope with keeping her at home. Bluma's spinal column and her ability to walk had deteriorated completely.

While my attorney colleagues were enjoying the Pesach recess, I was at the hospital day and night, and my office was not working. Two clients for whom I won a lot of money in their claims, took advantage of my distress and evaded payment. I was forced to sue them.

The feeling crystalized in my heart, and my mind formulated the decision, that it was no longer possible to keep Bluma at home, for both her own good and for mine. I began to inquire at various institutions and visited them, until the Gan Shalva sanatorium in Hod Hasharon caught my eye.

I saw many institutions, some of them in beautifully equipped luxurious buildings, but their rooms smelled of excrement, the nurses were cold to the patients who were cut off from an ordinary human environment. They were imprisoned on their floors. In another institution where I had tried earlier to hospitalize Bluma, I found her sitting on an ancient suitcase, waiting for me to come and take her home.

At the Gan Shalva sanatorium I saw that there was only one floor. The buildings were like in a kibbutz, in the first days of the State of Israel. The patients are taken out of their rooms in the morning, after seeing to their personal hygiene, and they eat breakfast. They are outside all day, see people moving around and visitors, they are employed as far as their cognitive abilities allow in handiwork, singing and traditional ceremonies. The main thing is that there are no odors characteristic of such institutions. Finally, my heart was captured by the number of employees who were running the place, the gardens, the flowers, the pretty seating areas with the singing birds and parrots all hours of the day.

At the time I decided that it would be the Gan Shalva sanatorium, Bluma was still hospitalized for an infection. I requested the director of Gan Shalva to come to the hospital to see whether he would be able to accept Bluma to his institution. He came, and advised me that he agreed and he told me the monthly fees. At that time I did not yet know what would be the results of my dealings with the Reparations Offices in Germany. My current financial position would not have enabled me to cover more than 30% of the hospitalization fees. My wife and I decided to move to Bluma's apartment, and to rent out our apartment, and to contribute the rental fees to Bluma's upkeep. Even then, we could cover only about 50% of the cost.

I reached the decision to take that road, whatever the cost. Three sayings reverberated in my ears: My father, Hanan, of blessed memory: "Yitzchak, you are in charge." The holy writings: "Do not fear, my servant, Jacob." Winston Churchill: "We have nothing to fear but fear itself."

After the director advised me that he agreed to accept Bluma, the seventh of April was determined as the date on which I would bring Bluma to the Gan Shalva sanatorium. That day was the second black day of my life.

Just like anyone else, Bluma did not want to leave her home. For Bluma it was not just something routine. She had lost the home of her youth, her parents' home, and the term "displaced person", homeless and insecure, had been assimilated into her soul at a very low threshold of stimulation. This was a woman who had begged me to come to her home to live together with her. Her home, until she became sick, was a museum, every object in its place, clean and shiny, the household utensils, bedlinen and clothes on the shelves emitting a pleasant fragrance, religiously starched and well-kept. The room where she raised her children was a holy temple.

What could I tell her? At that stage she still understood a little where I was about to take her. What explanation should I give her? These questions gave me no rest. I decided that the only way I could convince her to go to a place other than her home was to give her some good news. I thought a great deal about what I could tell her so that she would not object to my taking her to the sanatorium and not to her home.

"Mother, the Germans have heard what happened to you and they decided to give you recuperation at their expense at a luxurious rest home." I saw a smile of joy on her face.

I looked around to find someone to help me take her, a broken woman, with a walker, down from the hospital room on the seventh floor, which is about three hundred meters south of the elevators going down to the third floor of the underground parking space where I had parked my car. There was nobody to help me. I was forced to take her to the car on my own, slowly, a journey of about one hour along the hospital corridors. I felt at every meter I progressed with her to the car such heartache, that I, her only son in Israel, after everything she had undergone, was uprooting her from the home she so loved, which held her best memories and the nursery where she had raised her children, to a sanatorium with flowers and birds, which my father would have called a transit station.

I drove Bluma to the Gan Shalva sanatorium. On our arrival, we were received very well. It was the 7th April, 2008, the weather was excellent, the comfortable chair in which she was placed was next to the beautiful flowers of the garden, in the fresh air, with the chirping of birds and parrots and people moving around.

I started coming each day to check on her acclimatization and her treatment. Bluma released me from all my heartaches and conscience pains that accompanied me when I had uprooted her from her home to the sanatorium: "Yitzchak, you have brought me to Paradise. It is heaven here."

While I was sitting and talking to her, the nurses Olga and Cesarina, came over and kissed her and stroked her. It would be like that not only in my presence in order to satisfy me, that is how it was all the time. During my visits I felt the respect and warmth she received. They kept repeating to me that they had never met such a gentle and sensitive woman.

"Yitzchak", they said to me over the years, "We have never encountered such a woman. What a gentle, good-hearted woman, she always encourages the staff, compliments them, and most importantly she is pleasant, does not bother us, does not annoy or nag us like the others."

The nurse and the head nurse, Natasha, said: "Yitzchak, your mother speaks Russian perfectly." I knew that because she had studied at the Russian Gymnasium, but especially when she became sick with Alzheimer's the language began to return to her. I understood the reason – her memory had also been erased by the "first in last out" method.

At the beginning of her hospitalization the staff recorded many anxiety attacks and paranoid imaginings of persecutions by the S.S. and Gestapo at Birkenau. After about one year they stopped.

Two wonderful phenomena occurred due to the Alzheimer's disease, that I noticed after short periods of time. She began to smile and be happy. I had never seen her happy and smiling as I saw her at the Gan Shalva sanatorium. Her eyes expressed joy and warmth when we came to visit her. She praised the beautiful garden where she sat with the nurses. During my years of visiting her there I heard from quite a few nurses that Bluma would say to them, "Go and rest a little, you don't have to work so hard."

One day I came and told Bluma that the Germans had sent her a gift of $50,000 dollars to make her life easier. On the next visit I asked her: "Mother, what did you do with the $50,000?" She replied, "Yitzchak, I cannot walk. I am half the day on a wheelchair or I am helped to walk on a walker. I cannot go shopping in the stores. Look, Yitzchak, see all these poor people sitting around me. They envy me that I received the money, so I decided that to prevent their jealousy, I would distribute the money to them all. That is what I did. I gave them the money, so they would be happy."

When relatives of other patients would come sometimes accompanied by children, Bluma would melt with pleasure. Her love of little children and their laughter would cause her soul to bloom with joy.

In the first six years I visited her three times a week. I would also bring with me her relatives from the U.S. when they came to Israel and wanted to visit her. These visits with them were in addition to my routine visits. When Joan Weinstein, Corky, Elaine and Frances Weinstein came she was very happy. There were times when I told her that I would come later in the week with a relative from the U.S. and she often remembered about the visit. Edna, the daughter of Yehuda Ayalati, came from Jerusalem very often to visit her as long as she could. Emanuel also came a number of times, but his heart was torn because it was doubtful whether she remembered him.

While I was fighting in every way I could to improve Bluma's income to cover her expenses, her dear cousin, Mrs. Frances Weinstein, offered me financial help for her. I said that if required it I would let her know, and that I appreciated her offer very much. Only two or three months later, she requested her son Danny Weinstein to remind me that her offer still stands, and that if I needed financial help she would give it. Our cousin Frances Weinstein helped me most significantly with financing Bluma's stay at the Gan Shalva sanatorium.

Although I succeeded in greatly improving Bluma's income from Hannover, Lower Saxony and from Darmstadt, Hessen, these increments still were not sufficient to close the monthly gap. Frances' help did a lot to assist me in financing Bluma's stay at Gan Shalva for eight years and four months, until she passed away.

In my hundreds of visits to the sanatorium I saw many Alzheimer's patients. With some I made friends and saw that they were charming people. When cognition declines, a person's skill at maneuvering and concealing his thoughts and interests deteriorates. It is in these situations that his real personality emerges. They become like small children who are not capable of lying to camouflage their interests. The human body has the ability to heal itself, both physically and emotionally.

There are many studies today proving that Alzheimer's disease is much more frequent among those who suffered severe post-trauma or who lost the ability to absorb vitamins, but most important is the fact that the Alzheimer's disease and the loss of long-term memory, which evaporates layer after layer, erased for Bluma the horrors of the Holocaust and the anxiety, at least in the seven years after the first year of her hospitalization.

I discovered that my mother Bluma was an angel, good-hearted, generous, noble, considerate of the distress of others and able to hold out a helping hand. She never complained and was never a burden on others.

The Alzheimer's disease that had erased the memories of the horrors, enabled me to get to know the real Bluma as she was in her youth, when she was a human angel.

To see how the nurses from Russia and Ethiopia, the oriental Jews and the Arabs would kiss her was no light matter. When she was sick with Alzheimer's, for the first time in my life, I heard Bluma singing at the fortnightly meetings and singing with a lady who had been invited especially for her by the director of the institution, Mr. Giora Arenheim.

From April 2016 onwards a deterioration occurred in her condition, and she could no longer swallow. The situation worsened, and she suffered from repeated aspirations (a problem with the swallowing/breathing reflexes). I was summoned to talk with the Institution's doctor, and I came together with my son, Dr. Avinoam Borowsky. She clarified to me that the end was near, and that she could be transferred to a hospital. I did not agree to this at all, and we decided to enable her to leave the journey of her youth and adulthood with flowers and chirping birds, among people who loved her and respected her.

On August 25, 2016 I was in the cemetery in Holon where my father, of blessed memory, is buried, and alongside him there is a burial plot bought by my mother when he died. Since her demise was expected any day, after ten years of Alzheimer's, I went to make the arrangements required for her last respects, after her death.

While I was still at the cemetery, the Gan Shalva sanatorium, where she had been for the last eight years of her life, called to tell me that she had died without suffering, close to the hour of 11:00, a few moments ago.

I drove directly to the Gan Shalva sanatorium, and found there my mother, Bluma, lying on her back, without a wrinkle on her beautiful face, at the age of almost 92 years, while around her stood all the nurses, Jews and Arabs, with tears streaming down their faces. "Even among the Alzheimer's patients, we have not met such a noble and good woman," they told me.

Her soul returning to her Maker was accompanied by the odor of the burning flesh of a million and a half Jewish children, women and men, so that He should not forget how He had permitted this to be done by those purporting to be created in His image.

Made in the USA
Monee, IL
17 July 2023

39408457R00125